MW01633934

A DANGEROUS MAN (SPECIAL FORCES: OPERATION ALPHA)

AN APPALACHIAN STAR NOVEL
BOOK EIGHT

DEANNDRA HALL

CONTENTS

Dear Readers,

Welcome to the Special Forces: Operation Alpha Fan-Fiction world!

If you are new to this amazing world, in a nutshell the author wrote a story using one or more of my characters in it. Sometimes that character has a major role in the story, and other times they are only mentioned briefly. This is perfectly legal and allowable because they are going through Aces Press to publish the story.

This book is entirely the work of the author who wrote it. While I might have assisted with brainstorming and other ideas about which of my characters to use, I didn't have any part in the process or writing or editing the story.

I'm proud and excited that so many authors loved my characters enough that they wanted to write them into their own story. Thank you for supporting them, and me!

READ ON!
Xoxo
Susan Stoker

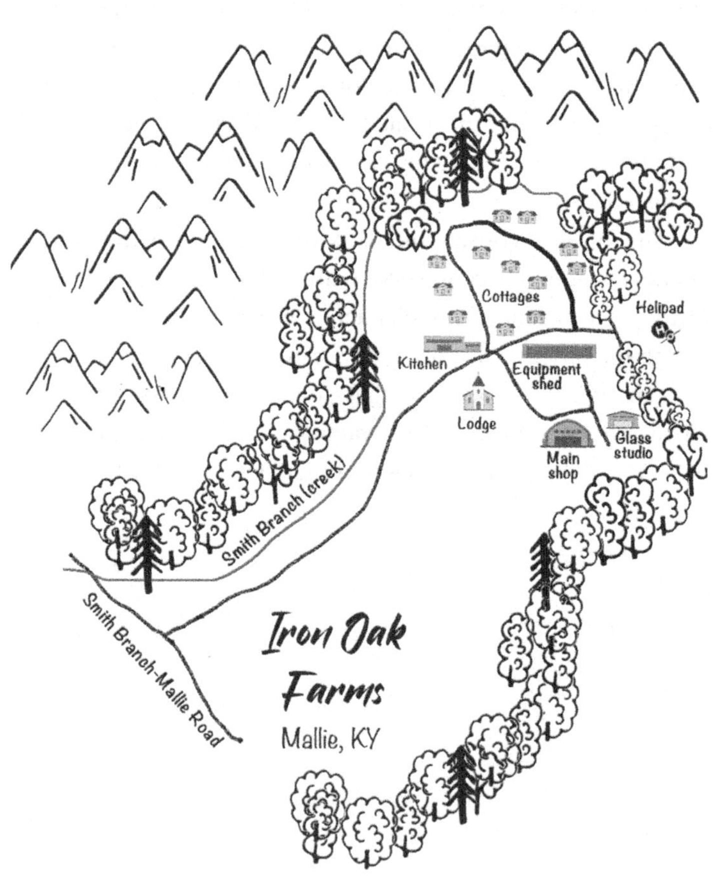

Cottages
Helipad
Kitchen
Equipment shed
Lodge
Glass studio
Main shop
Smith Branch (creek)
Smith Branch-Mallie Road
Iron Oak Farms
Mallie, KY

AUTHOR'S NOTE

The map of Mallie, Kentucky, is not an accurate depiction of the area, although Mallie does indeed exist. It is roughly 24 miles from Hazard, Kentucky; 13 miles from Hindman, Kentucky; and 20 miles from Whitesburg, Kentucky. It's also approximately 81 miles from Fallport, Virginia, the home of Susan Stoker's Eagle Point Search and Rescue.

CHAPTER 1

BEAR

THE REHAB FACILITY IS QUIET TONIGHT. IT ALWAYS IS IN THE evenings, but tonight it seems especially so. I'm not sure what the difference is. When I round the corner to the correct hallway, I can hear somebody singing. I have no idea who it could be. Probably somebody who thinks they're in church.

I said rehab facility, but it's not really. I mean, it is, but it's not. It's a nursing facility. Let's just be blunt—it's where old people go to die. Once they get here, they're never going anywhere else. It's a fact. The only reason she's here is because they have their own physical therapy department, so they can work with her every day, several times a day, all on the government's dime. I'm not complaining, mind you. That's as it should be. She was injured doing government work, so they should have to pay. Even so, a broken femur, broken fibula, and cracked pelvis make for some pretty serious rehab, so she's right where she needs to be.

When I get to the door, I almost don't go in. Why I keep thinking something will change is a mystery, but I keep hoping. I knock lightly and I'm answered with, "Yeah?"

"Just me." She's in bed, lying there stiff and still, head turned so she's staring at the wall. She's that way every night. "You okay?"

"Why do you always ask me that? No. I'm not okay."

"You're more okay than you want to be."

"That's bullshit. Am I going back to work? No. So I'm not okay."

"Well, right now, you're getting up and going for a walk with me." I don't even ask, just reach over and snap the sheet off of her. She's wearing a little tee shirt, some shorts, and her socks. "Come on. Let's go."

"I don't want to."

"And I don't care. You're going. I said let's go."

The look she gives me is murderous. "If I had a gun—"

"But you don't. No point fantasizing. Come on." I stand there and wait while she finally pushes herself up to sitting. "Shoes," I say and point to the slippers by the bed, so she slides off the mattress, slips her feet into them, and stands.

"Happy now?"

"No. I'm never happy. Not so long as you're in here." My attempt to take her arm is brushed off, as usual. "Get a move on."

"Yeah, yeah. Fucking slave driver." She shuffles past me and heads toward the door, but I'm right behind her. She's not as frail as she lets on, but I'm usually close in case she loses her balance.

Once we're out in the hallway, we wander past the nurse's station, and I slip a piece of paper to the guy there. He opens it and gives me a thumbs up, so we keep going. I wrote a simple note on it.

. . .

TAKING HER FOR A MILKSHAKE. BACK IN 30.

THEY DON'T CARE AS LONG AS THEY KNOW WHERE SHE IS, and if she's with me, they know she'll be safe. As we walk past rooms, this one and that one, I glance in. It's a depressing place, and I can see why she hates it. We've offered repeatedly to let her come out to the farm, but the government insurance won't pay for therapists to make home visits, so that's out. She's stuck here, and she has been for three months.

When we reach the front door, I turn so I'm between her and the keypad and punch in the code. "What the hell are you … How do you know the code?"

"I'm here every fucking day, Sela. How do you think I get out?"

"What is it?"

I give her a gruff chuckle. "Oh, not a chance in hell. You'd be gone in twenty minutes. I'm not that stupid. Come on."

"Where are we going?"

"Just down the road. Thought you might like a change of scenery." She's walking pretty damn good, so we head to Patch's truck, and I help her into the passenger seat. Once I'm behind the wheel, I turn and grin at her. "Here we go."

The drive-in is just a few blocks down, and I slide into a stall. "Okay. I figured you'd like a milkshake, so that's why we're here."

"Is that all I can get?"

I shrug. "What do you want?"

"What do I want? I want a fucking cheeseburger, that's

what. And a Coney Island dog. And some tater tots, and some fries, and some chicken tenders. And I want a diet lemon-lime soda, and a thing of fried cheese curds, and—"

"Whoa! Hold up, hold up! What the hell, woman?"

"I'm fucking starving! Do you know what they feed us? Pretty much nothing. I don't know what they're spending their money on, but it's not food, and it's sure as hell not décor." Until this moment, I hadn't noticed, but she's lost weight—not a lot, but too much for her frame—and there's some muscle wasting too. That's mostly because she refuses to get out of bed unless it's time to go to therapy. "And *then* I want a milkshake *and* a sundae. A brownie sundae."

"Okay. You order whatever you want and I'll pay for it. Anything and everything you want."

"You're not serious."

"I'm sure as hell serious. Anything you want. Better yet, how 'bout this? Order two things. When you're halfway through with those, we'll order two more. Because it's going to be hard to eat in the truck, plus some of it will get cold."

"You're right. It will. That's a plan. I want the cheeseburger and fries first, and the soda."

"Got it. What on the burger?"

"*Everything.* If they've got rutabagas, I'll take those. Melon slices. I don't care. I want that sonofabitch loaded."

"You got it." After I place the order, I sit back and turn to look at her. "And I want you to eat every bite."

"I will. I promise. I'm dying of hunger. That's why I don't have a roommate anymore. I ate the last one."

"Oh, lord, you're a hot mess," I say and rub my eyes. "What's your physical therapist saying?"

"That I'll never be able to do the job I used to do. And frankly, if I can't, I really don't want to live anymore."

"Stop saying that. It's bullshit. There are plenty of things you could be doing."

"Yeah. School resource officer. Nope. I don't think so."

"No. There are other jobs." I'm thinking of one, but I haven't had time to talk to the right person, so I don't know about that yet. "Most of the police departments would hire you as a detective. You'd do a great job."

"I don't want to be a detective!" she barks.

"Yeah, well, I didn't want to be in prison for thirty years, but here we are." That's not true. I did want to be in prison for thirty years. I wanted to do my penance, and I still don't feel like I really did all I should've. And I didn't trust people, plus I especially didn't trust myself, so I didn't want to be out in the world. Being outside the prison walls has been hard for me, even though I'm in the best place possible now.

"Yeah, and people like me put people like you away," she announces.

"No, local yokels put me away. There were no feds anywhere around, so you can quit puffing and blowing."

"Yeah, yeah. Whatever." Fuck, I hate that word, and I refuse to respond to it, so we just sit there in silence.

In about three minutes, she says, "Hey, you didn't order yourself anything."

"Already ate. Audrey made pork chops."

"Her pork chops are good," Sela says, and there's a tone in her voice that's the sound of longing.

"Yeah. They really are. I would've brought you a plate, but I didn't know if you'd already eaten."

"Whatever I had wouldn't have been enough to ruin that dinner, I can tell you that."

"Hey there," a cute girl who looks to be maybe seventeen says as she steps up to the truck window. "Loaded cheeseburger, fries, and a diet lemon-lime?"

"Yes, ma'am." I have my debit card ready in my hand, and we swap items. "Thank you."

"Thank you. I'll be right back."

Sela's already taken the bag out of my hand, and I swear to god, she's probably going to choke with the way she's gobbling down that burger. "Slow down," I warn. "You're gonna make yourself sick."

"Oh my god, this is so good. Best hamburger I've ever eaten in my *life*. And these fries are *perfect*," she says, cramming one into her mouth. "Juss perfeh."

"Let me ask you something. Do you do the same things in PT every day?"

She nods, then answers with her mouth full. "Yeff."

"If you were on your own, could you do the same things for yourself?"

"Athalully."

"Then please, Sela, come home with me. To the farm. You can do your own physical therapy. There's plenty of room to walk and hike and get your strength back. Audrey cooks, and we always have food around. This is ridiculous. It's totally absurd for you to be hungry and alone. Stupid."

She turns and stares right at me. "You don't want me out there."

"I do. I really do. I wouldn't ask if I didn't."

There's no telling what she's about to say when she drops her hands, food and all, to her lap and stares at me. "You've been coming to see me for three months now. I've never once told you thank you, or kiss my ass, or anything. I've been nothing but harsh and demanding and whiney and bitchy. And you want me to come out to the farm and subject you to that daily?"

"Yes. I do."

"Why the hell do you want that?"

"Because. Because I'm a fucking masochist, apparently." *Man up, Miles*, my brain tells me. "Because in case you haven't noticed, I care about you."

"Well, I don't care about you," she announces.

"So is that why every time I get even remotely close to you, your nipples get hard?"

"Oh my god! Oh my god, I cannot believe you just said that to me!" she shrieks, acting all offended.

"Oh, shut the fuck up, Sela."

"Being horny is not the same as caring! You should know that!"

"Yeah, yeah. You just stick with that. You're such a cold, uncaring bitch. Whatever." Fuck, it felt good to throw that back at her.

"Oh, now you're gonna whatever *me*? Uh-huh." She crams more hamburger in her mouth. "Can't wait until I finish this so you can take me back to the old-age home. You're getting a little clingy here."

"Fuck off. I've been very clear about how I feel about you, and you can't handle it. You're so afraid of letting anybody in. Nobody means you any harm, Sela. That's all in your head."

"It's all in my head, and you're up my ass every day. Right."

"Somebody's gotta be up your ass. Otherwise, you'd just sit around and feel sorry for yourself all day long every day."

Everything she has in her hands gets shoved back into the bag. "That does it. Take me back. Right now."

"Before your ice cream?"

"Yes. Now. Fuck you."

There are words on the tip of my tongue, but I decide to

hold them and instead, I drop my forehead to the steering wheel. She's impossible—totally impossible. "Let me ask you something," I say, straightening and staring directly at her. "Who else has come to see you while you've been in the hole?"

"Natalie. Patch. Penny. Audrey."

"That's it?"

"Yeah. Why?"

"You have family. Where are they?"

"Anywhere that I'm not."

"Do you treat them the way you treat me?"

"No, they treat *me* the way I treat *you*."

"Aha. Now I'm getting a clearer picture."

"Ah, yes. You're so perceptive," she snarls under her breath.

"More so than you realize. I figured you out some time ago."

"Uh-huh. Right. Nobody's ever figured me out."

"Sure. Of course. You haven't even figured you out. How can you expect somebody else to?"

Now she's dragging the food out of the bag again, but she tosses it right back in. "For some reason, I've totally lost my appetite."

"So no ice cream?"

She shakes her head and stares out the window. "No."

"Okay then." I'm tired. She wears me out. The constant bickering isn't fun, but I do it because I care about her. I have to believe she cares about me, but she'd die before she'd ever admit it. I just start the truck, back out of the space, and head back to the shithole she's been in all this time.

When we pull up, I stop the truck, turn it off, and take the keys out. She's already letting herself out on the other side, so chivalry is unnecessary. She's staring at me like I'm daft. "Why didn't you just leave the truck running?"

"And walk up here, only for you to turn around, run back to the truck, and take off? No way. How stupid do you think I am?" Before she can speak, I snap, "Don't answer that. I really don't want to know."

"You didn't have to walk me to the door," she says.

"Oh, yes I did. Otherwise, I'd turn my back and you'd ding-dong-ditch and hoof it out to the road to hitchhike."

"You really think I'd do that?" she asks, looking at me from the corner of her eye.

"I *know* you'd do that. I have every confidence that's exactly what you'd do." The door opens and I point inside. "Go. See you later."

"I'd thank you for the burger, but I didn't get to finish it because you're an asshole." Without another word, she saunters in and the door closes behind her.

It's not far to the farm, but it's dark now, and I'm paying close attention to the road. I hate driving at night. Funny, I don't remember it being a challenge before I went to prison, but now that I'm out, it's hard to see. Patch said he thinks I should check into getting glasses. Yay. Just another way to make me even less attractive. I really don't need help in that department.

I'm about halfway home when I decide to turn on the radio, but it's just an FM band thing, and it's not set to a particular channel. From what I can tell, I'm the first person who's ever tried to listen to it. I'm doodling with the dial and checking the road, and I think I've almost got it …

Something blinds me, and I look up to find a car heading straight toward me. Instinct kicks in—I yank the wheel to the right, and when I do, I realize there's a huge ditch. I'm jarred forward, and there's the sensation of something flying over my head …

* * *

SELA

I SWEAR TO GOD, HE'S ABSOLUTELY DETERMINED THAT HE'S going to make me feel something for him.

Problem is, I already do.

Bear is the closest thing to perfect that I've ever found. Good-looking, but not so good-looking that he's conceited. Taller, way taller, than me—believe it or not, a lot of guys aren't. Smart, a lot smarter than people give him credit for, and a lot smarter than he thinks I believe him to be. I'd never let him know that I think he's smart. He'd be unbearable.

But persistent? I swear to god, I've never met anybody more persistent than that motherfucker. He just doesn't quit. No matter how hard I try to run him off, he just won't go. I don't know if he thinks I've thrown down the gauntlet and he's accepted the challenge or what, but he cannot stop. His mind is made up that he's going to wear me down, and I do believe he'll keep going until I finally just kill myself to keep him from bothering me anymore. I mean, last night proved that this is a guy who isn't above plying me with cheese-burgers and ice cream. Sneaky bastard.

And then I think back to those two nights we spent together in the lodge. Holy hell, that guy's got a monster cock, best I've ever had. I'd never tell him that, but it's true. And he's one helluva lover. He knows exactly what he's doing, and how that's possible, given all the years he spent in the slammer, I don't know, but he really does know his way around a woman's body. Just thinking about it makes me so fucking horny that I can barely—

"Ms. Baldwin? Did you hear me?" Kimberly, the physical therapist, is staring at me like I'm mental.

"Uh, no. What did you say?"

"I said, we've got to work on your flexion and extension for your knees. Do you want to use the rowing machine, or would you rather do something else?"

"I'd rather do anything else, honestly."

"Yes, ma'am, I know, but we have to do it. I know you hate it."

"Hate is such a weak word. Loathe. Despise. Abhor. There are so many more powerful words that describe it, don't you think?"

"Ms. Baldwin, please. We've only got twenty more minutes, and I won't see you again until Thursday."

"Then let me go back to my room and read. I promise I won't bother you again for the rest of the week."

She rolls her eyes. "Oh, you're a funny one, Ms. Baldwin. Very funny."

"Yes. I am. Ha. Haha. I'm going back to my room now. Thank you, Kimberly. It's been an excellent session." I just get up and start out the door.

"But Ms. Baldwin …" I don't wait to hear whatever else it is that she's going to say because I really don't care.

By nine o'clock, I've had dinner, a shower, and I've watched the only three shows we can get on the TV here, since we don't have cable. And Bear's never shown up. That's weird. Maybe I finally managed to run him off. I might as well go to bed. Nothing exciting's happening here. Nothing ever does.

Unless a patient codes. And then at least we get to hear beeping.

BEAR

IT'S BRIGHT. SO, SO BRIGHT. I HEAR PEOPLE TALKING, BUT I can't open my eyes enough to see anything, just the brightness. And my head hurts. I'm going back to sleep …

CHAPTER 2

SUNDAY DINNER IS SOME KIND OF MYSTERY MEAT—I THINK it's supposed to be meatloaf—and mashed potatoes. All of the food is made for people without teeth. The bad part is that if you came in with teeth, by the time they get finished with you, you won't have any. No wonder everything they cook is soft. They're getting us ready for the inevitable.

Thank god for weekends. There's no physical therapist, so I don't have to mess with the ever-cheerful Kimberly. Sometimes I'd like to punch her lights out. Somebody's managed to find *Wheel of Fortune* on the TV in the game room, and there are like twenty people in wheelchairs in there, watching. It would be nice to watch, but I can't stand all the fucking togetherness, so I'm going back to my room.

Once I get there, I go to the bathroom, then climb back up on the bed. Four walls, off-white. Not a picture, not a poster, nothing. The curtains are drab beige. The ceiling is those stupid tiles with the holes poked in them, and they've got water stains on them everywhere. We won't even talk about the bathroom. It's beyond pitiful. I actually take my showers down the hall in the big communal bathroom where they shower the people in wheelchairs. Sure, I'm terrified of foot funk, but it's better than the shower in my room.

I've managed to drift off a bit, listening to some music on my iPad with my headphones, when I hear a sound and open my eyes. Someone's in my room, and when I finally manage to focus, I smile. "Hey!"

"Hi. I knocked, but you must not-a been able to hear me. You listenin' to some tunes?" Tinsley asks.

"Yeah, yeah. There's not much else to do around here, ya know. What are you doing here?"

"I just wanted to come see ya. The last time I seen ya, I was big as a house! Now I'm back to my little skinny self," she says and twirls.

"You look good! How's that baby?"

"Oh, he's amazin'. But I needed a few minutes away, and Bulldog said, 'Why don't you go check on Sela? You ain't seen her in a while.' So here I am! You doin' okay?"

"Eh. Good days and bad days."

"Yeah. I know all about bad days." She stops, and I get the feeling something's wrong and she's afraid to tell me. "Bad days all over the damn place."

Something in her tone sets off an alarm in my chest. "Tinsley, is something wrong?"

"I don't know how to tell ya this … Bear's in the hospital."

I feel a twisting sensation in my gut. "What? He's in the hospital? Is he sick?"

"No. He was comin' back from here Tuesday night and had a wreck. Guy was tryin' to pass another car comin' towards him and almost hit him head on. He took the ditch and flipped Patch's truck. Destroyed the truck. He's been …" A tear rolls down Tinsley's cheek. "He's been in a coma ever since."

"Oh my god." It's hard to breathe all of a sudden, and the room is getting spotty. "Oh my god, Tinsley. Oh my god. Coma? He's … He hasn't woken up?"

She shakes her head and wipes her eyes with the backs of her hands, smearing her mascara in the process. "No. They're watchin' him real close. We don't know if he's gonna be okay or not."

I am a bitch. The absolute worst bitch.

The idea that I may never see him again makes everything clear to me. What the fuck is wrong with me? To have gone through all he has, he's about the purest soul I've ever known, and I've treated him horribly. He came around when he knew I was going to eat him alive, and he did it anyway because he didn't want me to be alone. And now he's lying in a hospital room somewhere, between life and death, and I'm lying here feeling sorry for myself. Without another thought I blurt out, "I have to see him. Can you take me? Please? I have to."

"Honey, I don't think I can. I don't have time. I told Bulldog I'd run over here to see ya and then come back home. Hey, come to the farm with me. Somebody from out there can take ya to the hospital. I'll have to go nurse Patrick, but we can find ya a ride. Okay? Ya got some clothes?"

"Not much of anything. Mostly pajamas."

"Come on. You can wear somethin'-a mine if'n we can find somethin' that we don't have to worry about length, since you're way taller than me. Ya know, like a dress or somethin'." I haven't worn a dress in probably twenty-five years. "Ya wanna?"

"Yes. Yes, I do. You'll have to check me out at the desk."

"Consider it done. Let's go. Get yore slippers on and we'll head out."

The nurse working the desk starts to give Tinsley some trouble, but the little spitfire says, "Wanda, I 'member when ya didn't have a pot to piss in ner a winder to throw it outta. Ya gonna give me trouble 'bout takin' a friend to the hospital to see another friend? That's kinda low, ya know? Just gimme the damn sheet." A minute later, the sheet is filled out, Wanda is still scowling, and we're hurrying out the door.

She throws the cottage door open and the baby is squalling. "Where the hell you been?" Bulldog snarls.

"Talkin' this crazy woman into comin' back with me. Go raid my closet, honey. Find somethin' to wear. I'm sorry, baby. Let me have him. He's prolly hungry."

"Yeah, he kept trying to suck the buttons on my shirt. Not very productive."

"Nope. Not like Mama's knockers. Come here, little man. Got yore dinner right here." I can hear slurping and smacking, and then I wonder if the baby gets anything or if Bulldog gets it all. That thought makes me chuckle under my breath, especially since I hear Bulldog walk out the front door.

There's a dress hanging there, kind of like a long tee shirt, and that looks promising. "You got any leggings?"

"Yeah. Second dresser drawer on the left. Help yoreself."

I open it to find about two dozen pairs of leggings. Then I remember that she wears them to work just about every day. The dress is an odd green color, so I pick out a pair of black ones and pull them on. They only come about halfway down my calf, but that's okay. There's no way she has shoes to fit me. Her foot is tiny, and I wear a nine. Maybe whoever takes me to the hospital can run me by the discount store and I can get a pair of flats.

"Do I look okay?" I ask as I step out of the bedroom into

the living area. The baby is sucking like a maniac, and he's so adorable with his little fists clenched.

"Ya look fine. Somebody'll have a jacket you can wear. It's a lil' nippy out."

"Yeah. Fall's coming on like gangbusters," I answer.

"Ya want some jewelry? God knows I got plenty."

I shake my head. "Nah. That's okay."

"Suit yaself."

"Where'd Bulldog go?"

Tinsley makes a face. "Okay, I'm just gonna lay it all out here. Most-a the guys ain't real fond of ya."

No surprise there. "Why? Because I'm a strong woman who won't take their shit?"

"No. Because you're a strong woman who's pushed Bear back and forth like a bossy lumberjack with a two-man cross-cut. They ain't happy 'bout it."

At least she's honest with me. I'd rather have that than somebody who tells me they just don't like the way I chew my food or something. "Thanks for laying that out."

"Yore welcome. Honesty is the best policy."

Now I don't know what to do. Do I go over to the kitchen and see if anybody can take me? Wait for Tinsley to finish with the baby? There's a knock at the door. "Mind gettin' that? Kinda busy here," she says.

The door opens and I find Patch standing there. "Sure wasn't expecting to see you," he says.

"Oh. No hi or how ya doin'?"

"Hi. How ya doin? There. That's outta the way. And you're doing what here?"

"Trying to find a ride to the hospital."

"Why? You hurt?" I give him my best "fuck you" look. "I think that was a fair question, considering."

"Yeah, okay. Fine. I get it. Can somebody take me or not?

Because I can call an Uber … No. I can't call an Uber. This is bumfucking Egypt for all intents and purposes. So can I get a ride? I'm not going to beg, so—"

"Oh, I was so looking forward to that," he says with a smirk.

"Nope. Not happenin'. Taking me or not?"

"I know *he* would want me to, so yes. I'm taking you." Without another word, he turns and starts away.

"Guess I'm going. Thanks, Tinsley."

"Yore welcome, hon. I ain't been able to go to the hospital like I'd like, so please give him a kiss on the cheek for me."

"Yeah, okay. Bye."

Now I have to catch up with Patch, and he's walking pretty fast. Probably intentional. No, he doesn't look back to see where I am, so I *know* it's intentional. When I do catch up, I'm huffing and puffing. "Good to see you're on your feet, but it sounds like you should've done a little more PT to get some physical conditioning."

"I'm still in better shape than you," I counter, my breathing even more labored.

"You do *not* want to get into that pissing contest. Audrey said she's got a jacket in there that you can wear. It's hanging behind the door. Grab it and let's go."

I jet inside, grab the jacket, and slip it on as I close the door behind me. Patch is still standing there. "You look like you dressed out of a Goodwill donation bag." Unfortunately, I pick that moment to look down at my feet, and he does too. "Those the only shoes you have?"

"Unless you've still got some of my things over in the lodge."

He stops, cocks his head a little, and squints. "You know, we might have. I don't know if they cleaned everything out or not. You can look when you get back. Right now, we need to get going. Taking you to the hospital was not on my to-do list for today, so we're burning daylight." *Well, tell me I'm inconveniencing you without telling me I'm inconveniencing you, why don'tcha?*

As soon as I slip into the passenger seat of the big SUV, Patch turns to me. "Let's get something straight right now while it's just you and me. You hurt him and I will personally beat the holy hell out of you, and I've never hit a woman in my life, but I can promise you that."

"I can't hurt him. He's unconscious."

"They say patients can often hear what's going on around them. If he can, you'd better be decent or I swear to god, I'll drag you out of that hospital room and body slam you up against a brick wall so fast your head will explode. I'm not kidding."

"Aye-aye, captain," I say and give him a two-fingered salute.

"Don't be a smart-ass."

"I'm not! Shit. Guess I can't say anything right around any of you."

"Most likely not." He's already backed out and pulling out of the drive onto the road.

As we drive along, I remember something. "Hey, isn't there a Dollar Gentral up here somewhere?" I ask, mimicking Tinsley's name for it.

"Yeah."

"I could get some shoes there."

"They don't have much to choose from."

I take off one of my slippers and hold it up. "Anything they've got is better than this."

His nose wrinkles upward. "Put that damn thing back on. At least when it's on your foot I can't smell it."

A sniff tells me it doesn't smell. "Yeah, whatever." That

earns me an eye roll. "So, what's going on at the farm these days?"

"Bear's been coming to see you every evening, but you … Oh, yeah. You told him you didn't give a shit what's going on out there, so you have no idea. I'm right, right? Am I right?"

"Yes! Okay! You're right! Now, are you going to answer my question or not?"

"Fine. So Priest is with Aggie—"

"What's an aggie?"

"Not what. Who. She's a teacher over at the middle school. Nice lady. You'd try to rip her to shreds and she'd put your ass in place in about two seconds. Got herself shot too and still kickin'."

"Nice."

"And Reboot found out he has a kid who's now at the farm with us."

Well, there's a shocker. "Mr. Congeniality had a kid he didn't know about?"

"Yeah, a twelve-year-old boy."

"Holy shit! Well, hello, Daddy."

"Exactly. Lisa showed up a few weeks ago and dumped Tegan and Borden on Paddy, so he and Natalie have them now."

"What happened there?"

"Seems she'd been pressuring him about seeing the boys all these years so he'd take them when he got out. No one knew she and Luke had been having problems all along, and she just took off."

"Nat's gotta be losing her shit over that."

He shakes his head. "Nope. She's a natural. And she loves those kids."

"Wow. Lots of kids showing up. Hey, did they ever get that ratty-ass boat running?"

"It's beautiful, and yeah. Took it out for a maiden voyage a few weeks ago. Reboot's in heaven with that thing. Oh, and he and Mavis got married."

"Yeah? That's cool."

"Yeah, and Bulldog gave Tinsley a ring." Knowing that makes me hurt somehow. I just spent at least an hour with her and she never mentioned it or showed it to me. That's the moment when I realize something important.

Everybody at the farm hates me. I get that now. I was damn near killed trying to protect Natalie, but that doesn't count. "That doesn't count," I mutter under my breath.

"What?" Patch asks.

"What?"

"Did you say something?"

Fuck. "Uh, I don't think so."

"It sounded like you said, 'That doesn't count.' Is that what you said?"

Frustration. That's what I've been feeling the most of for the past three months, and now it's really hitting me. "Yes! That's what I said! I damn near died trying to protect Natalie, but that doesn't count for anything. Everybody at that farm hates me anyway."

"We don't hate you. Nobody hates you, Sela. We just hate the way you act, especially toward Bear. Look, we keep our mouths shut around him because we know he doesn't want to explain and doesn't want to admit he feels anything for you, because it's humiliating to him that he could care about somebody who treats him so badly. He's been afraid that if he told us how he feels about you, we'd all make fun and ask him why he cares anything about a raving bitch who's obviously using him."

"Using him? What about me? Don't you think he was using me?" I snap.

Patch's face is a blank slate when he answers, "No, Sela. I do not."

God damn it! Are they all trying to make me feel like shit? Because everything every one of them says to me does that very thing. I see the giant yellow and black sign up the highway. "Please, just let me go in there and get some shoes."

"Sure." He whips into the parking lot and throws the SUV out of gear. "Here. You'll need this. PIN is four three four five," he says and hands me his debit card. Good thinking. I have no money.

I run in to look around, and I find these canvas shoes that are knockoffs of Converse All Stars, so I grab a pair in my size, run to the register, and pay. Once I get in the truck, I hand back his card and start putting them on. They're not really comfortable, but at least they're clean and new. I've gotten them tied and I'm taking a good look at them when Patch says, "You're welcome."

"Oh. Sorry. Thank you."

We ride the rest of the way in silence. Talking to anyone exhausts me, especially since virtually everything I have to say has to be an attempt to defend myself in some way. The only person I routinely talk to is Bear, and we don't really talk, just sling barbs at each other or kinda grunt. When we pull into the hospital parking lot, I rest my hand on the door handle. "I won't be long."

Patch is already getting out. "Oh, no. You're not going into his room by yourself. I'm not having that."

"What? What's your point?"

"My point is that I don't want you saying anything to him that would upset him if he can hear you."

"What the hell do you think I might say to him?"

The veins on his neck are pulsing and I can see that he's losing patience with me. "Sela, we never know what's going to come out of your mouth, but we can usually bet on it being demeaning, degrading, negative, or hateful. I'm not having you talk to him like that. Nope."

That's a bit shocking. "You don't think I'd really do that."

"Honestly, I wouldn't put anything past you." He's out and slamming the truck door, so I open mine and slide out. Wow. Their opinion of me really *is* awful. If I'm honest with myself, I deserve it, but I'd rather lie to myself and tell myself that they're completely unjustified in their opinion.

The hospital is quiet for a Sunday afternoon, and we walk on past the main desk and to the elevator. This is a tiny hospital without a lot of amenities, but I guess if you're lying there in a coma, you're not using much in the way of resources. It has four floors, and apparently he's on the second, so it's a short ride up. When we step off, I follow Patch as he heads to the left, and we make our way down the quiet corridors, Patch occasionally nodding to a nurse or orderly as we pass.

He stops outside a door and says, "Mind yourself, Sela. I don't want to remove you from this room, but I will if I see the need." It's obvious from his tone that he means it, so I make the decision that if I have to fight him, a hospital room isn't the place. I'll do my best to behave until I can meet him on a better battleground.

Patch pushes the door open and I step inside. Why do people always look so small in hospital beds? He looks tiny. I step up beside the bed and I'm surprised. Bear's always worn a little scruff, but it's grown a good bit in the last few days, and it actually looks good on him. What am I supposed to do? His hands are lying by his sides, so I pick up the one near me and hold it. It feels cool until our palms meet, and his palm is warm, so I grip his hand and look down into his face.

"Surprise! Bet you never expected to hear from me," I whisper, but he doesn't move. "I would've been here sooner, but I didn't know. Nobody told me. So I'm sorry I haven't been here, but I'm here now. I thought I'd finally run you off! Wish I'd called. Or something." My free hand rises and I stroke down his cheek. "There wasn't anybody for me to torment, so I'm glad to find you. Please wake up. Please? It's okay. If you don't wake up, I'll be here anyway. But I want you to wake up. Wake up, damn it! Bear, please? Wake up!"

A voice from across the room says, "Sela …"

"No! He has to wake up! I have to talk to him. Please, Bear? Please?" I've never felt so helpless in my life.

"Sela, calm down." From behind me, Patch presses his hands to my upper arms and grips them tightly. "Calm down. Look, take this chair and pull it up to the bed. Just sit with him. That's what he needs now." When his hands disappear, I hear the scraping sound of the chair being moved, and I look up to see him pointing. "I put it over there so if they need to come in and do something for him, you're not in the way. You can just sit over there and hold his hand. He'd like that."

My legs feel wooden as I stumble around the foot of the bed, and I find the chair and plop down in it. Once I'm settled, I take his hand again. "You want something to drink?" Patch asks.

"Yeah. I'd like a diet lemon-lime if there is any."

"I'm sure I can find one. I'll be right back."

Once I hear him walk away, I stand again and lean down over the man in the bed. "Look, you big wooly mammoth, I … I'll miss you if you don't wake up, you understand? You need to wake up so I can actually tell you that. I know men never listen, but this is taking it to the extreme just a bit, don't you think? I'd really like to—"

His eyes fly open, and then they rotate toward me.

"Holy shit! HOLY SHIT! He's awake! Hey, somebody!" I'm looking for that call button thing, but I don't see it anywhere. It's probably under him. One of his hands rises and reaches for the ventilator tube. "No. Don't touch that. They'll get it. Nurse! NURSE! I need somebody right—"

"What's going on?" a woman in blue scrubs covered with cartoons of cats asks.

"He's awake!"

"Oh! Let me get the doctor. Mr. McMillan, we'll take out the ventilator tube, but the doctor has to be here. Let me get somebody, okay? Just hang on. It'll be all right. We'll get it out in a jiffy." And she hustles away.

His eyes are wild, and I know he's bound to be confused. "Hey, hey, it's okay. I'm right here." When I grab his hand, he locks mine in a death grip. "It's gonna be okay. They're coming back to take it out."

"They didn't have any lemon-lime in diet, so I … What the fuck have you done, Sela?" Patch screams at me.

"Nothing! He's awake! Look!"

Patch sets the drink on the credenza and crosses the room to look down into Bear's face. The big man's eyes are like saucers. "Hey, buddy. I'm here too. It's okay." He glances up at me. "Did you call somebody?"

"Yeah. The nurse said a doctor has to be here for them to take that tube out, so she's gone to find somebody. She'll be back in a minute." As I talk to him, my eyes never leave Bear. His grip on my hand conveys all the panic I know he feels. It's bound to be confusing. "Hey, it's gonna be okay. I promise. Just wait."

There's a rustling sound and a voice says, "Hi! I'm

Dr. Lindell. Mr. McMillan, is it? Let's see what's going on. Ella, vitals?"

"BP's one ten over seventy, pulse is seventy-five."

"Your vitals are good. Let's get this tube out and see how you fare." The doctor turns and looks at Patch and me. "Could you guys please step out into the hallway?"

Patch gives her a nod. "Sure." But my feet feel like they're glued to the floor. "Sela, come on." For the first time I can recall, I let somebody take my arm and lead me out of a room.

When I get to the hallway, I can't breathe. It's like the walls are collapsing in on me and smothering me. Patch's familiar voice says, "Sela, breathe. Just take a deep breath, hold it, count to three, and let it out. It's gonna be okay. He's gonna be okay. Close your eyes and breathe, honey." Even though he's not touching me, I can feel him right beside me, and my heartbeat slows a little. "Thatta girl. There ya go." From somewhere inside the room there's a monstrous amount of coughing. "Aha. They got the tube out."

I can hear them chatting and a few seconds later, the doctor appears in the doorway. "You can go back in now. He's going to be fine. He'll have a sore throat for a few days, and probably cough a bit, but otherwise, it's okay."

"Can he go home?" Patch asks.

"Not for a couple of days. We're going to need to do a few scans, see if we find anything still going on, but this is Sunday, so I'm going to say he'll probably get to go home … Wednesday? Yeah. Let's just say that and we'll see. But go on in. I'm sure he's glad to see you."

"Thank you, doctor," Patch answers, but I just dart past and head straight for the bed.

As soon as I reach it, I take his hand, and his head rotates toward me. "Hey. How ya feelin'?"

After a couple of attempts during which nothing comes out, he finally manages to whisper, "What happened?"

"Wreck. You totaled Patch's truck."

"Hey, buddy," Patch says as he steps back up to the bedside. "You okay?"

"Throat hurts," he forces out.

"I'm sure it does."

"What day is it?"

"It's Sunday," Patch answers.

"I'm … what? Sunday?"

"You dropped me off Tuesday and it happened on your way home," I explain.

It's like he's thinking about it, and then he says, "The drive-in. No ice cream."

"Exactly. You remember." Without even thinking about it, I reach up and smooth his hair from his face.

"The truck …" Bless his heart, he seems totally bewildered.

"They said you were driving down a straightaway and some guy coming toward you tried to pass the car in front of him. He was coming straight at you, and you took the ditch," Patch tells him.

"They said?"

Patch nods. "Yeah. The emergency workers. Took them a while to get you out of the truck."

"Truck? How's truck?"

"Gone. There's nothing left, but don't worry about that. I can get another truck, but there's only one you. And you were lucky you weren't hurt worse. But it doesn't seem like you broke anything. Just a pretty serious concussion that left you unconscious for all this time. We've been worried."

He lies there staring at the ceiling, almost like he can't believe what's being said to him, and I feel horrible for him.

Having gaps in your memory isn't fun, and I should know. I still don't know what was going on with me for the first two weeks after the fall. I just remember bits and pieces. It's weird, knowing you were alive but having no recollection of anything that happened. He interrupts my thoughts with, "You? Out?"

"Tinsley signed me out. Had to get rugged with the woman at the desk, but she did it. These are her clothes. I didn't have anything to wear." That's the understatement of the century. Everything I own is in my apartment in Atlanta, and I've been paying rent and utilities all this time for a place I can't even go to. I've got to remember to check at the lodge to see if the things I'd brought are still there, since Patch didn't know. Speaking of … I turn to look at him. "Could I talk to him alone for a minute?"

"Remember what I said," he cautions.

"I haven't forgotten. It'll be fine. I'll behave." That earns me another eye roll, but he steps outside the door and closes it, so I turn to Bear. "Do you want me to come and stay at the farm?"

"Told you before," he manages.

"Then I will if you still want me to. Somebody will have to get me out of the hellhole, but I'll come and stay there to be with you if that's still what you want." He nods. "Okay. I'll talk to Patch about it on the way back."

To my surprise, he reaches for my hand and clutches it tightly. "No. Don't go."

"I have to. They'll be looking for me at the torture chamber. But I'll talk to Patch and see what we can do. Maybe by the time you get out of here, I can be at the farm. And I'll be back. I promise. I don't have a car, but I'll figure something out."

"Guys'll bring you."

"Yeah. Somebody will, I hope. I should probably let Patch in before he has a stroke. He's just sure that I'm talking trash to you in here."

I head for the door, but just as I reach it, he calls out softly, "Sela?"

"Yeah?" I say, spinning to face him.

"I love you too."

Fuck. He heard me. Is that why he woke up? There's no point in arguing about it. He heard me, and he cut through all the clutter to hear what I was really saying. I just smile and open the door.

I'm so screwed.

CHAPTER 3

SELA

"Yeah, okay. I'll hold." For a government agency with a multi-billion-dollar budget, they have sucky hold music.

Just when I'm about to give up, the music ends and a voice asks, "Whaddya want, Sela?"

"You know what I want. You've talked to the physical therapist. So when can I come back to work?"

"I talked to the physical therapist, and she didn't have very good things to say about your recovery, Sela. Seems you haven't been following her plan of treatment."

"I hate physical therapy. I can do it myself."

"Unfortunately, that's not going to cut it."

"Why not? Why do I have to—"

"Sela, I'm going to be blunt with you. You're not coming back out into the field, not with your injuries. That's over." Uh-huh. I knew it. All my suspicions are now confirmed.

"When you get the all clear from your physical therapist, we'll start working to find you something in the—"

"Wait, wait. What do you mean, I'm not going back out into the field?"

"I think that's what I just said. I know that's not what you want to hear, but—"

"That's unacceptable, Andrew."

"It's just how it is, Sela. I've tried to tell you that in a roundabout way, but you won't listen, so I've just got to be plain. If you come back to the bureau, it'll be at a desk job or in a training position. You will *not* be back out in the field. End of discussion."

"What if I—"

"Sela, no. Nope. The decision has been made. We're coming up with a list of possible positions, but none of them will be in the field."

"I'll just talk to Markowitz and he'll—"

"He's helping to compile the list, so you'll get no backing there."

Markowitz has bailed on me too. My former partner doesn't have my back. Nice—real nice. "So I give the bureau the best years of my life, almost gave it my life, and this is how I'm thanked. Abandoned. Put out to pasture."

"It's not like that, Sela. We're looking for a position for you. Your expertise is valuable, and it can be utilized in a lot of different way, but not that one."

"What, are you afraid of me carrying a gun? Or that I've somehow forgotten what I'm supposed to be doing?"

"No. We're more afraid of a partner needing your backup and you being physically unable to provide it."

"Oh, so tell me you don't trust me to do my job without telling me you don't trust me to do my job."

"It's not about trusting you to do your job. It's about the

fact that we don't think we can trust your ability to do your job."

"Have I ever let you down before?"

"No, but have you ever come back from injuries this severe before? No. You haven't. So even you don't know how you're going to perform. And I think if you're honest with yourself, you'll admit that your physical abilities aren't what they were before the accident."

"Of course they're not! I almost died! But that doesn't mean I'm going to be in this shape forever!"

"From what the physical therapist says, you are, because you're non-compliant, so you're really not making that much progress."

I don't believe this. They're taking her word over mine? Like she's in this body. She has no idea how I feel or what I can do. "Okay, well, get back to me with that list of possibilities. And thanks."

"You're welcome. I'm hoping we can find something you'll be happy with. And do what that therapist tells you! Talk to you soon."

You know what I miss? I miss the ability to slam a phone receiver down on a cradle, because that's exactly what I'd do. Instead, I just hold my cell phone in a death grip and thrash around with my teeth clenched. God damn them! I was doing my job, I got hurt, and my whole world is gone. What the hell am I going to do?

I talked to Patch on the way home from the hospital yesterday, and he said if Bear wants me at the farm, I'm welcome to move in. But there's one call I have to make before I can do that. Her voicemail kicks in, so I just leave a short message. "Hey, it's Sela. Please call me back when you can. Thanks." There's time for a shower before dinner, but I really don't want to miss her return call.

When the phone rings, I give a little start. "Wow. That was quick."

"I'm leaving for the day. What's up?"

"I felt like I owed it to you to check with you … Um, you know Bear is awake."

"Of course! Everybody does."

"Yeah, well, um, he asked me if I'd move in with him out there at the farm. But I wanted to talk with you first."

"About?"

"Is that going to cause you any problems? PTSD? Flashbacks? Just having me around?"

Based on the hesitation before she answers, she sounds appropriately taken aback. "No. Why would it?"

"Because it was a traumatic experience, and I don't want you reliving that every time you see me."

"Sela, there's no way that would happen. You're the reason I'm still alive," Natalie says. "If anything, I'd be glad to see you there. But isn't that going to leave him in a bad place when you go back to work?"

Trying to explain what's going on with that would be a nightmare. "Um, I'm not sure when I'm going back to work."

"Have they determined that your disability is permanent?" she asks, and there's no way I'm going to tell her what Andrew Rosnick said to me.

"No. It's just that I'm thinking I need a change of pace." *That sounded pretty good. Just stick with that,* I tell myself. "I just wanted to make sure it wasn't going to be painful or awkward for you."

"Nope. You don't have to worry about me. With the boys there all the time now, I don't have time to dwell on the past. I have to keep moving forward."

"Okay then. As long as you're okay with it, I'll talk to him again. Thanks, Natalie."

"You're welcome."

Well, that settles that. Looks like I'm going to be the newest resident of Iron Oak Farms.

***

BEAR

"I'M NOT HERE BECAUSE I'M HAVING TROUBLE WITH MY JAW, my teeth, or my stomach. Could I *please* get some real food?"

The nurse isn't my type, but she's cute. And she's way too young for me anyway. "I'll see what I can do. I think they were afraid you were a choking hazard."

"Not unless they think I'm going to choke myself. Mashed potatoes would be fine. I just don't want another cup of broth or gelatin."

"Yeah, I think you need some real food."

From somewhere out in the hallway, a voice calls, "Hey, Christa, did that patient over in two eighty-one go home? I've got a dinner for him."

That makes my nurse smile. "Yeah. He was discharged this morning. Here—I'll take that," she says and steps to the doorway to take the tray from the other lady. Then she turns and winks at me as she heads toward me. "See? All you had to do was ask!"

"Thank you. I appreciate it."

"And a meal doesn't go to waste. I think it's a win/win, don't you?"

That makes me chuckle. "I do! Not a bite of it will be wasted, I can promise you that!"

"Good. Eat up. I'll pick up your tray later." And she disappears, leaving me there with a tray of hot food.

Let's see … I think that thing is supposed to be a pork chop. Oh, green beans! That's good. And sure enough, mashed potatoes and gravy. Finally! A decent meal. At least sixty-six percent of it is anyway.

I've taken the first bite when a voice says, "You must be feeling better if they're letting you eat."

"Hey! Grab a seat. I'm starving, so I hope you don't care if I keep eating," I say, watching Patch pull the chair up closer to the bed.

"No, you just go right ahead. I'm glad to see you able to eat. You're bound to be as hollow as a drum."

"I am. I needed this. What brings you here?"

"I wanted to check on you, for one thing. Doin' okay?"

"Yeah. Doing fine. Hoping they'll let me go home tomorrow," I say just before I poke a forkful of potatoes into my mouth.

"That would be good. Don't know if you could go back to work straightaway, but—"

"I don't know why not."

"You have a very dangerous job, and I'd hate for you to get hurt. That's the last thing we need. I'd rather you waited a week or two and got your feet back under you before you step back into the glass studio."

"So you don't want me to work?"

"No. It's nothing like that. It's just that I want you to be safe. That's all." His tone is calm and his face is smooth. He's not being angry or argumentative, and he's not challenging me. He's also not pitying me. I can tell that in his thinking, this is just a very matter-of-fact decision, and I'm going to take it as something he's doing for my good, or at least what he honestly thinks he needs to do. I get it. And that's fine. I'm not going to make a fuss over it, but it will put me weeks behind on my orders. I guess folks will just have to understand.

"I respect that, and I thank you for it." Maybe I'm wrong, but it seems like he wants to say something else. "Is something on your mind?"

"Yes. Do you really want Sela to move to the farm with you?"

"I do. What are you getting at?"

"She has it in her head that we all hate her, and we don't. At first, I thought maybe she hated all of us and she was projecting her feelings onto us, but now I'm not so sure. Might as well tell you that I told her we don't hate her, just hate the way she treats you."

"She loves me." There's no way for me to explain it. I just know it to be true like I know my own name.

"Could've fooled me."

"Yeah, well, she tried to fool me, but it didn't work. I've seen a side of Sela that you haven't seen."

"And I want to keep it that way," Patch says with a smirk.

"Not that side, although it's pretty impressive." The memory makes me grin. Those two nights we shared were something I'll never forget. The woman wanted, and I gave. After thirty years in prison, I was afraid I'd forgotten how with a woman, but it all came rushing back, along with all the stuff I'd read and watched in the meantime. And there was a lot. I wish I could recreate a couple of those porn videos. I know people say they're not real, but they were pretty spectacular.

"Look, I don't care as long as you can handle the rejection when she totally flakes on you."

That pisses me off just a little. "What makes you think she's going to flake on me? Am I all that bad? I know I'm not much to look at, but—"

"It has nothing to do with how you look, which, by the way, more than a couple of the women at the farm have indicated is, as they've said, pretty damn hot. Their words, not mine." He looks a little repulsed even saying it out loud. Looking for a straight guy? Patch Scott is definitely that guy.

This is interesting too. "Which women?"

"Nope. Not going there. Just know that they … I should just stop right here. The point is, it's not you. I'm just not convinced that Sela can … connect that way. Make a lasting bond. It's not about being faithful. It's about … being attached."

"Let me worry about that."

Patch shrugs. "Okay. As long as you can handle it."

"I can. I've handled a lot worse."

Patch shakes his head. "Nothing's much worse than being rejected by somebody you love."

"Like I said, my rodeo, my bull."

"Okay. It's up to you. She's welcome there. Of course, you'll have to spring her from the dungeon, and I'm wondering if you do that how the FBI will respond. If she doesn't finish that treatment plan, she probably won't have a job."

I'd already thought of that, and that's something she and I will have to talk about. I want her to do what she thinks she needs to do, but she's not going to sit around doing nothing and feeling sorry for herself. That can't happen. "We'll talk about it."

"Can you just tell me … How the hell did the two of you get together?"

I close my eyes and think back. We were all in the kitchen, eating dinner, and she was across the room. You know how it feels when somebody's staring at you and you can feel their eyes on you? That's how it was. I glanced up and our eyes met, and that was it. When everybody got ready for bed, I went back to the lodge and tapped on her door. The door swung open slowly, and she motioned for me to come in. As soon as the door closed, she dropped that robe and, holy hot hell, everything I thought I knew flew out the window. Her body is lean and hard, and she slid it up against mine perfectly. That first time, I fucked her so hard that she pressed her hands to the wall to keep me from slamming her into it. If there had been a headboard on the bed, I would've tied her to it. A woman that strong, that flexible, that sexy … damn, I want her so bad. But all I say to Patch is, "I'm not sure. It just happened."

"Uh-huh. Okay. Well, anyway, if she can handle you, I'm sure you can handle her."

That makes me laugh. "If she can't handle me, I'll sure teach her how!"

"You do that," he says with a grin, then rises from the chair. "I guess I'd better get back. Reboot volunteered to take Fiona over to the boarding stable to take care of the horse or I wouldn't have gotten to come see you. Everybody's busting their asses these days between work and the team and all these kids showing up out of nowhere." Before I can say anything, he blurts out, "Not that I mind. Not at all. I love having them all there. But it's all happened so fast, and we're all still trying to adjust, what with Paddy's two and now Martin and the baby … It's crazy around there."

Kids. Something I'll never have. I made my peace with that years ago. And something tells me that kids are something Sela has never really thought much about. Matter of fact, Sela being somebody's mother is just about as bizarre a thought as I can entertain. "I get it. If you really want me to take it easy for a week or two after I get out, maybe I can help pick up some of the slack, you know, drive kids around or babysit or something."

"I'm telling you, Sarah and Lenny have been godsends. They've decided all those kids are their grandkids, and they've come through every time we've needed them. And Tony and Nikki have been talking about coming and staying for a few days to get to know Borden, Tegan, and Martin a little better, and to do some training with Fi and her horse. I think Nikki wants to get her hands on that baby," Patch says and laughs. That makes me laugh too. Thinking about Nikki Walters fretting that there's a baby she hasn't gotten to hold is funny. Sounds just like something she'd do.

"You know she's probably worrying the shit outta Tony to bring her and let her see him," I say with a snort.

"You know it! Well, buddy, you eat that food there, if you can call it that—"

"Closest thing to real food that I've had since I've been here, so don't knock it!" I bark, laughing.

"Gotcha! Have fun with that! And if they kick you loose tomorrow, call and me or one of the guys will come get you." He lays a hand on my shoulder, and I press mine to the back of it. His hand pressed to my upper arm, or shaking hands with him, or just being around him … I'm always impressed with the strength, the peace and stability, the overall comfort I receive just from his presence. Patch is a man among men, the real deal, a person I'd like to be more like. Everything about him says honesty and integrity. He's the kind of person I strive to be every day because of the example he sets.

"I'll do it. Thanks, man."

"One way or another, I'll see you tomorrow. Night, bud. Love ya."

"Love you too. Have a good evening." I watch as he closes my door behind him and instantly regret his absence.

The dinner was … dinner. At least it was something that was chewable, not just something to swallow. I've about decided to take another little nap when the phone in the room rings. It's just close enough that I can reach it, and I grab it and say, "Hello?"

"Hey."

"Hey. Guess you called through the switchboard."

"Yeah. I don't have your cell number."

"That's okay. I don't have my cell. I guess it's in my cottage with my personal stuff. I think the hospital gave it all to Patch. Speaking of Patch, I talked to him about you coming out to the farm to stay. He's okay with it."

There's a deep sigh from the other end of the phone before she says, "Sure didn't sound like it."

"They're all worried about me, Sela. They're afraid you're going to chew me up and spit me out."

"Me? I'm such a powerful, controlling bitch that I could destroy you?" Then I hear her snicker. "With my pussy?"

Okay. I'm done with this. We're going to clear the air or she's not coming. "Look, I'm not afraid of you. You get that, right?"

That time she snorts loudly. "You should be."

"I'm not. I have the potential to hurt you as badly as you can hurt me."

That gets an actual laugh out of her. "Oh, really? And how's that?"

"You do realize I heard everything you said to me the other day, right?"

"And what did I say?"

"You said you love me."

"I did not."

"Let me explain something to you. One of the things I learned in prison was to read between the lines, and I do it very well. You were begging me to wake up because you had something to say to me, and I really don't think it was, 'I found a tick behind my left ear,' or, 'I had cabbage for dinner last night and 'bout ran myself out of the bathroom this morning.' I could be wrong, but I don't think it was either of those, and I sincerely doubt it was the price of milk at the store. So what exactly were you going to say, Sela? If you weren't going to tell me how you feel about me, what was it?"

Silence. For a few seconds, I start to think she's hung up until she says, "I have trouble with some words. They're hard to pronounce."

It takes everything I have to not start laughing. "Pronounce, huh? Got it. Do you do better with charades? You know, acting them out?"

From the other end of the phone comes a little chuckle. "Uh, yeah, something like that."

"Okay. Well, when I get out of here and you get to the farm, I'll let you do some charades and I'll see if I can figure out what you're talking about."

"Ohhhhh, uh, yeah. That sounds good."

Now I'm the one to chuckle. "Thought you'd like that."

"Yeah. When are you getting out of there?"

"Probably tomorrow. Somebody will have to come pick me up."

She hesitates for just a few seconds and then says, "I wish it could be me."

"You've gotta get out of there first. What's your physical therapist saying?"

"We can talk about that later." Uh-oh. That answer came a little too quickly. I don't know what the story is, but you can bet I'll be asking.

"Patch told me to just call and somebody will come and

get me. I hope they're not in a hurry. I've got a stop to make on the way."

"Oh? Where are you stopping?"

"To see you."

I'd like to think she's smiling as she sits there on the other end of the conversation, but with Sela, you're never really sure. "Oh. Well, that would be nice. Hope you can."

"If I can't, I'll just go to the farm, get a car, and come over there."

"And take me back with you?"

"If that's what you want. And they say you can come."

"I don't give a rat's ass what they say. I'll go if I want," she announces. And now I'm really concerned.

"Well, okay then. But right now, I think I'm gonna go. My head is starting to hurt a little and—"

"Are you okay?" The concern in her voice is genuine, and it surprises me a little.

"Yeah. The doctor said this might happen for a week or two. I got a pretty good lick to my head, he said."

"That's why you were out so long. I'm just … a little worried. That's all."

"Nothing to worry about. Just part of the healing process. Sleep makes it go away, so I'm going to try to get some shut-eye. I'll talk to you tomorrow, okay?"

"Yeah, okay. Make the headache go away."

"I will. And Sela?"

"Yeah?"

"I meant what I said. I love you."

"Uh, yeah, okay, I … should probably go start another load of laundry."

"You do that. Night."

"Night, Bear."

I drop the receiver into the cradle on the old phone and sit there, thinking. She really does have some trouble with pronunciation. Maybe it's not physical therapy she needs.

Maybe it's speech therapy.

GOD, I NEED A SHOWER IN MY OWN BATHROOM! I CALLED Patch to tell him I need a ride and some clothes, and he said he or somebody would be here in a little bit. In the meantime, I try my best to pull myself together, but I really have nothing to work with. Damn, I need a shave and a haircut.

An hour after I called, the door opens and a sight for sore eyes steps in. "Hey, honey! You ready to go?"

"Boy, am I glad to see you!" I hope she can see from my smile that I mean it. Mavis looks like an angel standing there with a duffel bag. "Did you bring me something to wear?"

"Yep! Sure did. I'll just step out and let you get dressed. All the paperwork is signed and everything?"

I nod. "I was just waiting for a ride."

"Well, you've got one! Your chariot awaits, kind sir. Meet me in the waiting area inside the doors and we'll be off." Before she leaves the room, she crosses it to me, rises up on her tiptoes, and kisses my cheek. "I've missed you. We all have. I'm so glad you're coming home."

For the first time ever, instead of just smiling, I open my arms and wrap them around her shoulders. She wraps hers around my waist, and I draw her in and hug her tightly. It feels so good to hug somebody, her warmth against me, and it reminds me of the way my grandmother hugged me when I was little. When I turn her loose, she steps back, smiles up at me, and then turns to go. I can't get my clothes on fast enough.

I just want to go home.

Five minutes later, as we pull away from the curb, I ask, "Do you have time to run me by the nursing facility?"

"Sure. You wanna see Sela?"

I nod. "Yeah. I do."

"Good. I've got plenty of time."

The sun is so bright that it hurts my eyes, and I'm glad she brought me a jacket because the air has gotten cool. We pull up to the nursing facility and I ask, "Do you want to come in?"

"Nah. I'll just wait in the car. Tell her I said hi." I get it. Sela's been so harsh with most of them that they really don't want to see her. I don't know what's going to happen when she comes out to the farm to stay.

She's lying on the bed, her back to the door, not moving. "Hey," I say as I tap on the door and peek in.

And I'm shocked. She sits straight up and pivots around, but I could swear she's wiping her eyes. "Oh, hey. You're out."

"Yep. Mavis came to pick me up."

Quick as a wink, she's on her feet. "It won't take me five minutes to pack up."

"What? What do you mean?"

Her eyes are wide when she spins to face me. "I'm going with you!"

"But Sela, don't you need to talk to your doctor and—"

"No. I'm going with you. Right now. Don't leave without me." She's hustling around, snatching things out of drawers and throwing them in the middle of the bed. When she's finished with that, she grabs a tote, disappears into the bathroom, and comes back with it. It gets dropped into the middle of the bed too, and then she takes the flat sheet, drags it together like a hobo bag, and turns to me with it clutched in her hands. "Okay. I'm ready."

"But Sela—"

"No. I'm going. Can you take this out to the car, please? I need to write a note." Before I can protest, she shoves the thing into my hands. "Go on. I'll be there in just a few seconds."

"Uh, okay." She's scrambling around, a pencil in her hand, so I head out the door. When I get to the car, I open the door and ask, "Can you pop the tailgate?"

"Sure." I hear it click, so I take the bundle and shove it in, then get into the back seat. "What are you doing back there?" Mavis asks.

"Sela says she's coming with me. She's writing a note or something."

A minute passes, and then two. At the five-minute mark, I let out a sigh. "I'm going in there to see what she's doing. I'll be right back."

Mavis just shrugs and says, "Okay."

Doesn't take me long to figure out what's going on. I hear her before I'm halfway to her room. "No, I'm done with this."

A woman's voice says, "But you're nowhere near where you need to be physically, Ms. Baldwin. You need to stay."

"I'm not staying here. I've had all I can take. This is my chance to get out, and I'm going."

"Your employer will most likely terminate you for non-compliance, and I have no choice but to tell them you left against medical advice. You know that if the doctor was here, he'd say the same thi—"

"I really don't give a damn what my employer does! I'm leaving. I've had enough of this hellhole. You're so damn concerned about my physical wellbeing, but honestly, I feel like I'm dying here. I really do. I have to get out of here while I still can."

My instinct was to stop right outside her door, and in an instant, she runs right into me. "Oh! I didn't know—"

"Sela, you should stay."

"No! I can't! I have to get out of here!"

"But your job—"

"I'll worry about that later. Right now, I have to go. If you won't take me, I'll—"

"We're parked right outside. But when we get to the farm, we *have* to talk. Do you understand?"

"Yeah, yeah. Just get me out of here," she says, almost running even with her limp.

"Oh my god, it's cold out here," she mumbles as soon as we're outside, and I realize that all she has are shorts. She came in here during really hot weather, and now that it's turned cool, her clothes are less than adequate.

"We'll get you something warm when we get there."

With me holding the door, she slides into the back seat, and I hear her say, "Hey, Mavis."

"Hi, Sela. Didn't realize you were coming with us."

"Nobody did. But here I am. Hope that's okay."

"Of course. It's fine. I'm glad to see you."

"Yeah, well, thanks. I'm … glad to see you too," Sela answers, but it's halting and stiff. I don't think she believes that anybody is glad to see her, and that makes my heart hurt.

Before we can even pull out of the parking lot, I've taken off my jacket and wrapped it around her. I figure if I try to wrap my arms around her and pull her up against me to keep her warm, she'll probably pull away, and she doesn't make any move to lean into me. For the first time since I walked out of the hospital, I'm feeling totally drained, and I have to imagine that she feels the same way. We don't talk, none of us, and I can't wait to get to my cottage, to my own bathroom, and to my own bed.

Mavis pulls right up to my door and stops. "Home sweet home," she says with a lilt in her voice.

"Truer words were never spoken," I reply, and I mean it. I've never been so happy to see home in my whole life.

"Need some help?" she asks, and I realize then that she's looking at Sela, who's sound asleep in the back seat.

"I'm not sure I need to try to lift her. Can you walk her in? I'll get our stuff out of the trunk."

"Sure. No problem. Hey, honey, we're here! Come on," Mavis says and takes Sela's hands.

"Whaaa? Oh. We're here. Okay." I watch as she slides out and stands, then lets Mavis take her arm and help her up the steps. I manage to slip around them with the key I keep under the doormat and unlock the door. I've got to find my stuff. I need my keys and my cell phone.

"Thank you so much, Mavis," I tell the small brunette as soon as Sela and I are inside.

"You're so welcome, honey. I'm just glad you're home." With a little kiss on my cheek, she turns to leave, then pivots again and smiles at Sela. "And I'm glad you're here."

"Thank you. I need sleep," Sela mumbles.

"Bye. You guys get some rest." The sound of Mavis' feet on the front porch dissipates and in seconds, we're alone.

"Come on. We can shower and all that later. Right now, I need to lie down," I tell the woman wobbling and weaving beside me.

"Sleep. I need some sleep. Real sleep," Sela whispers.

"Let's go." As soon as I clear the bedroom doorway, I throw the comforter back and point at the blanket. "Just lie down on top of the blanket and we'll cover up with the comforter. Get on in." For once, she doesn't argue with me and just crawls into the bed, sort of collapsing on the other side. I sit down on the side, take off my shoes, then reach over and pull hers off too. After they're deposited on the floor, I lie down, roll toward her, and pull the comforter over us.

Oh my god, it feels good to be in my own bed. A million things run through my head, but the biggest one is how thankful I am to be here in this little room. My gratitude instantly turns to the woman lying beside me. "You okay?" I whisper.

Instead of answering me, she rolls to face me and burrows into my chest. In that moment, I feel like the strongest, most powerful, and most capable man in the world. My arms wrap around her, and something happens that totally shocks me.

There's not a sound, but I can feel her sobbing. She occasionally sniffles. I would've questioned it if not for those sniffles, but she's actually crying. That's when I realize how frightened she must've been all these months, how alone she must've felt, how vulnerable, how defenseless, how weak and small she must've been made to feel. And how resentful and angry she is deep inside, angry at what happened, angry with her doctors, at how everyone out here has responded to her, and it makes me wonder: What's going on with her job? Has something happened? We'll talk about that and much, much more in the very near future.

But right now, I need some sleep. We both do. I don't know if everything will look better when we wake up, but it sure can't look much worse.

CHAPTER 4

WHEN I WAKE UP, IT'S LATE AFTERNOON AND BEAR'S STILL
sawing logs. I hate to get up, but there's something I need to
do, so I pull on my clothes, slip on my slippers, and head out.

There's nobody around at all, and that's unusual, until I
realize it's a workday and they're all working. An involuntary
shiver hits me, and I wrap the thin sweater tighter around me.
As soon as I step into the lodge, I'm warmer, and I'm
thankful for that. It's super quiet in there, and I'm wandering
down the hallway when somebody calls out, "Hey there!"

"Holy shit!" I bark.

"Sorry. Didn't mean to scare you," Sarah says, and I turn
to find her in her room, sitting on the side of the bed. "Didn't
know you were here. How ya feelin'?"

"I'm good, I guess," I lie.

"That's good. I'm glad you got here during the week so I
could see you. We're not here much on the weekends. We
usually go to Lenny's house then." Lenny? Who the hell is

that? Boy, some shit went on while I wasn't around, that much I can tell. "You here visiting Bear? I hear he got to come home today."

"I'm … I'm actually moving in with him," I explain. Oh, fuck, is she one of those holy rollers who'll have a fit when she finds out we're living in sin?

"Oh! Well, I reckon I'll see a lot more of you then! It's finally my chance to say thank you for saving Natalie. She's a sweet lady, and we really appreciate what you did for her."

"Just doin' my job. Um, do you by any chance know what they did with my stuff that I had here?"

"Far as I know, it's all still there. Nobody's moved it unless they did it on a weekend when we weren't here."

"Okay. Thanks. I'm going to get it. I don't have much, so it'll be nice to have some of my things."

"I bet. Need some help packing it over there? I can't carry a lot, but I'll do what I can."

I give her a smile. She really is a nice lady. "Nah, but thanks. I'll just take some and come back for more later. Right now, all I'm really interested in is some long pants. All I've had in the facility were shorts and I'm about to freeze to death."

"Oh, yeah! It's gotten chilly since you've been gone. So how 'bout this? You pull out everything you want to take in your bags and I'll help you pack it up. Plus I've got some totes for your bathroom stuff. How 'bout that?"

"That would be great! That would help a lot. Thank you. I'll just …" I say and throw a thumb toward my old room.

"Yep. I'll be there in just a minute." As I step down the hallway, I hear her rustling around.

What happens next is possibly the nicest thing anybody's ever done for me. Sarah sits on the side of the bed and folds stuff while I put it in my bags, and it's kinda fun, working alongside her and chatting as we pack. I didn't think I had much here, but by the time we're finished, I've got more than my bags would hold and we're stuffing some of it in totes. "Wow. I've actually got quite a bit here."

"You sure do. Not much of it is winter stuff, but you do have blazers and such that you can wear over tees. That'll help."

"True. Plus I've got a denim jacket and a couple of cardigans. Those will do nicely."

"And quite a few pairs of shoes too, and pajamas. I think you're just about set. Need the things out of your bathroom?"

"Oh, yeah. I do. Thanks for reminding me. I'll start gathering them up." It takes two more totes to get all that stuff packed, but when we're finished, the room is empty and my part of the closet at Bear's cottage will be full. "This is great. I really don't need to buy much. I've got everything I need here already."

"Sure do. You know, my old car is sitting outside. Why don't we load all of this stuff in the trunk and you can just drive it over? Sure beats making half a dozen trips back and forth."

"That's a good idea."

She's already rummaging around in her purse. "Here we go!" she says and holds up the keys.

Ten minutes later, everything is in the trunk, and Sarah hands me the keys. "Just bring them back at dinner," she says. Before I can get out of the room, she insists on giving me a hug, and that makes me a little uncomfortable, but I figure what the hell. The woman has just helped me immensely. Letting her hug me isn't like some huge sacrifice I'm making.

I pull up to the cottage, open the trunk, and grab a couple of bags. When I've set those two down in the living area, I go back and get a couple more. Pretty soon I've got everything inside, and I realize I'll probably have to buy some hangers. It's doubtful that Bear will have that many free in his closet.

"Hey, what's going on?" I hear a croaky voice ask, and I turn to find him standing in the doorway in nothing but his boxer briefs, his hair a royal mess and his eyes half closed.

"I got my stuff from the lodge. Sarah helped me. I guess after dinner I'll have to go get some hangers to hang everything up."

"I would've helped you if you'd asked. Half the dresser is empty, so you're welcome to that for underwear and stuff," he says, then staggers across the room and plops down on the sofa. "Damn, I was wiped."

"You were. You didn't even move when I got up."

"Come sit down. We need to talk."

I manage a sarcastic, lopsided grin. "Don't you need to wake up first?"

"I'm awake. Come on. Now." He pats the cushion beside him, so I guess I'd better take a seat. As soon as I'm stationary, he fixes me with a hard stare. "What's going on with your work?"

"Nothing. What? I don't know what you—"

"I overheard the physical therapist telling you that your employer wasn't going to like it when they find out you're non-compliant."

"They can just suck it. I'm not—"

"Sela, the only way this is going to work is if you, first, talk to me, and second, tell me the truth. Anything less is unacceptable. Now, I'm going to ask you again. What's going on?"

This conversation is one I really don't want to have. Just the thought of saying the words out loud fills me with fury. "Nothing. They're staying in touch."

"When are you going back to work?"

"I don't know."

"And what is your return to work contingent on?"

Whoo boy, here we go. "Me being physically able to do the work."

"And you're not."

"What the fuck do you mean, I'm not?"

"Sela, you're not capable of doing that kind of work right now and you know it."

"Oh, so now *you* know more about me than I do? I mean, really, what the everlovin' fuck does everybody think they—"

"Hey, slow your roll, Wonder Woman! I can't work right now either. Patch said he was too worried about me getting hurt because my job is pretty damn dangerous when I'm at my best, and as bad as I hate to say it, he's not wrong. I don't want to not work, but if he thinks it's best for me to sit back and take a little breather, then that's what I'm going to do. If they want you to take off for a while, that should be okay. You damn near died, Sela. A few weeks isn't going to kill you."

"We're not talking a few weeks here. They want to … take me out of the field." Fuck, it hurt to say that out loud.

"And the alternative?"

There's a shrieking in my head, and I feel like I'm going to throw up. "They're talking about making me some kind of trainer or some bullshit."

"That's good, right? You'd retain your seniority, your pension, your salary. Hell, it might even mean a raise!"

"So what? And be that agent? 'Oh, yeah, that's Sela Baldwin. She got hurt in the field and they stuck her behind a desk. SSA? Nah, she's not a supervisory special agent anymore. She's just a pencil-pusher. A has-been. Washed up. Finished. Just waiting for retirement.' I don't want to be *that* agent. No."

He turns sideways to face me, one knee up on the sofa and his elbow resting on the back as he props up his head with his hand. In that moment, I'm struck by how absolutely gorgeous the guy is. On top of being gruff and a little on the scruffy side, his body is hard and chiseled, and his shoulders are massive. I can see why people who don't know him would be afraid of him, but while I wouldn't call him meek, he's quiet and unobtrusive. Even when he's present, he's not an in-your-face kinda guy. Since the first time I met him, I've found his presence oddly calming, but the motherfucker knows how to tune me up in the sack. I'm staring at his pecs when I hear him say, "Sela? Did you hear me?"

"Uh, sorry. What did you say?"

"What if I had an idea for something you could do?"

"Unless I'd be carrying a gun, I'm not interested."

"You'd be carrying a gun," he says matter-of-factly.

"Then speak."

"Remember Steve McCoy? The Walters' attorney and friend?" Do I remember Steve McCoy? He looks like a fucking Viking prince. I couldn't forget him if I tried. His middle name should be Adonis. I nod at Bear's question. "He's thinking of expanding his security firm to Ashland. Remember Marshall who was here helping out?"

"Oh, yeah. Nice guy."

"Yeah. They're pretty sure Steve is tapping Marshall to head up the office. And I bet if he thought you'd come to work for them, he'd be thrilled."

"What all do they do?"

"They do security like you were doing with Natalie, but they also do investigative work, surveillance, things like that. I know their general manager helped to bust up a big sex-trafficking ring, and his second-in-command is a former Nashville police officer and does a lot of electronics work. He's got a technical analyst too, and from what they say, she's top notch. And I could be wrong, but I bet it would pay a lot better than the FBI. Better benefits too."

"You don't really think it would be better than a government job, do you?"

"I bet it would be *way* better than a government job. Would you be interested enough for me to talk to Tony and Steve for you?"

"Could I still live here?"

"That's something you and Steve would have to talk about. I can't say for sure, but I would think you could work something out. I mean, there would be assignments all over this end of the state, so having somebody who's somewhere other than Ashland would be a good thing, especially since you have enough expertise to be a supervisor and maybe even have a couple of employees working under you."

Me. A boss. I like it. "Hmmm. That's an interesting idea. Yeah, sure. Ask him. See what he says. The worst thing he can say is no."

"But if he does, what are you going to do?"

All I can do is shrug. "I guess go back to Atlanta until I can figure out what to do. I don't know."

"So you're prepared to leave," he says, and I can hear the defeat in his voice.

"I'm not talking about forever. I have an apartment there, and all of my stuff is there. No matter what happens, at some point, I have to go back there and pack up everything. If they decide to put me back out in the field …"

"Is that even a possibility?"

"I'd like to think so."

He dips his head and looks up at me from under his brow. "Realistically?"

It's the first time I've had to admit this, and as much as I hate it, I know the truth. Before I speak, I let out a deep sigh. I think that's what they call resignation. "No. Realistically, they're not going to let me back out into the field."

"Then I'll talk to Tony and Steve. Or Patch will."

"Why Patch?"

Something passes over his face, something I can't identify, before he speaks. "It should probably be Patch. I'm not … I don't feel like I can do that."

"Why not? From what I've seen, they'd probably like to hear from you."

"I just … I can't."

What's going on here? What am I not understanding? "Just call them up. You have their numbers, right?"

"No."

"You don't?"

"No."

"Why not? It's like they're the fairy godparents of this place, and you don't have their numbers?"

"No. I'm not …" And he stops.

"Not what?"

Now he's not looking at me, just at his lap. What comes out of his mouth next confuses me. "I'm not like them."

"What do you mean, you're not like them?"

"I'm not … like them. I'm not … I don't have family or people except here. I'm not a good person, and they're good people."

"What the fuck are you talking about, you're not a good person? You're one of the best people I've ever met."

"You don't know very many people then," he counters. I'm at a total loss. What is this bullshit?

"You're an amazing person. Hell, you're one of the most patient people I've ever met. If I were you, I would've kicked me to the curb, but you didn't. How can you say you're not a good person?"

Those huge brown eyes look up at me, and the sadness snatches my breath right out of my chest. I'm almost afraid to hear what he's about to say, and then he says it. "Sela, I killed a man."

"I know. That's how you wound up here."

"I killed a man who was just doing his job. He hadn't done anything wrong. I got stupid, got high on mushrooms, got all paranoid, and grabbed a gun and killed him." This isn't news to me. Natalie told me what he'd been in prison for, so I knew this already. "I was a dumb kid with parents who were decent, middle-class people, kept us in church, tried to do right by us. I finished high school and got a scholarship to community college until I did something so dumb that even now it's hard to believe. I remember absolutely nothing of the whole incident. Nothing. I don't remember smoking a joint, I don't remember drinking five shots of whiskey, and I don't remember chewing and swallowing those mushrooms, but I know I did it. I don't remember the gun, and I don't remember shooting him. I don't remember the emergency vehicles coming and trying to save him. I don't remember the police questioning me, and I don't remember what I said, but from what I was told, I confessed on the spot. I remember none of it, and I remember sitting in that cell and wishing I could just die because I didn't deserve to live. I still don't. I took a man's life, an innocent man who'd done nothing to me. And I live in fear that I'll do it again. I'm a dangerous man, one who doesn't deserve to even walk the earth. I'm just garbage. I don't deserve their friendship." By this point, I'm pretty sure he's not even talking to me. He's talking to hear his own voice condemning himself, recounting every horrible aspect of the whole thing, reliving it, and I'm powerless to help him.

I don't know what to say to make it better, but I have to at least try. "Tony and Nikki don't see you that way, and neither does Steve. The guys here don't see you that way. I don't see you that way. If anything, you should be proud of yourself. You've come a long way and you've done some really great things with your life. You've gotten a fresh start. A lot of guys don't. You have nothing to be ashamed of, babe. Nothing." It's the first time I've used a term of endearment with him and it feels strangely normal. "And you're most certainly not garbage."

"Tell that to the wife and kids whose husband and father I killed."

Now I understand, and I'd probably feel the same way. The guy I know, the patient one, the very calm and matter-of-fact guy, is slowly rotting on the inside with self-hatred. There's an ache in my ribcage just thinking about the pain he must be feeling. Does he talk to that Baxter guy about it? Or is he just quietly letting it eat him alive? "You can't bring him back. But the best thing you can do to honor his life is to live a better one yourself, and you're doing that. You're doing it. You're really doing it. And for what it's worth, I'm proud of you. I know I'm a bitch, and I don't deserve somebody like you, but I'm thankful that you're—"

"What do you mean, you don't deserve somebody like me? You're a fucking FBI agent, for chrissakes. I can't believe you'd even give me the time of day."

"All the more reason why you should believe in yourself. I said it myself—I put people like you away. But here I am. That should tell you something."

He lets out a little chuckle without a smile. "It tells me you're crazy."

That makes me chuckle too. "Maybe I am. Or maybe I just know a good person when I see one."

We sit there for a few seconds, neither of us talking, and he reaches over and swipes a strand of hair from where it drapes down my cheek and puts it to rest behind my ear. "What changed, Sela? Why did you all of a sudden stop fighting me and start believing that I have feelings for you?"

How did that happen? I haven't really thought about it. I just know how I felt the minute they told me he was in the hospital in a coma, and it wasn't good. "When they told me what had happened to you, I felt this …" I search for the word, and finally say, "Emptiness. Like everything good had been sucked out of the world. And I realized that in the whole world, you're the only person who seems to give two shits about me. Consistently, I mean. Don't get me wrong. I know everybody out here wanted me to survive after what happened, and they were glad I was going to be okay. But they weren't finding time to come to the hospital, or sitting with me when I couldn't even respond. That was you. I don't know why you did it—"

"Maybe because the sex was good?" he says, grinning.

"Yeah, it *was* pretty awesome, huh?"

"Very awesome."

"Be serious," I say and play-slap his leg.

That gets a laugh out of him. "Do I have to?"

"I'm baring my soul to you, and you're being all ridiculous and flippant?"

"Okay, okay! Sheesh! Sorry," he says, grabs my hand, and squeezes it.

"I'm just messing with you. I don't mind smiling a little more."

"That's good. I'd like to see you smile a lot more. But right now, we've got to get ourselves pulled together and get over to the kitchen for dinner. It'll be ready and we'll miss it."

After the horrible stuff I've been eating, missing dinner is not optional.

BEAR

EVEN WITH EVERYBODY'S ASSURANCES, SELA STILL FEELS like she's not wanted here. I'm not sure why. Nobody *doesn't* want her here, and everybody wants me to be happy. My eyes are constantly scanning in the big kitchen, looking for anybody who's staring at her funny or doing anything to make her feel unwelcome, and it's just not happening. No one is doing anything but trying to include her, but she's simply having none of it, or at least that's the way it seems. Natalie is sitting beside her across the table from me, and they're chatting a little, but I get the impression Sela feels weird being friendly with someone who used to be her responsibility. From time to time she glances up at me, and I give her a tiny smile, but that seems to make her uncomfortable too.

As soon as dinner is over, I start helping clean up, picking up plates and glasses, but Sela disappears out the back door of the kitchen. A female voice whispers to me, "I think maybe you need to go check on her," and I turn to find Natalie standing there.

"Yeah. Probably. Thanks." I set down the things I'm holding and make my way to the back door, trying to draw as little attention as possible.

She's sitting in a lawn chair out there, staring at the tree line. Instead of heading toward her, I let the door close behind me and lean back against it. "Whatcha doin' out here?"

Eyes never leaving the tree line, she answers, "It's going to take some adjusting."

"What?"

"Being around people after being alone for so long, especially in that nursing home."

"Rehab facility," I correct.

Her dark hair swings as she shakes her head. "No. It was definitely a nursing home. Me and dozens of old people. My roommate couldn't talk anymore. The old woman in the next room screamed all night long every night, so nobody got any sleep. Then I'd try to sleep in the day, but they were coming to get me to go to physical therapy and they wouldn't leave me alone, so I was so sleep deprived that I couldn't think. I pretty much decided they must like it that way. Compliance bred from exhaustion."

A sarcastic little chuckle erupts from my throat. "I'll have to remember that tactic."

She finally turns to look at me and her eyes bore into me like a couple of drill bits. "You'd best forget it."

"Nope. Filing that one away for when you get too sassy," I answer with a little laugh. "You about ready to go back to the cottage?"

"Can I watch TV?"

That strikes me as odd. "Of course you can watch TV, if that's what you want to do."

"I didn't get to watch TV in there. They only had a couple of channels, and the TVs were horrible. I've missed all of my favorite shows all this time."

"Oh, yeah? What are some of them?"

"*Criminal Behaviors, Murderous Masterminds, San Diego S.W.A.T.*, stuff like that."

"Then we should get along just fine. Wanna know what my favorite is?" She nods. *"Born to Protect and Serve.* It's my absolute favorite show."

Her jaw drops. "You've been in prison and you like cop shows?"

"Yeah. I like watching how they figure out who the bad guys are, but a lot of times, I figure it out first."

"How did they figure out who did your crime?"

That gets an eye roll directed to her. "Duh, I told them? Remember?"

"Oh, yeah. Solved your own crime."

"Kinda sorta did. Come on. Let's go see what's on."

To my surprise, after she rises, she reaches for my hand. "You have streaming services?"

"Do I have streaming services? Does the App STAR team have a helicopter? Of course I have streaming services! Pretty much anything you could ask for." Her palm is warm against mine, and I close my fingers around hers and lead her around the side of the building and out toward the cottages.

The cottage door closes behind us and I think of something I need to tell her. "Hey, before we turn on the TV, I wanted to tell you that I'm going to talk to Patch tomorrow about you working for Steve, see what he thinks. Is there anything special I should tell him to ask about?"

"Yeah. Ask if he has need of somebody who can do investigations. I'm pretty well-versed and I'd love to get into something like that."

"Will do. Now," I say, throwing a thumb toward the kitchen, "you want popcorn?"

"Not yet. Maybe in a bit. Come sit with me," she says and pats the sofa.

What follows is the most normal evening I've had in years, and by normal, I mean the kind of evening most people have. It's sweet and uncomplicated, and we watch TV, talk about the plots, guess at the bad guys and their motivations, use the internet to look up actors and actresses we think we recognize from other shows, and go through several soft drinks. I'm getting up yet again to grab one when she asks, "Can I have a beer?"

My question is automatic. "You taking any kind of pain meds?"

"Nope."

"Then sure." I grab her one, but I take out a diet soda for myself. "Here ya go," I say and hand it off to her.

"Thanks." She pops the top, takes a couple of swigs, and then asks, "Why did you ask me about meds?"

"Because alcohol and pain meds don't mix."

"So now you're my protector?"

I shake my head. "No. I'm trying to save myself some trouble with a woman who's both drunk and high."

"I'm not going to get drunk from one beer."

"You might if you're also taking pain meds," I point out.

"Ugh. Always with the logic," she snaps.

"Hey, I'm figuring out the plots of these shows before you are. Maybe my logic is actually good for something."

"Something other than bossing me around?"

"No. It's always good for bossing you around. But it's good for figuring out the shows too. Maybe we should call one of the networks and suggest that as a new game show: *Logic Bosses*. Could be a hit."

"Are you kidding?" she asks with a smirk. "Look around at the world we live in. They'd have trouble finding contestants."

"Yeah. That's true. Not a lot of logic and common sense going around these days," I answer in agreement. Well, there's not. I don't know if humankind is actually getting dumber, but it sure feels and seems that way. "Be right back," I tell her and head to the bathroom.

I've just gotten my fly zipped when I hear a weird sound outside the bathroom window. Then I hear voices. My shoes are by the door, so I head straight there. Sela goes from relaxed to red alert. "What's going on? What are you doing?"

"Something's going on outside." I've already got the door open, and she rises. "No. You stay here."

"I'm coming—"

"No! Stay here. I'll be right back." Before she can protest, I draw the door closed quietly and head down the steps.

The voices I heard are clearer now. One of them is Reboot, and the other is Ghost. As soon as I round the corner, I hear Reboot say, "Stop!" and I freeze.

"What the hell—"

"Shhhh!" Ghost says and points. There's something on the ground under my window, and it's whimpering.

"What the hell is that?" It's hard to focus in darkness this deep.

"Some kind of dog," Reboot whispers. I can see a light bobbing a little farther away. "Looks like Patch remembered his flashlight."

"What are you guys doing out here?" Patch asks when he gets close enough.

"Shine that beam over there, wouldja?" Ghost asks and points toward the sound.

The flashlight's brightness illuminates the entire area, and there, cowering under my bathroom window, is some kind of dog, a frayed, dirty rope hanging from its neck. "What the hell?" Patch whispers.

"It's a coydog. A lot of people kept them down where I grew up. This one ..." Reboot is creeping closer, and the dog begins to growl. "Looks like he's been beaten on.

Maybe kicked. Paw's messed up. Anybody got any lunch meat?"

"Uh, I think I've got a couple of hot dogs in my fridge," I answer.

"Go get 'em. Looks starved too," Reboot adds, so I turn and head back in.

"What's going on out there?" Sela asks as soon as I'm inside.

"Dog under my window. Beaten-up, bedraggled thing. I'm getting it something to eat." Before I've finished the explanation, I've got two hot dogs and two buns in my hands. "Be right back."

"What kind of dog?" she asks as I open the door.

"Reboot says it's a coydog."

"Need a gun to put the thing out of its misery," she says dispassionately, and I'm shocked.

"Nope. I'll be back."

I get to the corner and round it to find that Reboot is a little closer to the dog. "Do I just throw them to him?" I ask.

Reboot nods. "Yeah. Don't get too close. He's scared and hurt."

I pull a hot dog from the package and toss it in the dog's direction. For a few seconds, it seems too scared to go for the food, but I guess hunger takes over, because it snatches the meat with one step and the hot dog disappears. Then I toss it a bun, which was easier to get closer to it, and it wolfs that right on down. In a few seconds, the second hog dog and bun are both gone. "He was hungry."

"Yeah. Looks like somebody's been starving him. Shouldn't feed him too much right away." Patch is quiet for a bit before he asks, "Do you have some kind of shallow pan we could put water in?"

"Yeah. I've got a big bowl. Would that work?"

"Perfect. Just fill it with water and leave it out here. At least he'll have something to drink without having to try to make it all the way to the creek."

I head back in and grab the bowl and an old beach towel that's in the linen closet. This time, Sela says nothing. She kinda pissed me off with the execution order, so it's best that she stays quiet. When I come back, I step toward the dog until it growls, then set the bowl down. Once it's in place, I spread out the beach towel, hoping the dog will take the hint and find it a more comfortable place to sleep. "There ya go, fella. Maybe that will help."

"Let's just leave him alone for tonight. If he's still here in the morning, we're going to have to make some kind of decision," Reboot says.

Patch nods. "Agreed. He'll either be gone, or we'll have to figure out what to do next."

"I'll get him to a vet. That's a no-brainer," Reboot says.

Ghost's eyes widen. "You want to keep him?"

Reboot actually sounds pissed when he answers. "I promised my son a dog, and a dog has shown up out here. I'm not sending it away, if that's what you're thinking."

"Okay then. I'm going to bed. Y'all figure it out," Ghost says and turns toward his cottage.

"Me too. Let me know if I can help," Patch adds and heads away.

Reboot gives me this look that says he feels helpless. "I feel bad for him. Look at how torn up he is."

"Yeah. Me too. He's welcome to sleep here for as long as he wants. If he needs to go to the vet, I'm on the DL for a while, so I'll figure out a way to help you."

I see my friend's eyes soften. "Wow. Thanks. I appreciate that. I mean, this is an animal who's obviously been abused, but he showed up here at a place for humans, hoping for some help. He's not feral. He's just hurt and needs somebody. A second chance maybe."

"He came to the right place. That's what we specialize in," I answer with a smile.

"I think you're right. Hey, if you hear him whimpering or something in the night, call me, okay? I'll come see about him."

"Will do. Night, buddy," I tell him as I turn to go back inside.

"Night," he calls back.

As soon as the door closes behind me, Sela says, "Well, that was quiet."

"What do you mean, that was quiet?"

"Somebody got a gun with a silencer?"

A wave of fury breaks over me and I can feel every muscle in my body tensing. "No. Nobody's killing that dog. End of discussion."

I hear her snort as I reach for a bottle of water in the refrigerator. "Oh, so now you're an animal activist? PETA member?"

"No. I'm a human being who actually has empathy for other sentient beings. You should try it sometime." I'm getting angrier by the second.

"Why? So I can cry at those dumb ASPCA commercials? No thanks."

"No, so you can actually connect to something or someone in a meaningful way. I swear to god, Sela, you're one of the angriest humans I've ever met, and that's saying a lot, considering where I've been."

The look on her face is easily recognizable, because I'm pretty sure it matches mine. "Oh, I'm angry, huh?"

"You are! You do everything you can to slap a prickly paw at anybody who tries to get close to you, to be friendly to you, to spend time with you. You keep saying nobody wants you here, but I watched at dinner—*everybody* wants you here. Everybody's been friendly and kind to you. Everybody's gone out of their way to do whatever you need. And honestly, the way you've treated me, I'm not sure why I keep trying with you, because it's obvious that you're determined to care absolutely nothing about me." There. I've said it. I've been wanting to say it for a while, but now it's out there, I can't take it back, and she knows how I feel.

Ever smacked somebody in the face out of the blue? That's how she looks. "You think I care absolutely nothing about you?"

"It sure feels that way."

"Then what do you think I'm doing here?"

"I have no idea. I'm your ticket out of the nursing home?"

Any other time, I'd feel like I'd gone too far based on the expression on her face, that lost, hurt look, but this time, no. If I've learned anything from Shaggy, it's to be honest and talk about what's going on. "You really think that's who I am? You think that's what I'm doing here? Using you?"

"If it's not, you tell me what you're doing here, because I'm trying like hell to understand. You're so fucking edgy that nobody knows how to even approach you, and anything I do gets tossed back in my face. So tell me, Sela, what exactly *are* you doing here?"

She squirms slightly and doesn't look at me when she answers, "Trying to find a place to fit in. And it seems I've failed."

"You've failed because you *chose* to fail. Everybody here is trying, Sela, they really are, but you're not even meeting them a quarter of the way. Everybody here is here because they needed a second chance and a place to fit in when the world rejected them. What do you do? You swat at everybody who gets near and criticize a wounded animal who's terrified of humans but came to a human place for help because it was so desperate. Maybe you're not desperate enough yet. Maybe that's the problem."

It's like she's shrinking before my eyes. "You don't know me. You don't know anything about me."

"Yeah, well, how 'bout you enlighten me? I'm here, Sela. You can talk to me. You can lean on me. I love you—I *want* to love you—but you're making it almost impossible. I don't know you because you won't show me who you are, which is ridiculous because you know I won't turn away. It can't get so ugly or nasty that I'd turn away, and you know that's true because you know all about me. I know you do. You were probably briefed on all of us before you came here to work Natalie's detail, am I right?"

"Not really. What I know, I learned from being here with all of you."

"But you know who I am and what I did."

"I don't know who you were before all of that happened."

Instead of sitting on the sofa beside her, I pull up one of the dinette chairs and sit down to face her. "There's not a lot to tell. Average Midwest kid, lived in the same house my whole life, mom and dad worked in the community, older brother did too. Got decent grades, didn't get into a lot of trouble, played football—"

"No surprise there," she mumbles.

"Yeah, you could've guessed that. Made it to state—lost the championship game, but our little school had never been to state before, so it was super important. Graduated and wanted to go to the community college. Got through my first year and did pretty good. Second year was when everything went to shit. The kids I was with when it happened were all kids I'd grown up with. We were stupid. We knew nothing about psilocybins. Somebody's older brother sent them to him from college, and we couldn't wait to try them. Danny's mom was at work, so we all went to his house. And two hours later, you know what happened."

"And none of them got in trouble?"

"Oh, they got in trouble, but they didn't kill anybody. That was me—all me."

It's quiet for a couple of minutes before she asks, "Why didn't you ever get paroled?"

Even though I was sure she'd ask, I hate having to answer. "Every time I knew I had a parole board hearing coming up, I'd intentionally get into a fight and hurt somebody. That stopped the hearing."

"But why?"

"Because the guilt was eating me alive. I didn't want to get out. I was terrified I'd do something as equally stupid again and hurt somebody else. At least the guys in lock-up with me were just as bad as I was. Anything I dished out to them they probably deserved."

"At least you had a conscience. They were much worse."

"Yeah, I guess some of them were. I was one of the biggest guys in there, so nobody fucked with me and if they did, they wound up sorry. The day those bars closed behind me, I made it my mission to serve my thirty. That guy I killed had two little girls. He never got to see their dance recitals, or their graduations, or their weddings, or his grandkids. That was on *me*. I did that. And I didn't deserve to be out walking around."

"That's not true, you know."

I nod. "Yeah. Shaggy has—"

"Shaggy?"

"Yeah. Baxter. The counselor. He looks like Shaggy from Scooby-Doo. He's been helping me a lot. I'm trying to forgive myself, and doing things like I'm doing for that dog out there helps a lot. I feel like I'm making a difference to *somebody*, which is more than I was doing before."

"You make a difference to a lot of people." Her eyes have softened and she's looking straight into my face. "The guys here all love and respect you. So do the women. Natalie always spoke very highly of you."

That's a surprise. "Yeah?"

"Yeah. She said she always feels safe when you're around because she knows you'd lay your life on the line for anybody here."

Warmth spreads through my body. The people here love me. They respect me. I used to have a hard time accepting that, but now I want to enjoy that feeling, let it seep in and take up residence in my bones. "Thank you for telling me that. It means that all the hard work I'm doing on myself is actually being recognized, and it has definitely been hard." When she doesn't respond, I ask, "So, what's your story, Sela Baldwin?"

The shrug she gives me makes me wonder if she's going to shut down, but instead she says, "I wanted to be a police officer. But I was in college when an FBI agent came to speak to us in one of my criminal justice classes, and after that, being an agent was all I wanted to do."

"Yeah? How'd you get in?"

"After graduation, I got a call because I'd filled out an interest form. They said my grades were high enough that they wanted to talk to me. They offered me a job at entry level and I worked my way up from there after my twenty months at Quantico."

"What were you doing at first?"

"Field agent. Just your run-of-the-mill investigations helping local law enforcement when the crimes crossed state lines. But they found out I had a knack for seeing things others didn't, so they asked me to do more training and education so they could work me into the Behavioral Analysis Unit."

"You worked with the BAU?"

"Yeah. I'd been a field agent for eight years when they pulled that on me. Didn't last long."

"What happened?"

"Two years in, we were looking for a guy who'd killed three women. My partner and I walked up onto a porch in a neighborhood eight of us were canvassing. Guy opened the door, blew my partner in half with a sawed-off shotgun, grabbed me by the hair, pulled me into the house, and slammed the door shut. The other agents heard the blast, found my partner, and set up a perimeter. The guy held me hostage in the house for over thirty hours and tortured me while negotiators tried to get him to turn me loose. It wasn't until the local S.W.A.T. stormed the house that I got out. By then, he'd done a bunch of stuff to me that I really don't want to talk about."

"That's fine. You'll tell me when you're ready and if you never are, that's okay too."

"Thanks for understanding. Anyway, I asked to be transferred to protective details. I figured that was about as dangerous as I could handle. Garden-variety stuff. Couple of governors who were threatened. Woman who'd been abducted, got away, and was being stalked by her abductor."

"Did you catch the guy?"

"Eventually, but he was one of the sneakiest, most persistent assholes I ever saw. I got Natalie's detail and I really thought it would be fine. Never dreamed it would turn into what it did."

"I can imagine." It's clear I'm going to have to do it, even though I don't want to. "I get the guy who dragged you in and tortured you, but you're not telling me the whole story. Something happened between you and people you trusted. What was it?"

The pain I can see on her face is heartbreaking. Something horrible happened to this woman. If only she'd let me in, I … Hell, I don't know what I think I could possibly do to help, but I'd like to try. It seems like forever before she says, "It happened while I was at Quantico." Instead of speaking or asking, I just wait. She's got to want to do this. I've about decided she's not going to say anything else when she finally starts. "We had a test we had to do. Simulated attack. I scored highest of everybody in the class. Went to dinner that evening alone and when I went out to get into my car, three guys jumped me in the parking lot."

"Random guys?"

"No, Bear. Three of the guys in my class."

Holy shit. "You knew them?"

"They were wearing masks, but I knew their voices."

"But why—"

"They told me they weren't competing with me for spots and if I stayed, they'd kill me."

"Did they hurt you?"

"Broke my jaw and cracked a bunch of my ribs. Bruised my kidneys. Broke one of my occipital bones. Really worked me over."

"You wound up in the hospital?"

"Went, but didn't stay. I had to get back to training."

"Did anybody say anything? Instructors? Admin? Anybody?"

"Asked me what happened. I told them three random guys jumped me in a restaurant parking lot."

"Didn't you tell anybody?"

There's a wickedness in her grin that surprises me. "Nope. I just followed them, one by one. And when I'd catch one of them alone, I beat the holy hell out of him. The only reason three of them jumped me was because they knew they couldn't take me alone. I studied martial arts as a kid, plus I was quicker on my feet."

"Did you do them some damage?"

"Oh, yeah. One of them had to transfer out of Quantico and go into the private sector. I don't fuck around when somebody fucks with me."

"Jesus Christ, Sela!" I can't believe she's telling me this. "Didn't they report you?"

"What are they going to say? 'Hey, the woman the three of us almost beat to death beat me up.' You think that's likely? Nope. They'd never admit it. But I did watch my back from then on." She stops for a second before she says, "So now you know. They drummed into our heads that we had to be there for each other and other agents, and then they did that to me. I never trusted *anybody* after that. Not really."

As much as I hate it, that actually explains everything. They taught her to distrust everybody in a five-minute timespan with a lesson that didn't fade in her mind. My brain is trying to figure out what to say when I manage, "Sela, I'm so sorry."

"For what? You didn't do it. Had nothing to do with you. Had nothing to do with Quantico. Had everything to do with me being a woman in a man's world."

"It *does* have to do with me. For too long, guys like me haven't held these men accountable. Of course, I wasn't in a position to, but I will now when I get a chance. Won't hesitate."

"Good. Because the good ol' boys' network in law enforcement sure is still alive and well."

"I can tell you that if you go to work for Steve, he won't put up with that bullshit. Somebody gives you trouble, he'll squash it. I haven't been around him much, but he's a straight-up guy who does the right thing every time. He has to be like that. Otherwise, he wouldn't work for the Walters."

"I hope you're right. I'm afraid if I beat the piss out of an agent who works for the Walters' attorney, my days will be numbered. You know, Italian mafia and all that," she says with a shrug.

That makes me laugh. "I've got news for you. I don't know who told you that, but Tony Walters is about as far from the Italian mob as anybody can get."

"Oh, you don't think he can make things happen?"

"I *know* he can make things happen, but there's no mob involved. He knows how to pull strings in all the right ways."

We sit there for a few minutes, silent, until she finally asks, "So you still think I'm a waste of your time?"

"I never said that, babe. I just said I wasn't sure why I was bothering because you didn't seem to care. Do you? Care, I mean?"

"Of *course* I care. I was scared out of my mind when I found out about your accident."

That makes me grin. "Yeah?"

"Yeah." She's chuckling when she says, "You're the best fuck I've ever had. Sure don't want to lose that!"

"Okay, you run with that, bitch babe. C-Y-A. See if it deters me." The smile fades, but the feeling doesn't. "I wasn't lying. I love you. I really do want to be with you, but I can't stand any more of the abuse. Are we past that?"

Her head dips before she lifts it and she smiles into my face. "I'm trying to trust."

"That's all I'm really asking for, honey. I don't want the moon. I'd just like a little of its glow, that's all."

"You're gonna get a lot more than that." There's not a chance to say more before she climbs up to straddle my lap, facing me. "A lot more." I just rest my hands on her thighs and wait to see what she's going to do.

There have been a lot of kisses shared between us, but for the first time, I think I feel some kind of emotion in it, at least more than I'm putting into it. Her palms press against my cheeks and even through my beard, I can feel their warmth. When I feel her tongue press against the cleft in my lips, I wait, wondering what she'll do if she senses that I won't open to her, but she just works more insistently until I finally part them just a tiny bit.

She forces her tongue in and it's game on. There's no holding back now. Mine meets hers and it's almost like a wrestling match, thrashing together, wrapping around each other, and I'm smothered by the sensation of her hands stroking down my chest and the feel of her lips against mine. I vaguely remember the sex I had with girls back in high school, but that was nothing compared to fucking this woman. Everything about her is tight, firm, smooth, muscular, and strong, and I want her naked and in my bed now—right now, not a minute later. It's a struggle to get her to turn loose. "Hey, get in there and strip. I'm right behind you. Go," I bark at her and point toward the bedroom.

"Aren't you supposed to sweet-talk me or woo me or something?" she asks with a chuckle as she heads that direction. I'm already unzipping my jeans.

"Seriously? Wouldn't you rather I just fuck you?"

"Actually, yeah. Why waste time?" she asks, and turns to make sure I see her as she strips off her bra. "Just bone me hard. That's what I'm really looking for."

It's hard to get my briefs down with my dick this rigid,

but I manage. "You realize we're gonna make love someday, right?"

"Yeah, but that day is not today." She's already on the bed, legs spread and one knee up. Everything is open, wet, and blush pink, glistening in the low light. My cock starts to throb as I watch her run a finger from the entrance to her pussy up to her clit. "Hungry kitty," she hisses.

"It'll be full," I growl as I roll on a condom.

"Good. It needs feeding."

No time for a grand entrance. I just slam into her and listen to her cry out as her back arches. "Oh, fuck! Yeah. Hard, babe."

"Be careful what you wish for. You might get more than you really want." Her weight seems like nothing as I slide my hands up her back and grab her hair, pulling it hard to force her head back. With it tipped that way, she's almost totally helpless except for her arms. And that leaves me in my favorite position.

I hunch into her like a madman. In my mind, she's a bitch in heat and I'm taking her my way, fast and rough. I feel her hands between us and realize she's stroking her nub herself, trying to get off, but right now, I don't care if she doesn't. My body needs to slam into her, my dick smacking home over and over, the head abrading the end of her channel, her tightness around me driving me on. "Oh! Oh, damn, Bear! Oh, fuck me," she cries out.

"Miles. Call me Miles when I'm fucking you." I ramp it up, and I can feel her legs churning, trying to dig into the top of the mattress and failing. "I'm gonna fuck you until you pass out, you hear me?"

"Oh, damn. Oh, fuck me, Miles. Harder. Faster. Yeah. Oh, yeah. I need it so bad." She's whining, and I like it. Whining, begging, crying out, screaming, I don't care. I want her to make a lot of noise, because I want to tear this thing up. Love-making is for later. Right now is for fucking like the stallion that I am, fucking my mare into oblivion under me, making her shriek. "Oh! Oh, god! Damn it, Miles! Oh, fuck, fuck, fuck …"

I have to bow my back harder and stretch my arms out straight, but I manage to pull a nipple into my mouth, suck it hard, then give it a nip. "Oh, fuck! Miles!"

"Get that finger busy, girl. I want you pulsing around me," I bark into her skin.

"Oh, oh, oh, ohhhhh …" she groans as her hips start to churn. I'm hunching into her so fast that my knees are burn-ing, and I don't care. Fatigue is setting in and I'm wondering if I can keep going when I feel myself hardening a little more, that burning sensation taking over, and I fill the condom, everything inside me groaning with the release. I give her three more hard stabs, hesitating inside her with each one, until I'm sure I'm finished.

She's limp underneath me when I grab her hips and roll her. "What are you doing?" I hear her whimper.

"I'm taking what I want. And when I'm finished, you can do to me whatever you like. But right now, you're my toy, Sela. And I plan to play with you until I'm finished." My hands grip her hips and pull upward until she's on her knees, her torso slanting away from me and her face buried in the mattress. I've already started stroking myself again, and I roll off the condom and reach for another one. The small bottle of lube I keep in my nightstand drawer for jacking off is plenty for this, and the minute I dribble some onto her dark star, she whines. "You know what's coming," I say, my voice low as my free hand keeps stroking my shaft. "You'll likely pass out before I'm finished with you."

"Do your worst, devil," she mumbles into the sheets, and

I very nearly come undone. With the head of my cock lined up at her rear entrance, I give a mighty shove and send my hardness straight into her.

The little squeal she lets out almost makes me laugh, but it feels so damn good that I couldn't laugh if I wanted to. All I can do is moan, pull back, and thrust into her again. I watch her slap the mattress with her hand and I know it's getting to her, so I just ramp up the speed and the force and listen to her cry out. And that's the moment that I realize something odd.

I'm not enjoying this. I'm really not. My gaze falls on the woman in front of me, resting on her knees, face down, my rock-hard dick in her ass, and I feel a little sick. All I really want is to have a relationship with a woman, the kind of relationship Patch and Penny have. Like Paddy and Natalie. Like Priest and Aggie. And instead, I feel like I'm fucking the hell out of some slut I paid fifty dollars to bare her ass to me. It's not what I thought I'd feel, or how I want to feel.

Then it occurs to me that she seems to be enjoying it. And if that's the case, what is this? Does she understand what I'm really looking for here? Probably not. And she most likely doesn't care, if past experience continues. Am I just a hard cock for her to ride? Does this mean *anything* to her? Do *I* mean anything to her?

No. I can't. There's no contemplating it—I'm already going soft. My ears are buzzing, but I hear her ask, "Bear? What's wrong? You're getting soft on me. What the hell?"

As soon as the tip of my cock clears her ring, I slip off the condom and head to the bathroom. From behind me, I hear her say something, but I just mutter, "No," and keep walking. When the bathroom door closes, I toss the condom in the trash can and sit down on the toilet. It's clear to me that I can't do this. She says she loves me, but there's no tenderness, no softness, no connection. And I'm not the animal I used to be. Even when we were together before she wound up in the hospital, I never behaved like this. Right this moment, I don't know what to think or how to feel. I only know that this feels wrong somehow.

There's a tap on the door and I hear her say, "Bear?" When I don't answer, it changes to, "Miles?" What am I supposed to say to her? How can I explain what's going on in my head? Whatever it is, she's not going to like it. She wants to be a balls-to-the-wall bitch babe. That's all she's comfortable with. There's no … vulnerability. Maybe that's what's missing. I don't know. All I know is that what we were doing a few minutes ago, it's not what I want. It's not what I need. "Miles, please. What's going on? Talk to me. Miles? You okay?"

"Yeah. Yeah, I'm fine. No, I'm not. I don't …" Nothing is making sense.

"Please come out. I don't understand."

Instead of answering, I just sling the door open and she almost falls into the bathroom, naked and confused. "I don't understand either."

"You mean you've never had … *that* problem before?"

"It's not that."

"Then what is it? One minute you're giving it to me like a bronc and the next—"

"And that's the problem, Sela."

She rolls her eyes and lets out a big sigh. "What's the problem? I don't get it."

"Me either." As I drag toward the living room, I pick up my briefs and draw them on, then drop onto the sofa. When she steps into the room, she's got the sheet off my bed wrapped around her. I'm at one end of the sofa, and she sits on the other, waiting. I really don't know what to say to her right at this moment.

Five silent minutes go by before she says, "Okay. Tell me what happened in there. I thought we were having fun."

"We were. Until we weren't."

"We weren't?"

"I wasn't."

"Because you lost it."

"No. I lost it because …" How do I explain? After another full minute of my scrambled brain shredding every thought, I come out with, "I lost it because I wasn't happy with what I was doing."

"I was fucking ecstatic. What weren't you happy with?" There's a pause before her eyes lock with mine and a look of horror spreads across her face. "You mean you weren't happy with me?"

"No, no. Yes. But no. That's not …" Somehow I've got to say this without sounding like a total nut job. "Look. I love you. You know that. I've told you that."

"Yeah. I know. And I told you the same."

"Right. But I want to love you. I mean, *love* you. I mean, I don't want to use you like a fuck puppet. Yeah, okay, maybe sometimes. Occasionally. But that's not the kind of physical relationship I want. I want a real one."

"Bub, that's about as real as it gets," she says with a snort.

"That's not what I mean. I mean, I want a real relationship, like, you know …" That's a sentence I'm not brave enough to finish.

"No. I don't know. Spell it out for me."

"Like, um, not like fucking. Like, um, uh, making … making love."

I can't interpret the look she's giving me. "Making love? Like huggy, touchy, kissy stuff?"

"Yeah."

"That's not what I do."

"I was afraid you were going to say that."

"So that's a problem?"

I nod. "Looks like it."

"But guys like to fuck."

A breath involuntarily huffs out of my mouth before I can stop it. "Well, yeah, but not all the time."

"Hasn't been my experience."

"Then you've been with the wrong guys. Because some of us want deep, passionate, meaningful relationships where we enjoy cuddling, long kisses, things like that." Damn, I sound like the biggest pussy on the planet, but right now, I don't care. Baxter keeps telling me to be true to myself and express my feelings, and by damn, I'm trying. It's not coming out the way I want, but I'm still making one helluva pitiful attempt to explain.

"Uh-huh." That's all she says, but her face is saying it all. Her mouth is set in a straight line, her brows are furrowing inward, and her eyes are slitted. I think this is probably over.

There's nothing else for me to say. I've verbally shot my load, so I stand from the sofa. "I'm, uh, gonna go get dressed and go over to the lodge to sleep. That'll probably be best. We can decide what to do in the morning."

"Please, Bear, don't—"

"You don't have to feel bad about this. It's just best if—"

"Miles. Please." As I try to pass her on my way to the bedroom, she reaches out and takes my hand. "Please, sit back down, okay? Please?"

"Why? We don't see eye to eye on this, and I don't think we ever will. It's just who we are, Sela. You don't know how to be anybody but you, and I don't know how to be anybody but me. And I can see that's not going to work."

"But you could be wrong. Sit back down. I have something I need to say." Well, there's a switch, Sela sharing without somebody practically squeezing it out of her. Can't wait to hear this, so I sit down and wait. "I fuck like a bitch in heat. But I've always done that because that's what all the guys I've ever been with wanted. And you acted like that's what you wanted, at least the times we've been together."

"Damn, girl, it had been over thirty years for me! Of course I wanted to fuck like a racehorse! I was making up for lost time." So it was partially my fault. I see that now. "And for making you think that's all I wanted, I apologize. It was total excitement after all those years."

"I get that, and I can totally understand that. Teenage boy in the back seat of Dad's Buick and all that."

"Exactly," I say with a nod.

"But, Bear," she says, then stops. "Miles," she says as she starts again, "I was just doing what I thought you wanted me to do. You wanna try to make love, sure. Let's. Nobody's ever wanted to do that with me, but the way I feel about you … I don't want to lose you over this. Of course I have needs, but you do too. I'll try it your way. I'm glad to. However you want to do that. But please, don't give up on me. Even though I'm rough and tumble, I'm still a woman. I've never been romanced in my life, and sometimes I'd like to see what that's like."

If you want to see what shock looks like, you should get a load of my face at this moment. I'm sure I look like somebody just goosed me, because I definitely feel that way. I couldn't be more surprised. "Really? You want to be *romanced*?"

"Sure. That would be nice for a change. I'm certainly not opposed to it. I just find it odd because nobody's ever done that with me before."

"I've never done it with a woman before, but I'd really like to. Flowers, candy, gifts, dinners out, all that stuff. It would be nice. Closest I got was giving my high school prom date a corsage, and that's *not* the same thing."

She lets loose a little laugh and all of a sudden, I feel like things just might wind up being okay. "No, it's definitely not the same. So can we try this and see what happens?"

"Yeah. I'm game if you are."

"I'm game. Want to start now?"

I squint one eye. "Aren't you a little tired?"

"I'm not *that* tired!" she says and laughs.

It's hard to believe that she'd try to meet me halfway. Sela Baldwin, who knows how things should be and wants them that way, even if it's all in her own mind. Who wants to be in charge. Who doesn't want to give an inch if she doesn't have to and really doesn't give a fuck what anybody else wants as long as she gets her way. Holy shit. It dawns on me instantly that there's a lot of pressure on me now to do this right or we'll never do it again.

I think I can.

When I lean across the sofa and reach out for her arm, she scoots toward me, sheet and all, and crawls until she's across me, her hands on the sofa arm. Then she spins and lowers herself onto my lap. My arm's already around her back, and I let the other hand rest on her knee. Her dark hair is a mess, and her lashes are thick and dark around those smoky, deep hazel eyes. "Damn, woman, you're so fucking beautiful."

As her eyes fly open, the lashes fan out under her brow bones in surprise and she whispers, "Nobody's ever said that to me before."

"Nobody? Because you are, Sela. You're beautiful. Your skin is so soft and your eyes just sparkle."

Her wicked grin is adorable. "And you like my tits."

"Okay, I'll admit, I do like your tits. They're gorgeous too." This is not a lie. She unwraps the sheet and there they are, small and firm and upright with nice-sized, hard, rosy nipples. The hand I'd rested on her knee comes up to palm the left one, and I rake my thumb across the peak to watch it harden even more. An instant later, I lift my hand, take her chin between my thumb and forefinger, and pull her face to mine.

Of all the kisses we've had between us, this one is different. Our lips meet and I kiss her softly, just pressing mine to hers, then tip my head slightly to make them fit together better. Her arms encircle my neck and I pull her closer to me, my hands lightly grasping her shoulders, holding her there, relishing the feel of her soft skin and taking in the scent of her shampoo. Everything inside me wants to draw her in and make her mine, and I kiss her even more deeply, still reining in my tongue, letting that feeling of simplicity take over.

Kissing from her lips across her jaw and over to the soft spot beneath her ear, it makes my heart skip a few beats when she tips her head to the side to give me more access. God, she smells so fucking good. When I nibble her earlobe, she giggles softly. "Like that?"

"Tickles," she murmurs.

"Mmmm." That makes me suck it between my lips, and I can feel her shiver in my arms. "I'm so glad you're here with me," I breathe against her skin.

"I'm glad I'm here with you. This is nice."

"Yeah. It is." My lips find hers again, and this time, there's a heat between us that hadn't been there before. Instinctively, I close my arms around her and feel hers tighten around my neck. We're locked there, and when she breaks the kiss, her eyes are dewy. "I just want to hold you."

Instead of answering me, she turns her face toward my neck and drops her head onto my shoulder, her cheek resting there, arms loosening and slipping down to encircle my ribs. I just hold her even more tightly, and the elation I feel is something I can't describe. Lost in my thoughts, I'm pulled out of them when she whispers, "I do love you, Miles."

"I love you too. This is what I've dreamed about, babe. Just sitting with somebody I care about, holding them, listening to the sound of them breathing and feeling the warmth of their skin. And you're that somebody, Sela. You're bringing my dream to life." There's a bit of sadness in my heart when I ask, "But can you ever trust me?"

"I already do."

It's hard to contain my emotions, even though the words slip from my tongue so easily that I can tell I've waited my whole life to say them. "Sela, I need you like I need breath. I swear to you, from this moment forward, anything I do with you, to you, or for you, I do it out of love. I don't want anything but love between us. There can't be room for anything else."

That gets me a nod from her. "Same."

The kiss I drop on her lips is quick and sweet. "Can we go back in there and start again?"

Instead of answering, she stands, takes my hand, and drags the sheet behind her as she leads me back to the bedroom. I don't know what's about to happen, but whatever it is, I'm sure it's going to be amazing.

CHAPTER 5

EVERYTHING ABOUT THIS MAN'S BODY IS PERFECTION. There's no doubt in my mind that he worked out while he was in prison, and I'm guessing he's found some way to do it here too. Somehow, with really no gym equipment here to speak of, just a couple of pieces, he's managed to stay fit and hard.

And speaking of hard … He had to be really unhappy earlier, because he's never had any trouble keeping it up before. Every time we've been together, he's been like stone. Is he big? Eh. Plenty big enough. I've had smaller. I've had bigger. But for a guy who hasn't been with any woman except me in a long time, he knows what he's doing, I'll give him that. As I stroll toward the bed, I toss the sheet on it, then climb up and sit down. Bear is right behind me, and he drops his briefs and crawls across the mattress toward me, his dick like a flagpole.

Instead of practically mauling me, he leans in and kisses me. Something about this kiss is different from before. It has a soothing quality that I really like, and when my hands wind into his hair, he wraps his arms around my waist and gently leans me back until I'm lying under him, his cock pressing into my belly. His lips are soft and a little salty, and when he exhales, his breath enters me like a whisper or a song. No one has ever kissed me this way, and when he tips his head to the side and crosses my mouth with his, a fire blazes deep in my belly. What is happening? This is something I don't understand, but I like it.

A trail of warmth is left behind as his hand slides from my waist up my ribs and stops to cradle my breast. It's almost like he's checking its weight, and then brushes the pad of his thumb across my nipple. Everything inside me lights up like a fire set by a flare gun, and it ignites something I don't completely understand. In that instant, I want this man inside me, not moving, just still, our bodies one, something linking us together like a mystery unfolding. "Bear, I—"

"Sela, please. Call me by my name. Be the one person who really knows me. Please?" It's not like a request. It's more like a prayer, and right now, I'd do anything his soul asks of mine.

"Miles, please. Please, just … be inside me. Please?" Begging is something I don't do, but I'm begging him. I need him. Everything inside me is screaming for his touch and his hardness.

There's pressure, and then a stretching sensation with just a touch of a burn. His forearms rest in the hollows of my shoulders as his hands stroke up the sides of my face. "So beautiful. You're so beautiful, *banrigh*."

"BOWN-ree?"

"*Banrigh*. It's Scottish. It means queen. You're my queen, Sela. Never forget that." His body is resting on mine, no movement, no thrusting, just the two of us lying there connected in the most intimate of ways, the room quiet and still. I'd forgotten—his last name is McMillan, so somebody in his family must've been Scottish.

"Did somebody in your family teach you that?"

His lips brush against mine once more before he answers. "My grandpa. He called my grandma that every time I saw them together. He'd say, 'Mac, if'n ye treat yer woman like a *banrigh*, you can never go wrong. Unnerstan, aye?' I never saw two happier people than my grandparents. I want that, Sela. And I want it with you."

I have questions, but this isn't the time to ask them. Instead, it's time to let all of these foreign feelings sweep over me and settle in. Can I trust this man? Is he really what he says he is? Does he really feel for me what he says he feels? And do I even know enough about love to know if I feel it for him? Before I realize what I'm doing, I blurt out, "Miles, what is love?"

That smile. It's incendiary, but it's also gentle. "Hell, I dunno, babe. Nobody's ever asked me that before. Ummm … So if something happened, if I died in the night, how would you feel?"

"I'd be sad."

"But what about tomorrow? Or the next day?"

I'm not good at these kinds of things. "I dunno. I'd be sad. But I'd miss you. A lot. What about you? How would you feel if I died in the night?"

"The truth?" I nod. "I wouldn't want to go on. I'd want my life to end. The idea of you not being in it is so painful that I can't imagine it. Knowing I'd never see your face again, never touch you again, never hear you call my name again, I don't think I could do it. I'd rather die myself than go on without you. But I'd be concerned about you if I died, because you'd have to go on without me." He stops and stares down at me. "And you don't feel the same way, I see."

"No! It's not that. It's just that … I'm trying to imagine what it would be like if you weren't here anymore. Like, if I woke up and you were gone, and nobody knew where you were, and you didn't come back, I'd be so fucking pissed. But I'd miss you. And I'd always be looking for you, watching crowds, searching roadways as I drove past. I'd always hope that you'd come back. But if you died?" My brain is trying to wrap around that idea. "I can't even think about it. I don't know how to imagine that."

Deep down, I'm lying and I know it. When I was a kid, my dad's mom died suddenly, and I remember every Christmas after that, thinking about how I didn't even really like the holiday anymore because Nanna Jo wasn't with us. It colored everything I felt about every holiday or celebration after that, and they've never been the same.

And in that moment, I understand. If something happened to Miles, that's how I'd feel. The world would be a colorless, gutted place, filled with nothingness and uselessness, no purpose and no meaning. *Man up*, I tell myself. *Be honest with him. He's being honest with you. You owe him that.* "I'm sorry. I just lied. I know exactly how I'd feel."

His eyes are sad, and that's surprisingly hurtful to me. "Yeah?"

I nod again. "My life would have no meaning. Nothing would ever be the same, and waking up wouldn't be worth the effort. I … This is all new to me, but please, don't give up on me? Can you just do that? Don't give up?"

That gentle smile stretches his lips wider again. "I'll tell you again. I'll never give up on you, *banrigh*. Never. You're mine and I'm yours."

I'm unprepared when his hips draw back and he slides

back into me slowly. Never in my life have I felt as whole and complete, as wanted and cherished, and I know I let out a little groan because he chuckles under his breath. "Fuck, you feel so good, baby. Is that good?"

"Oh, yeah. Very."

Still buried deep inside me, he rises up on his knees and spreads my legs wider. I'm about to ask what he's doing when his fingers find my tenderest spot and start to circle it slowly. Everything inside my belly coils, and the room heats up by ten degrees. By bowing his back just slightly, his long arms can reach up until the fingers of his free hand pinch one of my nipples and I suck in a breath. "I want you to come for me, *banrigh*. I wanna feel you pulse around me." That tweak he just gave my nipple turns into a twist, and I feel my skin ignite. "Yeah, that's tuning you up. I can feel it. You clamped down on me."

The fingers circling my clit grow more insistent, until he's stroking it aggressively. "Oh, fuck. Miles, babe, oh … Damn, baby. Oh, damn." It's taking everything I have to hold off.

"Why are you fighting it, babe? Let go."

"No. I … I want it to be strong. Really strong. I want you to make me crazy with it."

"Baby, I'm gonna do that. You'll come but I won't let you stop. Hear me? Sela, let go. Do it." Every muscle in my belly is quivering, and I can feel it building, that pressure and heat. "Sela …"

The spasms hit, and my hips start to buck. I thrust, unable to stop myself, and I could swear I feel him grow harder and longer inside me. Before I realize what's happening, the hand that's been tweaking and twisting my nipple pulls it out sharply, twisting at the same time, and I cry out, but I can feel that building sensation again, his fingers stroking me faster. "Do it, Sela. Do it. Come again for me.

It's gonna be crazy, babe. I want you screaming. Sela, turn loose …"

I have never in my life felt like this. My back bows and I shake all over, everything out of control and pulsing. There are sounds coming out of my mouth that I've never heard before, and it's as though I'm hearing them from someone else's perspective, like I've left my body, a body that's spasming unbearably. "Stop. Oh, god, please, Miles, stop. I can't take anymore. Please …" I'm just mumbling because I can't talk. His fingers are driving, driving, driving, leaving my limbs shaking and my body jerking.

And then he stops. The room is still and quiet, but I know what's coming. Without even thinking, I reach up with both hands and start twisting and pinching my nipples myself. "You need this as much as I do," he whispers before his lips land on mine and he draws back.

The thrust he gives me nearly sends me into the headboard, and he begins to hunch me, keeping his body close to mine, his chest almost flattening my hands against my breasts, but he's powering into me rhythmically with an intensity that terrifies and thrills me. His hands slide down my lower back and cup my ass, and we're moving together, this huge, mighty man using me like I'm just a wisp of a thing. Something about it really turns me on, makes me want him more, makes me want him to pound into me, to claim me and ruin me for other men. "Fuck, Sela, you're perfect. Everything about you is perfect, from those soft, sweet lips, to those round, perky tits, and this hot, wet pussy. Damn, babe, you make me glad to be a man."

When this man pulls out of me, I will cry. The way we're moving together in this moment feeds my soul like nothing else ever has. I belong with Miles McMillan like he belongs with me, joined in the holiest of ways. "Oh, god, Miles, fuck me. Keep goin', babe. I need it so bad."

"I know. I can tell. Your body is amazing. This was meant to be, Sela. I know it was meant to be. Oh, damn, girl, I'm gonna come, and I really don't want to. I want to make this last. Fuck, fuck, fuck. Oh, no-no-no-no, damn!" There's that heat and wetness I hoped I'd feel, a man who's filled me up in every way. And then reality sets in.

"Are you wearing a condom?"

He presses himself up, his eyes go round, and his mouth gapes for a second before he says, "Oh, shit. I thought you …"

"Yeah. I am. I just figured … Thought you'd want one."

"Why? I haven't been with anybody. You been with anybody?"

"No."

As soon as he drops on top of me, I wrap my arms around his shoulders, and his hands slide up to encircle my waist. I love the feeling of his weight on top of me and his essence dripping from me. "Then I think we're fine. You like me bare?"

"Yeah," I answer and nip his shoulder.

"We're good. This is our world, babe. We get to decide how things go in it. And right now, it's all good. Sela …" He presses himself up again, and one hand comes up, his knuckles brushing my cheek. "I'm so in love with you. No matter what. It can't get too dirty or complicated for me. I know you might not feel the—"

"I do, Miles. I do. Our world. We move forward together." My eyes take in his face, the tiny lines by his eyes, that shock of wild hair, his beard, those kiss-stained lips. "I'm in love with you too."

There's a funny, wistful quirk to his lips and his eyes are

bright. "Are you telling me you just made love with a man for the first time?"

That makes me laugh. "Yeah, I guess I did!"

"So I popped your lovemaking cherry. Sweet!" He's laughing too, and I realize that above everything else, when I'm with Miles, I actually have fun. He's so many things. So many.

And he's everything to me.

BEAR

WE FALL ASLEEP STILL JOINED TOGETHER. YEAH, I'LL SOFTEN and slip out, but for a little while, it will be like we're frozen in time, and I like that. Along with feeling sexually sated and extremely emotionally connected, I'm exhausted too. I meant to wear her out. Wearing myself out was a byproduct, and I'm not unhappy about it. Not at all.

When I do wake up, I glance at the clock and find it's ten before two in the morning. Sela is sleeping peacefully beside me, her arm draped across my chest. My bladder is full, and I figure if I can get out of bed without waking her, I should run to the bathroom. That doesn't seem to be a problem—she doesn't even move when I lift her hand and lay it on the mattress beside me.

As soon as I'm finished, I clean myself up a little and head back out to the bedroom, but I hear something outside and I wonder about the coydog. Is it okay? The sounds are odd, so I drag on my briefs, tiptoe out of the bedroom, and head to the front door.

And when I round the corner of my cottage, I get a huge

surprise that scares the living shit out of me. "Son, what are you doing out here?"

Martin looks up at me, his eyes wide and a little frightened. "Um, I just … I, um …"

"It's okay. I'm not mad. But what are you doing?" It's not like I can't see. I just can't believe my eyes. "Does your dad know you're out here?"

"No. I was worried about him. He's out here all alone and afraid." He's sitting on the ground, back leaned up against my cottage, and the coydog's head is across his lap. Holy hell, if I make one wrong move, that dog might snap his face off. As I watch in wonder, his hand comes up and strokes down the dog's head. The big animal seems to relax with every swipe of his small hand.

"Hon, we don't know anything about this dog. It might have a disease or something, and if it bites you, you could get really sick." How can I get Reboot out here without causing a commotion and setting the thing off?

"He's not going to bite me. He's been around people before. Can't you see? He came to us for help, Mr. Bear. He wants to be here with people."

"Martin, you don't have to call me mister. Bear is fine. And I know he came here for help, but he's really scared and skittish, and that can be dangerous."

"Well, he might be scared and skittish of you, but he's not scared and skittish of me. See?" With no way to stop him, I watch in horror as he leans down.

And the damn dog licks his face.

Well, son of a bitch. I don't believe it. "I think he likes you," I murmur. Hmmm. I should test this. "Let's see what he does." Ever so slowly, I reach out a hand, and the dog leans out and licks my fingertips before depositing his head back on Martin's lap with a plop. "Huh. Not the vicious wild animal we thought."

"He's not. I need to get this rope off his neck, but I'm going to wait until tomorrow. Maybe he'll trust me more then." Gotta give it to this kid, he's got a good head on his shoulders.

Sounds come from the other cottage and I hear a loud whisper call out, "Martin, what the hell are you doing?" Before Reboot can take two more steps, I throw my hand up, palm toward him, to stop him in his tracks. Thank god he gets it and freezes.

"It's okay, Reboot. Everything's fine. Just take it easy and go slow." Reboot's in his pajama pants, his feet bare, and he steps very carefully toward us. "I think Martin's got it under control."

"Yeah, Dad. Everything's fine. He was alone and afraid, so I came out to sit with him. He's okay." He's still stroking the big dog's head, and we watch the animal's eyes close. "See? He likes it."

"I see that. But you need to come back inside and go to bed."

"But Dad, can he come too? He'll be good and—"

"I think that's a little early, bud," I tell the boy before his dad can say anything. "He needs to stay outside for a couple more days until we really know more about him. And maybe until we can take him to the vet, don't you think?"

"Yeah, I guess that would be best. Can he sleep on our porch?" he asks Reboot, his little eyes sad.

"Sure. See if you can get him to come and bring his towel with him. Maybe he'll bed down up there."

"Okay. Come on, Elmore," I hear the boy say as he scoots away from the dog and stands. Instantly, the canine rises and shakes himself hard.

"Elmore?" Reboot asks.

"Yeah. That's his name."

"Why?" I ask.

"Because he said that's his name, and I believe him." With that, Martin turns toward Reboot and Mavis' cottage. "Come on, Elmore. Let's go back to bed." I watch, slack-jawed, as the boy and the dog head across the space between the cottages, leaving Reboot standing there with me, just as shocked as I am.

"Well, I'll be a son of a bitch," he whispers.

"Yeah. Kids and dogs. Ya never know." There's something about watching that child and that dog stroll across the grass that makes my heart sing. Little things. Our lives are made up of the little things, the little moments, that make life worth living. "I gotta get back inside. Good luck. Looks like you're going to need it," I say and slap Reboot on the shoulder.

"Yeah. Lucky me. Night, brother," he says as he picks up the bowl of water, then turns to follow the child and the dog.

"Night, brother." I start back toward the door, but when I get to the porch deck, I stop to watch. Martin spreads the towel beside their front door and, as if he'd done it a hundred times, the dog—whose name is apparently Elmore—lies down and curls up there. Reboot places the bowl at the edge of the porch near the dog, and the boy gives the dog one more stroke before he steps inside the open door. Reboot doesn't attempt to pet it, just follows Martin inside and closes the door.

I've barely made it to the bedroom door before Sela's sleepy voice asks, "What's going on?"

"I'll tell you in the morning. Right now I need to wipe off my feet and then I'll be right there." That's when I realize I've been outside in nothing but my boxer briefs.

Oh, well. There was nobody to see me except Reboot, Martin, and a dog named Elmore. And I don't think any of them paid one bit of attention.

———

Sela

I WAKE TO THE SOUNDS OF THE SHOWER AND REALIZE MILES isn't in bed beside me. In a couple of minutes, the water turns off and he's standing in the bathroom doorway with a towel around his waist. "Hey, better get up and get moving if you want breakfast."

"But you're not working."

"I know, but I'm eating! I'm going over to see if there's anything anybody needs me to do today. I want to stay busy, you know? I hate just sitting around."

"There's definitely something you can do. I've got a doctor appointment. Can you take me?"

His eyebrows shoot up and he smiles. "Sure! Of course! I'd love to. When is it?"

"Eleven?"

"Want to get lunch or something?"

"Sure. That would be great. I need to go to the discount store too."

"We can do that. Just get showered and dressed and we'll set out after breakfast, okay?"

He doesn't have to tell me twice. I'm up like a rocket and headed to the bathroom. "You always that free about running around naked?" he asks as I clear the bathroom door.

"Why not? You've seen it all."

"I have. And I like seeing it again," he announces from behind me.

"Yeah?"

"Oh, yeah. I can think of some things I'd like to—"

"Keep that up and I'll miss my doctor appointment," I tell him, squirting toothpaste out onto my toothbrush.

"Yes, ma'am. Don't want that." That makes me smile and I turn to say something, but for the first time, I catch a look at his back.

It's covered in scars. All kinds of scars, all sizes and all shapes. I knew he had a couple on his ribs and one on his abdomen, but this … "Miles?"

"Yeah, babe?"

"Your back."

His brow furrows like he's not sure what I'm talking about, but then I see the realization hit. "You hadn't seen them before, had you?"

"No. There are a lot."

"Yeah. I got into a lot of fights."

"No, babe. What I've got is a lot. That's … I've never seen anything like that."

"Yeah, well, you haven't been an agent for thirty years, but that's how long I was in prison. So I had a lot of time to collect these."

"I see." This is not really the time to talk about all of that stuff, so I brush my teeth and think about it the whole time. What has he seen? How badly has he been hurt? I'll get my answers, but they don't have to come now. I remember his words: *This is our world, babe. We get to decide how things go in it.* There will be time for all my questions, I'm sure.

We walk hand in hand to the kitchen, and it feels weird and middle schoolish to me, but still good. I'm in love with somebody, and he's in love with me. Hard to believe.

"Hey, good morning!" Audrey calls out from across the kitchen, and several of the other occupants of the kitchen turn and smile.

"Mornin'. Smells good in here!" Miles calls out.

"It *is* good. Nobody cooks as good as my woman," Hollywood answers him as he passes by Audrey and leans out to give her a kiss on the cheek.

"And nobody knows how to squeeze a buffalo nickel until it shits like my man," Audrey quips back, and everybody laughs.

Having people to eat breakfast with seems odd to me. After all, it's been years since I lived in a family unit. One of Paddy's boys looks up and smiles. "Need a seat, Miss Sela? You can sit beside me," he says and pats the chair.

"Oh! Don't mind if I do! Tegan, right?" He nods and his cheeks turn pink. "Thank you."

"You're welcome. I'll get you something to drink. What do you want?"

"Just black coffee. Sure you won't get burned?"

"Nah. I'll be careful. Be right back."

Miles leans down, I assume to kiss my ear, but instead he whispers, "I think somebody's got a crush on you."

That makes me crank my head toward him and stare. "Me?"

He chuckles under his breath. "Why is that so hard to believe? You're beautiful." Then he's off and gone toward the food.

"Here you go, Miss Sela. Just like you like it. Plain." Tegan sets the coffee cup beside me. "Anything else I can get for you?"

"No, but thanks. I think Miles is getting it."

He stares at me. "Miles?"

"Oh. Bear. That's his real name."

"Cool." The boy plops down in his chair beside me and picks up his fork. "So do you like to read? Because I do. And I'm reading a really good book."

"What is it?"

"It's called *The Absolutely True Diary of a Part-Time Indian*. Have you ever read that?"

"No, can't say that I have."

"You really should. It's about an Indian boy. You'd like it."

I nod and smile. "I'll have to look it up. Thanks!"

"You're welcome. Do you need more coffee?"

I haven't even touched my cup. "Nah. But thanks." I think Miles is right. This kid does have a crush on me. That's weird—adorable, but weird.

"Here ya go. I remembered that you liked this." A plate appears in front of me with some kind of casserole on it, along with some fruit and a muffin.

"Oh. Yeah, I remember this from when I was staying here with Natalie. It's delicious." I can't wait to cut into it.

Natalie and Paddy sit down across from us, and we all sit and chat. It seems easier somehow with Miles sitting next to me. At first, the idea that I was going to be Natalie's equal felt odd, like I should still be telling her what to do, but now it feels a bit more natural. We're almost finished eating when her phone rings, and she looks down at it, then jumps up. "I've got to take this." I hear her feet as she jets across the kitchen and steps outside.

"Must be work," Paddy says, never looking up from his plate.

In a flash, a hand falls on my shoulder, and I hear her voice say, "I need to speak with you outside. Now."

I can't jump up fast enough, and I follow her outside. As

soon as the door closes, she turns to me. "That was the FBI Kentucky field office."

"What did they want?"

"Something's going on with the cartel. They want to talk to me at the office today."

Every red flag in my arsenal starts to snap in the breeze. "Did they say what?"

"No, but they're making a trip to Pikeville, so it must be important."

"Did they say anything about me?"

"Wanted to know if I knew where you were. They want to talk to you too."

"When will they be there?"

"Close to eleven."

"Damn, Nat, I've got a doctor appointment."

"Don't worry about it. Go to the doctor. If it's important, they'll hang around."

"Okay. Um, okay. Yeah. Okay." I've already started to pace, a response from my years at the bureau. "Okay, I'll go to the doctor, but you call me if I need to come to Pikeville, okay?"

"I will. I promise. You getting better is your top priority now. I'll tell them that. They probably already know."

"Yeah. Probably. Okay. Thanks. And be careful."

She nods her understanding. "You too."

I return her nod and head back inside. By the time I'm sitting back down, she is too. "Everything okay, sweet pea?" Paddy asks her.

"Yeah. We'll talk later." And she goes back to eating. That's my cue to do the same. I can feel Miles' eyes on me, but I'm not saying anything in here at the table.

Just as I'm finishing, Patch wanders by the table. "Hey, you doin' okay?" he asks.

He must be practicing to be a server, because I have a mouthful of food. My hand comes up to cover it and I answer, "Yeah. Good."

"Great." His hand pats my shoulder. "I'm glad you're here."

"Me too," I say as I swallow my last bite.

"Everybody," he calls out from right behind me. "Two things. One, I'm glad Sela's here, and if you haven't told her the same, please do. We need to do everything we can to get these two back to one hundred percent so they can go back to work. I know it's driving Bear crazy to be on the bench, but it won't be like that forever, buddy," Patch says and reaches over to squeeze Miles' shoulder. "Second, Tony and Steve will be here tomorrow. The farm down the road, the old Pettit place, is up for auction tomorrow, and Tony will be coming to bid on it. He wants to buy it and deed it to Iron Oak so our land mass will be larger. He says land is the number one best investment anybody can make, and that will make our acreage much larger."

"I've never been down there," Bulldog says. "Dwellings? Outbuildings?"

"If you remember, that was the property where the barn that we pulled Penny from is located." I've heard Miles talk about it, and apparently that was a really scary day. "There's also a small house, plus a springhouse up the creek, a nice summer kitchen, and a very nice garden patch. We've talked about it, and Tony wants to approach Eastern Kentucky University to see if they're interested in doing an interpretative farm there to show how former slaves and free Black people lived immediately following the Civil War. That would probably mean their archaeology department would come and do some excavating near the buildings, and their history and Black studies departments would probably have students work as guides and interpreters. In other words, a living history farm. That could bring in some tourism to the area, which—"

"Would definitely help us," Ghost interrupts.

"Bingo. I'm excited about the idea, but they have to win the auction first."

"Tony won't even break a sweat," Hollywood says.

"Don't say that. He's a sharp businessman, and he's not going to pay an enormous amount over what he knows it's worth. So fingers crossed. But what they'd be using for the exhibit would be just a tiny portion of the farm. The rest would all be wilds and fields and things we could use over the years, and if we ever found ourselves in dire straits, we could probably sell parcels and still have a lot of room. Plus by letting them do that with the university, we'll probably get a tax break."

Good. Tony and Steve will be here tomorrow. Maybe we can talk about a job for me. Under the table, I feel Miles' hand close around mine, and I know he's thinking the same thing.

Patch gazes around. "Anybody else have anything?" When no one says anything, Patch claps his hands together loudly. "Okay. Time to go to work. As usual, thanks for the delicious breakfast, Audrey, and everybody be safe!" Everybody in the room echoes the sentiment, and soon they're all scattering for the day.

"Guess I'd better get going. Gotta get to the office," Natalie says, leaning down to kiss Paddy. When she straightens, her gaze turns to me. "We'll talk." I just nod.

"Boys, it's time to go," a female voice says, and I look up to find Aggie standing there.

"Awww, do we have to?" Tegan grouses, and I can see

Borden grinning at him. Yeah, his older brother has figured it out too.

"Come on, butthead. Time to go," Borden orders and heads toward the door.

"Bye, Miss Sela. See ya later," the younger boy says and falls into step with Sarah and Martin as they head toward the parking area.

Everybody's clearing out, and pretty soon we're alone in the kitchen except for Audrey and Izzy, who are cleaning up. "Wanna tell me what's going on?" Miles asks, his voice low.

"Yeah. Something to do with the cartel. Feebs are going to see Natalie today in Pikeville."

"Sounds serious."

"Yeah, they wanted to see me, but I've got that doctor appointment. She's going to call me though."

"Okay. You keep me in the loop, you hear me?" His voice is stern in a way that I've never heard before.

"Of course. Wouldn't dream of not."

"Good. Come on. We need to head out." Just as we reach the door, Miles turns and calls out, "Hey, Audrey!"

"Yeah?"

"Did anybody take that dog something to eat?"

"Who, Elmore?" she answers with a laugh. "Yeah. We had some leftover stew, so I gave it to Martin to take to him."

"Thanks. I'll pick up some dog food while I'm in town."

"Oh, can you get some syrup? We're about out."

"Sure. Text me the kind and amount and I'll pick it up."

"Great. Hollywood will reimburse you."

"Nah. I eat it too. Have a good day, sweetheart," he tells her and waves.

"You too, both of you."

"We will," I call back, and we're out the door. "You got something to drive?"

"Yeah. Patch slipped me the keys. We're taking one of the SUVs. I need to just buy a car. Hell, I need to buy him a truck, since I wrecked his."

"That's what insurance is for, babe," I remind him.

An hour later, we're pulling into the parking lot of the big box store in Hazard, and I'm looking at the list of things I need to get. While I pore through the health and beauty stuff, Miles grabs a cart and heads out to get syrup and dog food. What a combination. I'm starting to get a little crazed with trying to hold everything when I look up and see him rounding the end of the aisle. "Thank god. I need to put this stuff down."

"At your service, m'lady," he says in a fake accent while I drop everything into the cart. "Hey, whaddya think? I like them." He holds up two items—a collar and a leash, both in camouflage print. "And they've got a reflective strip on them too."

"Good choice. It'll look good on the mutt."

"He's a sweet dog, Sela. You weren't out there with him."

"I'll take your word for it." They're going to have to prove it to me. Otherwise, I won't believe it.

We wander on through the store. I've still got two hours before I have to be at the doctor's office, so we've got time to kill. We're strolling down an aisle adjacent to the lingerie department, and I reach out and pick up a bra and panty set, a lacy thing in fuchsia and black. "Whaddya think?"

"I like it. It'll look great on the floor too," he says and winks. I lean over to put it in the cart when a voice stops me cold.

"Agent Sela Baldwin?"

That makes me spin toward the sound, and I find two men in dark suits, white shirts, and ties. There's not one doubt in my mind.

They're feebs.

"Yes?"

"I'm Supervisory Special Agent Morreau, and this is Supervisory Special Agent Landrum. We need a word. Now."

"I'm listening." For an agency that's treating me like they're never letting me come back, I'm a bit surprised that they're turning up here.

"Could we go somewhere a bit more private?" Morreau asks.

"You want to go into a dressing room?" I ask and point, feeling a little too sassy. Yeah, I'm flirting with disaster, but I'm sick and fucking tired of male agents playing god over me.

Before I realize what's happening, Landrum reaches over and grabs my upper arm. "Let's go."

As soon as I shake off his hand, he reaches again, and I sidestep and grab his arm, then wring it behind his back. "You put your hands on me again and I'll take out both of your kneecaps."

"Agent Baldwin?" I hear Morreau say.

"Save it, asshole. I've been dealing with you guys since Quantico. You're going to be polite or you're going to be flat on your faces, and if you've read up on me, you know I can take both of you at once."

"Not in the shape you're in right now," Morreau says. To his credit, Landrum has shut up.

"I wouldn't bank on that, sir," Miles says, pointing at me. "I'm twice her size, and I'm not fucking with her. She can definitely take you both down, but she won't have to, because I'll help her if you touch her again, and I'm not kidding."

There's a tense moment while I wait, until Landrum finally motions, palm down, that he's backing off, and I release his arm. Just as I do, I lean forward and whisper,

"And do not think that I took no pleasure in doing that, because I did. It delighted me. I'm looking forward to doing it again if you can't keep your hands to yourself."

He nods. "My apologies. We're just concerned for your safety."

"I get that, but you can be concerned with it with your hands on the butts of your guns, not on my body."

"Agreed. Can we talk now? Somewhere more private?"

I nod at Landrum. "Sure, but I don't know where."

"This store has a break room. We'll find it," Morreau says, and Miles and I trail them toward an employee. Morreau pulls out his badge, flashes it at the wide-eyed young man, and says, "You got a break room here?"

"Uh, yes, sir. We do. I'll take you."

"Thanks." He turns to make sure we're still following, and our whole little entourage heads for the back of the store. The young man ushers us into a room not much bigger than Miles' bedroom and as soon as the door closes, Morreau turns to me. "Does he need to be here?" he asks, motioning to Miles.

"Absolutely." He opens his mouth, but I add, "Because I said so, and that's the only reason you need."

"Fair enough." Morreau rests his ass on the top of a chair and folds his arms across his chest. "Two other agents went to talk to Judge Anderson."

"I'm aware that they were planning to do that."

"You don't have your bureau phone turned on."

"Why would I? Your bosses won't let me come back to work, so I'm using my personal phone."

"Right, right. Look, we didn't come here to tear your world apart or remind you that things aren't the way you'd like."

"Things aren't right—period."

"Whatever."

That makes me furious. "Do not fucking whatever me. I was injured in the line of duty. I know it frosts you when you get a hangnail, but some of us have given a lot to be part of the bureau, and we're not happy when you treat us as second-class citizens because we have vaginas."

"Look, we got off to a rough start. Can I call you Sela?"

"No, you may not. I'm Agent Baldwin until I'm told I'm no longer Agent Baldwin." Someone touches my arm and I lash out, assuming it's Landrum.

"Hey, just me," a soft male voice says.

"Sorry. I thought it was asshat over there," I say and point at Landrum.

"Can I, um, speak to you privately for just a second?" Miles asks and points toward the door.

"Sure. Back in a second. Y'all check your underwear," I tell the two agents as I follow Miles out. When the door closes, I look up into his face. "Yeah?"

"Let them say whatever they've come to say so they can leave us the hell alone. Please. I hate having these guys around, and the sooner they're gone, the happier I'll be."

"Gee, didn't realize you had such an aversion to feebs," I say in a low growl.

"I don't. It's specifically the two of them."

"Why? What did they do to you?"

"*Banrigh*, whatever they do to you, they do to me, and I'm simmering under this calm façade, okay?" That's when I notice it. His face is smooth and seems carefree, but there's a fire burning behind his eyes. I can see it in the glare he's fixed on me.

"Yeah, uh, okay. They're as good as gone." His presence

is right behind me as I step back into the room. "Okay, talk fast. I don't have all day. I've got somewhere to be."

I watch as they glance at each other, and then Landrum locks his gaze on my face. "We got intelligence that the cartel leader has—"

"Don Julio Alphonso."

"Yes. Those two men who went over the cliff with—"

"Bluff," I correct.

"Yeah, okay, bluff. Those two men … The one Natalie took over the edge with her was Don Julio's nephew. But the one you took down with you? That was his son."

Shit. This is not good.

"Word is out that he's hired a pair of hitmen to hunt down you and Natalie for retribution," Morreau explains.

"That makes no sense. We didn't go after them. We were trying to get *away* from them. If they hadn't been chasing us, that never would've happened. How is that our fault?"

"You know as well as we do that things don't have to make sense to a cartel leader. He's just got a reputation to uphold, and the appearance that two women killed his nephew and his son … well, the optics aren't good."

"Okay, so now what are we supposed to do with that information?" Miles asks.

"You'll be assigned agents to watch you," Landrum explains.

Miles' frustration is palpable. "We live on a farm with over a dozen other people. Kids too. What are we supposed to do about that?"

Morreau shakes his head. "I don't know, but nobody is safe until we get these assholes handled. I know it's inconvenient, but …"

"Does anybody know where these clowns are now?" If I know where they are, I can avoid them.

"All we know is that they're here in the states somewhere. The field office chief wants us to bring you into custody and let us put you in a safe house so—"

"Oh, no. I'm not going to a safe house. First off, I'm not being separated from everybody. And second, I've seen that safe houses are anything but safe. So no. I'm safer where I am."

"With a bunch of ex-cons who can't own guns?" Landrum blurts out. That was a mistake on his part. He's just full of wit and wisdom.

"Let me just assure you that we can protect our own, and if we can't, we have help," Miles barks.

"Let me guess. You believe in the twenty-one foot rule," Landrum asks, his grin lopsided and cocky.

"No, what I believe in is that if I'm brave enough to let somebody get within arm's length of me, I can cut them faster than they can shoot me. And I'm not afraid to let them get that close." Miles' voice is like ice. "I'm not some pussy depending on a badge and a gun to protect me and mine."

"Okay, okay, let's just dial it down, everybody. Okay? Shit. Y'all gonna give me a stroke," Morreau says, pinching the bridge of his nose. He's getting a headache. Good. "Look, Baldwin, we can do this the easy way or the hard way."

"If the hard way means forcing me to go, you can go fuck yourself." He lets out an irritated huff. That tells me I've won. "And let me guess. Judge Anderson said pretty much the same thing." I watch as he and Landrum glance at each other. "Uh-huh. Just as I thought. Look, thank you for making us aware, and yes—we'll take all the intel you can drum up. But I'm not putting my life on hold to let the bureau solve my problems. They've caused me more than they've ever solved. So I'm going on about my business, being my usual cautious self, and we'll see what happens. Got it?" I glance down at my watch. "Shit. I've got a doctor's appointment to get to. Y'all can see yourselves out." Without another word, I head for the door, and I can hear Miles right behind me.

We don't speak as we make our way to the front of the store. Thankfully, they've got self-check stations, which I usually hate, but this time, it lets us check out and get the hell out of the store. Once we've gotten everything loaded up and we're in the locked SUV, I say without looking at Miles, "If you want out, now's the time to say something."

"Not a chance in hell, *banrigh*. I'm in this for the long haul. They shoot you, they will have shot me first, because as long as you're standing, I'm going to defend you."

Still not looking at him, I reach for his hand. "Thanks, babe."

"You're welcome. Thank you. Now, let's go to that doctor's appointment and when we get back and Natalie gets home, we'll all sit down and figure out what to do next."

"Sounds good." Having somebody I can rely on is a foreign concept to me, and yet I feel oddly comforted. Anyone with ears could tell that Miles means exactly what he's saying. I have no idea if he realizes what protecting me might entail, and we're going to have that conversation back at the farm.

My doctor's appointment goes okay, but not as well as I'd hoped. Based on what he saw in the x-rays they made down the hallway, things aren't going as smoothly as he wanted. Me? I guess you could say I'm devastated. When we get back into the SUV afterward, I don't know what to say. "Your brain is going ninety miles a minute, Sela. Tell me what you're thinking."

"I'm thinking I'm fucked."

"You may well and truly be, but let's not forget that you

have options. We'll have a chance to explore those tomorrow."

I'd forgotten that Tony and Steve were coming to the farm. "Think they're going to spend the night?"

"I can't imagine that they won't."

"Is Tony's wife coming?"

"Nikki? Probably. He doesn't go very many places without her. Steve's wife? Probably not. They've got the little girl at home, so I don't know if she'll come or not, but Nikki probably will. The idea that he'd come and she wouldn't get to see all of her grandkids at the farm? Nope. She'll probably spend some time with Fiona and that horse of hers, and probably a little extra time with Martin, since he's new and doesn't know them that well. She's such a sweet person. I wish we could clone her and keep her clone with us when she's not around."

"She's always seemed really kind and friendly."

"She is. If you need somebody to talk to, she's the right person. Definitely. Now, ready for some lunch? I hear this place has really good sandwiches." He wheels the SUV into a parking lot and parks in front of a little place called Marley's. It's cute, with a light blue and white striped awning, lime green paint on the trim, and a pink door.

He holds the door for me and as soon as I step inside, a girl in a short white dress with a pink-and-white-striped apron yells, "Welcome to Marley's! I'll be right with y'all. Sit where ya like." I point to a table in the window, so Miles nods and we sit down. We've no more than gotten ourselves pulled up to the table when the same girl appears, pad in hand. "Hey, y'all! Welcome to Marley's. So today we've got cream of tomato bisque and chicken and noodle delight for our soups. Our special of the day is a brisket panini with white cheddar and smoky mustard. Comes with kettle chips and a dill spear. Otherwise, here's our menu." She points to a board on the table. "Do you know what you'd like to drink?"

"I'll have a diet cola," I tell her, and wait while Miles orders. "What sounds good to you?" I ask as soon as she's gone to fetch our drinks.

"I'm having that panini. What about you?"

"Panino."

"What?"

"It's a panino."

"Panini."

I shake my head. "No. It's a panino. I've been to Italy. Ask Tony. It's a panino. Panini is more than one."

"Yeah, okay. Panini, panino. I'm having that."

"Think I'm getting the turkey club wrap. It sounds good. It comes with kettle chips too."

"Yep." We sit there for a second until she comes back with the drinks, then give her our order, and she disappears again. "Sela, listen. I just want you to know that last night … It was like a dream come true for me. I've never felt this way about a woman, and you're it for me."

"Yeah. That's what I want, Miles. That kind of relationship. Nobody's ever been there for me, and I've never felt as close to anybody as I felt to you last night."

"So are we committed? I mean, is there anybody else you want to go out with, or somebody you'd already been seeing, or—"

"Nope. I'm happy right where I am. And I'm really happy about being out there at the farm with you. It's perfect. I love being there and I feel like I'm home in your cottage."

"Then let's start calling it our cottage, okay? Because I want it to be your home. But you've still got to decide what you're going to do about work and all that."

"Maybe tomorrow will make it clearer." I sure hope so.

It seems like my career with the bureau is likely over. All I can do is move forward. I don't know what I want to move forward into, but I know who I want to move forward with. That's not in doubt anymore. Not one bit.

CHAPTER 6

BEAR

DINNER'S ALMOST OVER WHEN I HEAR MY NAME. "NATALIE, Paddy, Sela, Bear—stay behind." Uh-oh. He got wind somehow.

When the kitchen crowd clears, Patch wrangles us all into a circle. "I heard."

"How did you find out?" Natalie asks.

"Sheriff Stafford said they came around asking questions of him. He called me to find out what was going on. Were you planning to tell me, or were you just going to keep me in the dark?" Patch asks, and he seems pissed off. I guess he's got a right to be.

"No. We didn't know what was going on until earlier today ourselves. Hell, they went to her work so I didn't really know what was going on until she got home," Paddy says and points to Natalie.

"And they accosted us in the discount store earlier before

her doctor appointment. We haven't had time to tell anybody anything," I add, tipping my head toward Sela.

Natalie speaks up. "Yeah, I knew this morning that they were coming to talk to me, but I didn't know why except that it was about the cartel."

"Stafford called me to find out why I hadn't warned him. I had to tell him I didn't know, so I looked like an idiot," Patch says, his tone a bit huffy.

Sela shrugs. "We didn't know either. You can't tell somebody something you don't know anything about. And I'm sorry it got sprung on you, but it got sprung on us too. Wasn't something we wanted. It just happened that way."

"Okay. I've got a clearer picture now. What did they want? I mean, what's going on?"

It takes us a few minutes to explain to Patch what we were told. Sela ends with, "And I'm not going to one of their stupid safe houses. I know from experience that if you need to be safe, those are some of the least safe places in the world to be. There's always some jackass at the bureau who's on the dole to some cartel boss and spills the beans. Somebody shows up and massacres everybody, the person in safekeeping, the agents, everybody. So much for safe."

Patch nods as if he's thinking, and we all just wait. "Tony and Steve will be here tomorrow. Does the bureau know where these guys are right now?"

"No. They said they don't. But I don't trust them," Sela says again.

"Then we talk to Tony and Steve tomorrow and go from there. In the meantime, stay alert."

"We will. Thanks," Paddy answers.

None of us hang around. Paddy and Natalie disappear into their cottage, knowing the boys will be there waiting for them. As we head to ours, I see Reboot open the door and say something to Martin, who's sitting on the porch with Elmore. When he sees me looking his way, he waves, then says something else to the boy before closing the door. Martin grins and waves too, so I wave back. "Thanks for the dog food, Bear!" he calls out to me.

"You're welcome, buddy. Did you like the leash and collar?"

"Oh, yeah! They're really cool. Elmore likes 'em too, don'tcha, boy?" He scratches the dog's head and I can see the animal's tail wagging.

"Good deal. Don't stay out too late, okay?"

"I won't. Night, Bear."

"Night, buddy."

"Night, Miss Sela!"

"Night, Martin," the woman beside me calls back, and I smile. I hope by now she's seeing that everybody wants her here, even Martin and the dog she wanted to put a bullet through. When the door closes behind us, I hear her say, "That dog has really surprised me. He might actually turn out to be a good companion."

"Martin sure loves him. That little boy has been through a lot. If that dog makes him happy, I'm glad the dog is here."

"Me too. His mom died, right?"

"Yeah. He was in foster care until they found Reboot. Sad days for him."

"Natalie said Reboot didn't know he existed."

"She told you right. Soon as he found out, he couldn't get Martin here fast enough. Jumped right in. I have to tell you, I have mountains of respect for Reboot. He's one of the best people I've ever met. Funny as hell too. Guy's a nut, but he loves everybody, and he'd do anything for you. And Mavis took that child in and loves him like he's her own. They're amazing people."

"I got that impression." She's already stripping off her clothes as she walks through the cottage. "Ready for bed?"

"As in ready for bed or ready for bed?" I ask with a chuckle.

"Ready for bed, not ready for sleep." I can hear her moving around in the bedroom, so I grab a bottle of water and lock the doors. "Unless you're sleepy."

"Not me," I answer.

"Good. Because I'm not either."

Five minutes later, we're wrapped around each other like honeysuckle wrapped around a fence post, and every stroke into her makes me happy to be there and in her arms. "I'm so thankful for you, *banrigh*." The scent of her skin fills my head and makes my heart beat even faster. "Oh, girl, what you do to me. Damn, babe. I'd do anything for you."

"I love you, Miles. I only want to be here with you," she whispers, her hips pumping against my pelvis as I rock into her, lost in her softness and the deep hazel of her eyes.

When we're both spent—her first, always—we lie there in the darkness of the bedroom, her molded to my side and lying in my arms, her hand lightly stroking the hair on my chest. Out of the blue, she says, "They're going to kill me, you know."

"Not as long as I have breath," I tell her, my free hand rising to trail down her cheek. "No one's going to kill you. We're going to finish out our lives together, Sela. I promise you that."

"Then we're both going to die, because they will kill me. Natalie too. These people, they're ruthless. They don't care who they hurt as long as they do what they came to do." There's a weariness in her tone that I've never heard before, and it worries me.

"They've never met the men at this farm. We won't let

that happen, babe. Not happening. Stop worrying about it." That's easy to say, but much harder to believe.

Because I can say that, for the first time in my life, I really am scared.

THERE'S AN AWFUL LOT OF ACTIVITY OUTSIDE WHEN I WAKE up, and I glance over to find Sela still sleeping peacefully. I swear, that woman could sleep through a world war, volcanic eruption, earthquake, hurricane, and tornado, all happening at the same time. The floor is chilly when my feet hit it, and I stumble into the kitchen and peer out the blinds on the door.

I don't know why I'm surprised at the racket. The Walters are here. I can see Tony and Nikki talking to Patch, and Steve is talking to Bulldog. As I watch, Tinsley steps up to him, and the attorney takes the tiny baby in his arms, talking to the little guy the whole time. I never pictured Steve as being a baby person, but then I remember that he's got a little girl, and I can definitely see him being the quintessential girl dad.

I wake Sela up on my way to shower, and by the time I'm finished, she's picked out her clothes for the day and is ready to take her turn. I dress, make some coffee, and when she's finished and dressed, we sit down for a few minutes, drink the coffee and chat, and then head out.

Everybody's obviously in the kitchen, so we wander that way. When the door opens, there's laughter and chatter everywhere. The kids are running around, Taylor in the lead, and Fiona is yelling at them to sit down and eat. Elmore is rumbling along behind them, stopping here and there to see if somebody will give him something from the table, but they all tell him no—Reboot's orders. Smack in the middle of the racket are Tony, Nikki, and Steve, laughing and talking with everybody who says anything to them. They all look up as we step in, and Tony rises and heads straight for us. "Bear! Good to see you!" he says, all smiles, and when his hand comes out, I take it for a one-sided bro hug. "You doin' okay? Heard about the accident."

"Yeah, I'm fine. Trying to keep up with her," I say and throw a thumb at Sela.

"Sela, honey, you doin' okay?" he asks, his hands gripping her upper arms lightly as he looks into her face.

"Yeah, I'm okay. Not as good as I'd hoped, but good enough."

He pats her upper arms and smiles. "It'll be fine. Just takes time. But you look good! Come on over and say hi to Nikki. We've been thinking about you ever since, well, the thing with Natalie."

"Thanks. I appreciate it."

"Hey, babe, look who's here!" Tony says and moves aside so Nikki can see my girl.

"Sela! Oh my god, I'm so glad you're here!" The tiny blond runs straight to Sela and gives her a big, warm hug. For the first time I can ever remember, I see Sela hug her back. She usually recoils like somebody's trying to stab her, but I've never seen anybody reject one of Nikki's hugs. "You're lookin' good, honey! Are you here full time now?"

"Uh, yeah. Moved in with Miles, um, Bear."

"That's great! Isn't this a wonderful place? And you fit right in! So you're doing okay? Need anything? Are you still going to therapy?"

"No. I hated therapy. They put me in a nursing home and—"

"Oh, good lord! You sure as hell didn't belong there! I bet we can find somebody who'll come out here and work with you so you don't have to drive to find somebody. Don't you think so, Tony?" she asks her tall husband.

"Oh, I'm sure we can. You two can work on that while we're here, I bet. Baby, don't forget to make arrangements with Fiona to pick her up at school and go over to see the horse" he says with a grin.

"Oh! Yeah, I need to do that! Guess I should talk to her and Sarah. We'll catch up in a little bit, okay?" she says and pats Sela on the shoulder. "I need to run to stop them before they leave!"

"She's sure cheerful in the morning," Sela says just loudly enough that Tony and I can hear her.

"She wakes up that way every morning. I thought she probably always did, but she told me that since we've been together, she's excited to wake up in the mornings because she's just sure the day will be amazing. It isn't always, but she's always hopeful that it will be. Gives me hope too. That woman is the only reason I'm still breathing." He's watching her go, and as soon as she clears the doorway, he sighs. "Guess I'd better get ready. We've got to be down the road in an hour for the registration at the auction. I sure hope Steve remembered my bank letter or we're screwed."

"Sounds like a busy day. Better eat before you have to go," I tell him and point at the stove.

"Miss Audrey's cooking? I'd never leave without eating whatever she's made! Y'all have a good breakfast. I'm going over there to fill my plate."

As he walks away, I glance over at Sela, then lean in toward her and whisper, "Are you checking out his ass?"

"Jesus, that man is fine. I mean, you are too, and younger, but holy hell. I think he's just about the prettiest thing I've ever seen." That makes me laugh. "Well, he is! Damn fine-looking man."

"His brother is prettier."

"Shut up! You're lying. That can't be."

"You've never met Vic, so you just don't know. Hell, I'm a man and I recognize how fine-looking he is. I thought Bulldog was going to turn wrong side out the first time he saw Vic."

"Bulldog? What do you mean?"

I lean even closer and whisper directly in her ear, "Bulldog's bi."

Sela yanks her head back and looks up at me, head tipped sideways and eyes cut. "You're not serious."

"I am. Turns out that's why he was so hostile to Hollywood when they both came here. He thought Hollywood was the cutest little piece of ass he'd ever seen, but he didn't dare say anything. We thought he was pissed off about the whole silver spoon thing, but it turns out he was just really, really frustrated because he was attracted to Hollywood but knew it could never happen, not if they were going to live and work together out here. Thankfully, Tinsley came along and caught his eye, and Hollywood had already met Audrey. Bulldog's been very clear that he adores Tinsley, but he had a rough time for a while there, and nobody but him knew why."

"Wow. I never would've … wow. I mean, *wow*."

"Yeah. Shocked us all too. Never would've guessed, but yep. And now you know."

"On that note, I think I'm going to get some breakfast."

I'm laughing. "Me too." Nothing like shocking the shit outta your girlfriend first thing in the morning. I have a feeling I'll live for a chance at it in the near future.

Twenty minutes later, Patch does his usual morning talk. "So I guess by the end of the day we may have a lot more property than we do now, thanks to family over here at this table." He gestures toward Tony, Nikki, and Steve, and everybody applauds. "And that's all I've got for today. Anybody else?"

Reboot stands. "Bear, is there any chance you could take the dog to the vet? Doesn't have to be today, but maybe sometime this week if you—"

"Know who you want to take it to?"

"No. Anybody know a good vet?"

A woman's voice pipes up. "We made arrangements for a Dr. Lindsey to see Fiona's horse. Might want to call them. I'm not sure if he does small animals, but he does big ones," Nikki says.

"Will do. Thanks."

"If he can't, call animal control. They'll know somebody good," Priest offers.

"Good idea. Thanks." Guess I'm taking Elmore to the vet.

Patch gazes around. "Anybody else?" No one says a word. "Okay, time to go to work. Let's all have a good, safe day." Everyone heads out, but I grab my phone. As I'm scrolling through, I feel a presence near me and look up to find Nikki standing there.

"Is this the guy?" I ask and show her a page.

"Yeah. That's him. Nice fella. Tell them that you're one of my friends and I think that'll get you right in today. So, this dog—"

"Coydog that wandered up. Martin's in love with that dog."

Nikki smiles. "Yeah. I wondered how it came to be here. Got a messed-up paw, I noticed."

"Yeah. I'm hoping we can get some answers. Not everybody is crazy about him, but so far he's been friendly and sweet, and Martin adores him."

"Martin needs somebody who doesn't talk to him, somebody he can just ramble to and they'll listen. I think that dog is perfect for that reason. Does he have a name?"

"Yeah. Elmore."

"Like Elmore Leonard." I keep wondering where I've heard that name before, and I guess I give her a weird look. "You know, the guy who wrote the book that *Justified* came from. The Raylan Givens series."

"Oh! Yeah! I kept thinking I recognized the name!"

"Do y'all watch that around here?"

"Actually, we do."

"Then I bet that's where he got it. Cute name for a dog," she says, grinning.

"Agreed."

"Call over there and see if they can get you in. I'd better catch up with Tony. I want to be there when they start the bidding. He's the one who takes care of that stuff, but if I give him a funny look like I think he's going too far, he'll back down in a heartbeat. I don't want him second-guessing himself on this one. You fellas need that land, if for no other reason than an investment." Her hands land on us, one on my shoulder and one on Sela's. "Have a good day and we'll see you in a bit. And Sela, I really am glad you're here," she says as she turns to walk away.

"Thanks." As soon as she's out the door, Sela turns to look at me. "She's like a little tornado, isn't she?"

"Yep. More like a fairy godmother in a tornado. Tony's always looking out for the big picture, and Nikki sees the details. They're a great pair."

"Seems like it. Hey, call that vet and see what's going on so we know what the rest of our day looks like."

Ten minutes later, we're putting the leash on Elmore and coaxing him into the SUV. Once he's in, I wonder what's going to happen when we start rolling, because he sure didn't want to get in the vehicle. But I shouldn't have worried. Two miles down the road, I've put the window down about eight inches and his muzzle is out, sniffing the air. "He seems to like riding. But shoooo-wee, we need to find a groomer to bathe that thing. He's rank," Sela says, fanning her nose.

"Yeah. He really is. Wonder if somebody at the vet's office can do it. Sometimes they do."

"Gah. Let's ask. Ugh. It's getting worse."

I reach out to the dash. "Here. Let's turn on the air conditioning and see if that helps." A few minutes later, the stench is getting worse. "Not helping much."

"No. It's not. Can't wait until we get there to get some air."

I pull up and park, and Sela hops out to retrieve the dog. Before I can get around the SUV, I hear her say, "Holy fucking lord. Oh my god."

"What? What's … Oh, fuck me."

There's shit everywhere. I mean, *everywhere*. The seats, the door panels, the carpet. This dog has shit all over the back seat, and he's got it on him too. His feet, his sides, his tail. It's … My god, I can't believe it. "What the hell do we do?" Sela whispers.

"I don't … Stay here." I hit the office door running, and a startled receptionist looks up. "Hi, um, I'm Miles, and I have an appointment for Elmore, and we've got him outside, and there's been this, um, I dunno, *explosion* in the back seat, and he's—"

"Let me guess. Not familiar with car rides and he pooped everywhere."

A miniscule bit of my panic slips away. "Yes."

"I'll come out and get him and walk him around the back. We'll clean him up a bit before we take him in for an exam."

"That's amazing. Thank you. Thank you so much. I mean, really, thanks so much."

"Hey, it's okay. Don't worry about it. We'll take care of it."

"Oh, god, thank you. I've gotta go tell Sela … Do I—"

"Somebody will be out there in just a minute. Don't worry, Mr. McMillan. We've got this." I don't care what these people charge. Whatever it is, it'll be worth it.

Sela's standing there, her hand as far from her body as she can get it, holding the leash, trying to keep the dog away from her. "What the hell do I—"

"They're coming to get him."

"Thank god. This is awful."

"Yeah. So if I give you some money, will you take the car to the car wash and try to clean it up while I'm in there with him?"

"Sure. Yeah. Dog shit is my specialty. I live to scrape it off everything."

"Sela—"

"Just being an asshole. It's fine. Go."

"So I hear we have a little fella here who … Oh, wow," a young woman who looks to be mid-twenties says. "He really outdid himself, didn't he?"

"I'd say. I've never seen anything quite like this in my life," Sela responds. I'm with her. This exceeds all of my experiences, and I was in prison for thirty years, so that's really saying something.

"Come on, boy. We'll get you all cleaned up and Dr. Lindsey can give you something for your tummy." We watch as she disappears around the corner of the building with Elmore.

"Okay. Here's …" I'm scrambling through the contents of

my pockets. "Um, forty dollars, and, oh, here's another five, and some change, and—"

"I've got it. Just go with the dog and I'll be back in a bit. Gotta stop at the dollar-type place and get some towels I can throw away. And then take another shower when we get home."

"Okay, if you're sure?" I say, trying to sound apologetic. Honestly, I'm glad I'm not the one doing it.

"Yeah, yeah. You're gonna owe me though," she says as she climbs into the driver's seat.

Me owing Sela. Yeahhhh. Somehow I think I might be better off doing the cleanup myself.

Sela

I SWEAR TO GOD, IF I DON'T GET THIS THING TO THE CAR wash soon, I'm going to be cleaning up puke too. I'm gagging. All the windows are down, and the stench is so horrific, I'm sure people around me can smell it. At the traffic light, a car stops beside me, and before the light can change, I see the guy's nose wrinkle up as he sniffs and figures out where the stank is coming from. I just give him a palms-up shrug and mouth, "Burritos." He frowns and hits the gas as the light changes. Nosy motherfucker.

Thankfully, there's nobody at the car wash when I roll up. I stop the big GMC in a bay and get to work. Not only did I buy towels, but I got a squeegee too, and I start by scraping all I can off the seats. That's only marginally effective. Then I wet down some cloths and start wiping. Did I mention I bought rubber gloves too? Yeah. No way was I touching this mess.

But I only seem to be smearing it around. I really need some professional help, like car detailing professional help, but yes, professional therapy will come into play after this too, I'm sure. I can't imagine I'm going to forget this anytime soon. There's a guy working at the car wash, cleaning and stuff, and he comes over to where I'm working. "Whew! You drew the shit job today! Literally!"

"Yeah, no shit. And that phrase doesn't work here either. You work here. Got some advice?"

"Truth?"

"No, lie to me. Of course, the truth."

"Truth is, your best bet is to let it dry and then scrape it off. Using wet stuff just makes it worse."

"And how do you propose that we don't throw up constantly while we're waiting for it to dry?"

"Hmmm. Hey, I've got an idea. Let's see if it works. Pull around here in the auto wash bay. Don't worry—I'll turn everything off. But if we can get you to the other end, open all the doors and windows, and turn on the dryers, maybe we can get enough air through it to dry everything out. Four cycles is about two minutes, but it might work. Wanna try it?"

"Buddy, at this point, I'd opt for a propane torch, so yeah. I'm game."

I drive the giant shit box into the bay and he motions to me to pull forward, then to stop. "All the windows and doors open. Step out here. Otherwise, you'll look like you've been in a tornado."

"Can't look much worse than I do right now," I grouse under my breath as I step outside the concrete block enclosure and stand out by the vacuum stations. And that's when I see it.

There's a car across the street, facing the car wash. It was behind me when I was driving here, and now it's sitting over there. And there are two men in it. That makes me sit up and take notice. I look at my watch, and I have no idea how many times this dryer thing has run, but I know it's run at least once and started again. The boy wonder from the car wash is checking on it occasionally, and that leaves me free to stare at the car out of the corner of my eye. They're not moving, just sitting there.

Watching me.

Now there's no doubt what I'm seeing. "How's it coming?" I yell to the kid as I step back toward the vehicle.

"Looks like it needs four more cycles, but then it should be good." I give him a thumbs up and go back to leaning against the vacuums. Yeah. The guys are still there. When I finally hear it cut off, I step back up to the GMC. "Tell you what. I've got another squeegee in the booth. Pull over there to the vacuums and get started and I'll grab it and help you. Just scrape and vacuum, scrape and vacuum."

"Okay. Thanks." Once I've pulled up to the vacuums, I get to work and, damn, that kid was right. The stuff is crumbling off the seat, door panel, and up from the carpet, and when I've gotten a big area done, I grab a vacuum hose and vacuum up the dried crud. He's come up on the other side, and he's working along too. In ten minutes, it looks pretty good.

We scrape and vacuum for another ten minutes before he stops and takes a long look. "Hey, this looks all right."

I straighten and look at it. "Yeah. It actually does. Thanks!"

"Okay, get a couple of rags, wet them, and let's wipe it down. That should finish it off nicely." Sure enough, he's right. Another five minutes, and you really can't tell that anything happened in the car. There's a little bit on the back of a headrest, but that wipes right off. "Hang on. I've got something else. Just a sec." There's a box of something under his arm when he returns from the control booth. "Let's put these around under the seats. That'll help." They're cinnamon air fresheners, and in a few minutes, the soothing scent starts to permeate the car.

"Oh, this is nice," I murmur.

"Yeah. We did a good job."

"I owe it all to you. Can you guys take tips?"

"Uh, yeah, I guess." I hand him a twenty, and he smiles. "Oh, wow. Thank you! That's great. I really appreciate it."

"And I appreciate you. You have a great day, okay?"

"You too! By the way, if you ever want to talk or just have a burger or something … Could I have …"

"I don't think my boyfriend would like that very much," I tell him, trying to make my face seem apologetic.

"Oh. Did he do that?" he asks and points to the back seat.

That makes me laugh so hard I can barely talk. "Yeah, he's got a spastic colon! If I get to the point where I can't take it anymore, I'll come back and look you up. How's that?"

"Cool! Okay. Here's hoping he shits himself blind then!" he says with a snicker as I start the SUV, a huge grin on his face. Yeah, little man, you just keep on dreamin'. Wait until I tell Miles about this.

I pull out of the car wash onto the street and look in my rearview. At first, I don't see them, but by the time I've gotten to the third light, sure enough, there they are behind me. Now I'm wondering when they picked me up earlier. Were they waiting outside the drive to the farm? Or did they see me up here at the vet's office and follow me? I wasn't driving, so I really wasn't paying attention, and that's my fault. I know better. Of course, the smell from hell distracted me, but that's no excuse. When I pull up to the vet's office, Miles isn't outside, so I park and step inside.

"Hi," the same twenty-something girl says. "They're right back there if you want to go back."

"Sure." The hallway runs behind the reception desk, and she points to the correct room when I reach it.

Elmore is on the table, and the vet is feeling all over him. He seems to be enjoying the attention, and there's no sign of the goo that he was wearing when he got out of the car. "How's it going?"

"Good. He's really well-behaved," Miles says and scratches under the dog's chin.

The vet sighs. "He really is. Helluva sight better than the golden retriever I had in here earlier. That dog was crazy."

"So is he really a coydog?" I ask, hoping the vet will know.

"Yeah. Absolutely. I can see all the markers, and he's built right too. We have more of these around than you'd think. Matter of fact, got a guy who used to raise them. I think he got arrested for alligators or some such nonsense. Rumor has it that he gave away the coydogs, but he kept a few and left them tied around his property to starve. If I had to guess, I'd say this one is one of them."

"That's totally fucked up," Miles mumbles.

"Yeah. It really is. Fish and wildlife went out and put a bunch of them down, but some had chewed through their ropes and gotten away."

"He was wearing a dirty, ragged rope when he wandered up at the farm, so that's probably where he came from."

The vet nods. "Yeah, he's been beaten, but not too severely. The foot has been broken and left to heal incorrectly, so I'm not sure we can do much with it, but I'll try. Probably put a boot on it and see if he tolerates that. And a couple of the pads have deep cuts, so we'll take care of that too. I'm sure glad his tummy seems to be empty. That smell … That was pretty horrible."

"You should've been the one cleaning it up," I tell the vet, my nose wrinkled up.

"Did you actually manage to get it all out?" Miles asks.

"Yeah. Kid at the car wash helped me with it or I'd probably still be there. He tried to ask me out, but I told him I have a boyfriend."

Miles' eyebrows shoot up. "Oh, yeah? And what did he say?"

"He asked me if you made that mess in the back seat."

Now he looks really alarmed. "What did you tell him?"

"Of course I told him you did it! I told him you have a spastic colon. Not passing up a chance to say something like that, dude," I say, the vet laughing the whole time.

Based on his expression, I'm unsure how Miles feels about that. "You told him I shit all over the back seat?"

I nod purposefully. "I did. I told him if I ever got tired of cleaning up after you, I'd come looking for him. Gotta give the kid some hope."

"Holy hell. Be sure to tell me which car wash it was. I can never go there."

"He didn't see you. He won't know it was you. Oh, wait! I showed him a picture of you," I lie.

"You … You showed him a picture—" he bellows. The vet has given up and is hee-hawing.

"Calm your tits, babe. I didn't. I'm just messing with you." It's taking everything I have to keep from shrieking with laughter.

"Good lord. Last time I take you anywhere."

"That's okay. It's the last time I take *him* anywhere," I answer and point at Elmore.

Miles nods. "Gotta say I'm in agreement with that."

"You probably won't have more of that trouble with him. I think he had stomach upset brought on by new food. Feed him tonight but don't take him anywhere. He'll adjust to it pretty soon. Might want to give him a little cottage cheese with the food. That'll help his stomach. But other than looking emaciated, being tired, and having a bum paw, he looks to be in pretty good health. Good teeth, skin's good, ears are clean now, he's had all his vaccinations and he's been wormed, which may also upset his stomach a little, so give him plenty of time outdoors for the next few days. I'll set you up with some heartworm, flea, tick, and internal parasites medication and he'll be all set."

"Thanks, sir. I appreciate it."

"You're welcome. Sorry you had such a rough trip here. Oh, and can you please tell Mrs. Walters that the horse over at Gus Erickson's place is doing great. I hear she's in town."

"Will do. Gladly. Thanks so much."

"You're very welcome. Just pay Christine on the way out and we'll give you a tag for him and all of his papers."

I take the dog outside while Miles pays the young woman at the desk. Poor thing is appropriately subdued now. I'm guessing he's in shock from the poop and the bath and the vet visit. "Hey, pup," I whisper and reach down to stroke his head. "Everything's okay. The car is clean, you're clean, and we can go home now. You'll get to see Martin! It'll all be fine." As soon as I straighten up, I look around like I'm looking for Miles, but I'm really scanning.

Yep. They're across the street.

In a few seconds, he joins me on the sidewalk. "Ready?"

"Yeah. Hey, I bought a blanket at the store too and put it in the back seat for him. Thought it might protect the seat."

"Sure can't hurt. Okay, boy," Miles says as he opens the

door. "Up you go." It's interesting to note that he doesn't balk like he did at the farm, just hops right up in the back seat. "Well, that was easy enough. You drivin'?"

"Nope." I hand him the keys and round the SUV to get in. As soon as the doors are closed, I turn my head with my back to the window and say, "Look straight out the front windshield. Do not turn and look. There's a gray car across the street with two men in it."

"Okay."

"It followed me to the car wash."

There's no change in his expression but he says, "Okay. And now they're here."

"Yeah. I don't think that's a coincidence."

"How long had they been following us before the car wash?"

"I wasn't driving, so I don't know if they picked up our trail in Mallie, or in town somewhere, or what. But it's no coincidence that I've now seen them several places I've been."

"No. It's not. I'm going to pull out. That will give me an excuse to look that way." I watch as he checks traffic, but his eyes are scanning. "Yeah. I see them over there."

"So I'm not imagining it."

"No. Definitely not." There's a wicked gleam in his eye. "Let's have some fun with them," he says as he pulls out onto the street, and I can see in the rearview on my side that they're pulling out of their parking space.

"What are we doing?"

"We're gonna confuse the hell outta them. Just make sure you're buckled up." He takes off, and I see them a couple of cars back, trying to catch up. As soon as he gets to a corner with no stoplight and a building right on the side of the street, he turns right and makes an immediate U-turn, but he doesn't pull up to the stop sign. They turn the corner, and we take off, turning right and heading back out on the highway. By the time they pull back out, we're a block in front of them, and he takes a quick left, drives half a block, turns left into an alley, and then left on the next street and to the stop sign. We see them drive past to turn at the next corner, and he pulls in behind them. They apparently don't notice us, because as they turn left, he sits down on the horn and flips them off out the window, then guns the big SUV. Now they've turned down the side street and we're still headed toward Mallie.

"Holy shit, this is fun," I say, looking behind us. I can see them way down the street, sitting there at the stop sign to our left, waiting to get out on the street. As soon as they do, Miles turns right again, then left at the next corner, then another left, and back out to the main street. We watch as they turn where we turned initially, and he drives across the main street and down another side street, then turns left. I know what he's doing. He's hoping to meet them head on.

"Here. Look up Preston and hit his contact, then put it on speaker," he says and tosses his phone to me.

I do what he says, and someone answers, "Hey, Bear! How's it goin'?"

"Hey, Preston, I'm in Hazard and—"

"Oh! Wanna grab a bite?"

"We've got somebody tailing us."

"No shit?"

"No shit. Can you help me out?"

"You got it. Where are you?"

"Um … I see a building that says Carter's Tires."

"I know exactly where you are. On my way." And the phone goes dead.

"Who was that?" I ask, bewildered.

"Preston Ramage. He's a city police officer."

Oh, wow. I think these guys are fucking with the wrong ex-con. In a couple of minutes, I hear a siren and the phone rings. I just hit ACCEPT and then speaker. "Bear, you hear me?"

"Yeah. You're somewhere behind me."

"Do you see them?"

He stops at the stop sign and, sure enough, there they are—facing us. "Yeah. They're directly across from me on the other side of Main Street."

"Look in your rearview." I turn just as Miles looks up in his mirror and sure enough, there's a Dodge Charger cruiser right behind us. "Sit still. I'll take care of this. And when I do, you drive straight to Mallie."

"Roger that. But be careful. We have reason to believe they're from a cartel."

"Shit. Wish you'd told me that earlier. I've got it under control." And the phone goes dead again. Before I can speak, the cruiser passes us and faces up on the car. We can see Preston on the radio, so I'm not too worried. As Miles turns out onto Main Street, I can see three more cruisers, one behind us and two in front, coming our direc-tion. Miles just keeps moving, picking up speed a little, and in three minutes, we're out of Hazard and on the open road.

We pull into the farm and straight to the equipment shed where the vehicles are parked. I hop out and open the back door, and Elmore drops to the ground, whimpering only slightly at the boot the vet put on his foot. I can see Ghost coming out of the kitchen area, and I realize they just finished lunch. "What now?"

"Now we go to the kitchen to eat and hope Patch is in there." With Elmore between us, we set out for the kitchen. And we're halfway there when a black sedan roars up and slides to a stop in front of us. "Oh, joy," Miles mutters. "Can't wait to hear this."

"What the fuck do you think you're doing?" Morreau screams our direction.

"Do you see cartel members here?" Miles asks calmly.

"No."

"Then I did a good job."

"We were watching them!"

"Then you know the Hazard Police Department stopped them and talked to them."

Morreau folds his arms across his chest. "And what did they say to them?"

"Well, I don't know," Miles answers in the snarkiest voice I think I've ever heard. "Why don't we ask them?" Phone in hand, he hits a contact.

"Hey, big guy! Well, that was fun!"

"Yeah? What did they have to say for themselves?"

"Said it must've been a coincidence because they were just here sightseeing. You guys okay?"

"Yes and no. Yes, we're fine. No, we've got a pissed off feeb standing here yelling at us."

"Oh! Am I on speaker?"

"Yep."

"Hello, Agent Morreau! How are you this beautiful day?" Preston asks, and it's all I can do to keep from laughing.

"What the fuck? Who is this?"

"Lieutenant Preston Ramage of the Hazard Police Department. I realize you're shocked that I know who you are, but you have to understand, in this area, we all have each other's backs, so I've known you were here ever since you talked to Sheriff Stafford."

"Bunch of redneck bumpkins," Landrum grumbles under his breath.

"Hey, you need to show some respect. You're strangers in these parts. If you can't be respectful, you won't get an ounce of cooperation, and your boss isn't going to like that at all," Miles says.

"And I'll be sure to call him and tell him," I add.

"Of course you will. Look, Ramage, leave those guys alone. We're taking care of this," Morreau orders.

"You work with us. We don't work for you. You best remember that, Morreau. I'm going to do what I think is necessary to take care of the people of this town. We're not going to have a pissing contest," Preston warns.

Morreau glares at me. "I don't even know why we're doing this. We should just let them have you, but they'd take Judge Anderson too, and she's our real concern."

That statement washes over me like sulfuric acid. "So you don't give two shits about me anyway. You're here for Natalie, and I'm just extraneous work."

"Extraneous. I like that word." Landrum grins at me. "You said it. We didn't."

"No, you definitely said it in all the ways that matter. Get in your car and go. You're not welcome here," Miles says, his voice smoky and low. "And if you ever show up out here again, I can't promise you that you'll be safe."

"You threatening us, convict?" Morreau asks, his voice snotty.

"Nope. Not a threat. It's a promise. I can't have a weapon, but I don't live out here alone."

"No. He doesn't," a voice says, and there's a sound behind me that I recognize. It's a round being racked into the chamber of a handgun. "It's actually legal for me to have a weapon, and I just might have to use it. Get off our property. Now," Reboot orders.

"You're kidding, right?" Morreau says, his eyes wide.

"No. But you'd be surprised how fast I can draw this thing if I have to. You're not welcome here. Go." I can see the outside of the shop building just well enough to see Hollywood crossing the grass with a shotgun, and Bulldog's got one too. "Now would be the time for you to make your exit."

They both seem to understand that nobody wants them here, and they turn toward the car. As they reach it, Morreau glares at me. "You realize you're now on your own."

"No, I'm not. I've got a family here, and I'll be fine without the likes of the two of you," I bark. "Get the hell outta here." We all stand and watch as they turn the sedan around and take off, throwing gravel as they go.

"What the hell was that about?" Patch asks as he steps up to us.

Miles is still talking to Preston, and I've already pulled my phone out and hit the contact. "Good afternoon. You've reached the office of the FBI Protective Details Division. How may I direct your call?"

"Valerie, it's Sela Baldwin. I need to talk to Andrew."

"Sure. You doin' okay? Been missing you."

"Yeah, I'm fine. Just need to talk to him."

"Uh, okay. Hang on." There's that sucky hold music again. Really? It's awful. They should change that.

I hear some sounds and a voice answers, "Sela?"

"Andrew, what the fuck? We just chased Morreau and Landrum off the property out here."

"Why did you do that, Sela? They were sent there to make sure you're safe."

"The fuck you say!" I scream into the phone. "They just told me I'm extraneous!"

"What does that even mean?" he asks, and I can tell he's confused.

"They told me the only reason they're here is because of Natalie because I'm *extraneous*! That was the exact word they used! You want somebody out here, you need to get somebody out here who doesn't call local law enforcement redneck bumpkins and tell me I'm extraneous!"

"Calm down, Sela. I'll get to the bottom of this and in the meantime, I'll find somebody else."

"Yeah, well, they need to be respectful and want to work *with* us, not run roughshod *over* us. That won't work here. And in the meantime of your meantime, I'm going to work on it from this end. I'm not without resources."

"Resources? What kind of—"

"Thanks, Andrew. Hope to hear from you soon." I just hang up. No more words from him. They mean very little anyway.

Patch's voice is stern. "We need to have a sit-down. All of us, later, when Steve and Tony are back."

"Yes, sir," I answer, not even thinking about what I'm saying. It just comes naturally with him. Patch is the authority figure here, and no one questions that.

"Speak of the devil," I hear Bulldog murmur, and we turn to see Tony's big black Yukon Denali pull in and two of Steve's men open the rear doors. As soon as the tall Italian man's feet hit the ground, he jets straight for the little group standing on the lawn, Steve right beside him.

"This doesn't look good. What's going on?" Tony asks as soon as he reaches us.

"Long story, but we all need to talk about it. How'd the auction go?" Patch asks.

"Farm is yours. University reps were there and they're on board. There was only one other person bidding against us, and he ran out of money real quick."

"Do you know who he was?" Miles asks.

"Yeah. I do. We had a discussion afterward and I'm giving him ten acres on the far side of the farm. He's the grandson of the Pettits, but he really didn't have the kind of money that size place would go for. He asked about moving the house and keeping it, but I took a good look at it and it would never survive a move. Giving him the spot it sits on wouldn't work for the interpretative farm. But we can build him something new and nice for not a lot of money. According to him, the sale was his uncle's idea, not his, and he wanted the house, but the rest of the family wanted the money from the sale. This guy should be rewarded. He wanted to keep his family history alive, and they just wanted dollars, so I'm going to give him what he needs. The university rep told him he would be instrumental in helping them with the history of the place and the story of his grandparents, and he seemed really excited about that." Tony hesitates for a minute, then says, "I hope that's okay with you guys, giving him a parcel. I felt like it was the right thing to do."

"Oh, no, that's totally your call," Patch says. "I think that's a great gesture. We don't preserve enough of African American culture in this nation, and this will go a long way, at least in this area." And now I get it, Tony being Italian and all.

I didn't realize the Pettits were black. Did I mention my Grandma Irene was black? Can't tell it by looking at me, but yeah. After hearing her stories as I was growing up, I definitely get it.

"So what's going on here? Gotta say, I've never been greeted this way," Steve says with a sneer.

Patch rubs his temple. "Long story. We'll talk about it after dinner. You guys are staying, aren't you?"

"To eat Audrey's cooking? Hell yeah. Not going

anywhere." Tony turned to glance behind him. "Anybody see Nikki? I thought she was right behind me."

"Saw her head into the kitchen," Reboot offers.

"Of course. She'll be right in the middle of it. Guess I'll go over to the lodge and watch a little TV. You guys finished for the day?"

"Nah. We've got a couple more hours," Bulldog says.

"Mind if I tag along? I'd love to watch some of what you do."

"You're more than welcome. Steve?"

"Yeah. I'll come too," Steve adds, and they start en masse toward the shop.

Just as they reach the shop door, Patch wheels and stares out our way to call out, "Sela, watch your back! Bear—"

"I know. Eyes on her," Miles calls back to him. Patch gives him a thumbs up, and they all disappear into the shop. When I turn to look at the man beside me, I can see his fingers twitching, and I smile. "What? I want to go back to work."

"I know. I'm sorry." All of a sudden, I realize I'm really hungry. And Elmore is still standing there between us, placid, his tail wagging slightly when I look down at him. "Let's see if there's anything left to eat in the kitchen and take this poor doggo to get a drink." With a little tug on his leash, he stands, and I head toward the kitchen. "Come on, boy. We'll get you some water."

Nikki's the only one left in the kitchen when we step in, and she's making sandwiches. As soon as she sees us, she smiles. "Figured the guys might be hungry. Where'd they go?"

"They're over in the shop with the rest of the crew."

"You two haven't eaten, have you?"

"No, ma'am. We haven't," Miles answers politely.

"Then here. You eat these and I can make more. I'm making myself one too. I haven't had lunch either. Mind if I sit with you?"

I shoot her a smile. "Of course not! That would be great."

"Oh, here." I watch as she ransacks a couple of cabinets, comes out with a big bowl, and fills it with water. "Here, pupper. You look a little ragged." When she sets the bowl down, Elmore steps up to it and starts to drink deeply. "Bless his heart. He was thirsty! Oh, wow. He smells good." As he drinks, Miles unclips the leash and hangs it on a hook by the door, but the dog doesn't flinch, just keeps drinking.

In a couple of minutes, we have Nikki screaming with laughter when we tell her about our escapades that afternoon with Elmore. We sit and eat and chat, and time flies. Nikki is really amazing. She's easy to talk to, fun, and she seems to really care about people. Natalie told me that there's nothing even remotely fake about Nikki and Tony—what you see is what you get. I see that now just from talking to her.

The sound of the door opening behind us makes us turn, and we look up to see Tony and Steve striding across the room. Nikki starts to laugh. "Hungry?"

"Starved. Forgot to eat. But watching them was really cool. I think Steve picked out something," Tony says and heads to the refrigerator.

"Yeah. Bulldog's going to make me a claymore sword," the big attorney says.

"Claymore. Scottish?" I ask.

He nods. "My name *is* McCoy."

Tony takes over the conversation as soon as he has his sandwich in hand. "So, what was up with the black sedan rolling out of the drive? I know a fed when I see one."

"Caught that, did you?" I ask, grimacing.

"Yeah. Couldn't miss it. What's the story?"

I set about telling him what I know, and he really doesn't react. I'm not sure what I was expecting, but it's not happening. When I finish, I look at Miles and he pats my hand under the table.

"Sounds like you need some help," Tony says dispassionately.

"I could use some."

He glances over at Steve. "McCoy, take care of this, wouldja?"

"Sure thing. How many people you think you'll need?"

I shrug. "I dunno. Maybe ten?"

Steve nods. "Let's shoot for fifteen. Hey, boss, maybe Angelo could help us out."

"You know, that's a good idea," Tony says just as he starts to take another bite.

"Who's Angelo?"

Mouth full of food, Tony nods to Steve, who picks up the question. "Tony's cousin, Angelo Cabrizzi. He's former AISI. Italian version of our FBI. Did a stint with the AISE—their CIA—and did some undercover work as SISMI. That's terrorism. He's private security now. Mercenary."

"So he's in Italy? What could he do for us?"

Tony swallows and snickers as he looks at his sandwich. "What *can't* he do? The guy can get information that nobody in our country can. I've seen him do it. Headed up a strike against a blackmail and assassination ring led by a guy who'd faked his own death and took them all down. My uncle, Vic's father. He's dead now, but we'd thought he was dead years earlier. Angelo actually managed to infiltrate his operation and broke it down from the inside. Guy's amazing."

"So you think he could get information on the cartel?" I'm feeling a lot more hopeful.

"If he can't, nobody can. He's got contacts all over the

world—every country, Interpol, Scotland Yard, CIA, Secret Service, French DST and DGSE, everywhere. You got a problem you need solved, Angelo's the guy to see, a man who's not above walking the line between ethical and unethical to get the job done." And he takes another bite of his sandwich, totally unconcerned. Holy shit. I feel like I'm in the presence of greatness, and he's just a guy in a tee shirt and jeans sitting across the table from me. "I'll call him up later and see what he can do. Steve, you got any people in this end of the state yet?"

"Not yet. Hoping to pretty soon." Oh, damn, I feel my chance coming on. "Getting Marshall up here and getting him set up, finding a little office location in Ashland, finding more people—"

"Would you consider Sela as one of those people?" Miles asks before I have a chance. I hate when somebody else takes words right out of my mouth. Fucker.

"Why? You interested, Sela?" Steve says, staring at me.

Be nice. Miles was only trying to help. Don't bite the hand that feeds you, I tell myself. "I might be."

"You willing to leave the bureau?"

Oh, fuck. This is hard. "I think the bureau may have left me."

"Because of your injuries?" I nod. "Motherfuckers. Yeah. I'd definitely like to have you on board. Could you relocate to Ashland?"

"I'm sure I could." Miles' face isn't in my range of vision, and I'm glad. He's probably frowning.

"Maybe it would be best if you were here. You know, get a couple of employees under you and—"

"You'd consider that?"

"You were FBI. You're far more highly trained than most of the people I can hire off the street, except maybe for other law enforcement types. You could set up a training program and cover this whole region. Marshall in the northern part, you in the southern ... perfect."

Well, hell, that was easy enough. I glance over at Miles and he winks at me. There's just one thing bothering me. "You think we'd really have enough work?"

"I can guarantee we would. There's all kinds of weird, crazy shit going on in this end of the state. No question. There's no one else doing what we'd be doing on this end of the state. Yeah, we might catch a few cheating husband cases, but there are a lot of businesses in this end of the state that could use our services, and politicians, and other ... things."

I chuckle. "You mean nefarious operations?"

Tony laughs. "What? Steve? Nefarious operations? You've got to be kidding, right? Because no one would ever believe Steve would do anything nefarious. Right, Steve?"

"Uh, yeah. Right. Nothing nefarious. Ever." And the blond attorney rolls his eyes. I like these two. They're my kinda people.

"Then it's settled. Steve is going to hire you and you're going to be management at Citadel Security. And you're going to have plenty of help and protection. And we're going to stay a couple more days to get everything in order, and by the time we leave, you'll have paperwork and all that shit. Right, Steve?"

"Absolutely. Paperwork and everything. I'll call Marshall and ask him to come tomorrow. He's been here before, but I left him behind to finish up something."

Tony hums before he asks, "Ummmm, that thing with the guy?"

Steve nods. "Yeah. That's the one."

"Think he'll shoot the asshole?"

"I'm pretty sure he will."

"Got a plan to take care of that?"

Steve leans back and frowns as he looks at Tony. "Don't I always?"

"Yep. So that's good. Nice work."

"Thanks," Steve says. "We're tidy." Shit, I really like this guy. I can hear Nikki chuckling down the table, and he leans over and asks, "What are you laughing about?"

"I can picture Marshall at the hardware store, buying plastic sheeting, rope, and duct tape."

"No. I have that shit delivered by the truckload," Steve says, taking another bite of sandwich.

"Don't let him fool you. He's a cheap-ass. He sends them to Walmart with his cash-back credit card," Tony says and side-eyes Steve.

"Oh, you know me so well," Steve declares and crunches a chip.

Miles throws a thumb in my direction. "I can tell right now that she's gonna fit in just fine."

"Why? Are you full of shit too?" Tony asks me.

"Well, you can't tell it because my eyes aren't brown, but give me a couple of weeks working for him," I say as I point to Steve, "and I'm pretty sure my levels will go up until they change."

"That's the spirit!" Steve crows, and we all laugh. I think everything's going to be just fine. Right this second, I feel better than I have in weeks, knowing that I'm going to have purpose in my life again.

That's if some cartel asshole doesn't kill me on the first day.

CHAPTER 7

*B*EAR

WE WERE STILL LAUGHING WHEN WE LEFT THE KITCHEN earlier, and even now, when I think about the conversation, I start to laugh. I love being around that bunch. They're so funny. I was especially impressed when Tony went to the door and told the two security agents outside to quit staring at the trees and come in for some food. Their names are Royce Hopkins and Charles Waters, and they're both just as funny and friendly as Steve, Tony, and Nikki. I love how the Walters treat everybody like family. It makes me proud to know them.

The rest of the day is uneventful. Dinner is a treat; Nikki starts cooking at about four o'clock after she comes back from taking Fiona to see the horse, and we have a huge Italian feast, with four kinds of sauce, all kinds of pastas, beef and cheese cannelloni, a beautiful salad, focaccia, and cannoli stuffed with strawberries and a light, fluffy cream cheese concoction. Tony brought about a dozen bottles of wine, and we laugh and eat and drink until we're all stuffed.

By the time we finish helping with cleanup and get back to the cottage, it's late. "Think I'm gonna take a quick shower. I feel a little grubby."

"Yeah, me too," she replies.

"Wanna shower with me?"

"Nah. I'll wait until you're finished." Sela drops onto the sofa and picks up a magazine. It's some kind of science publication—I like those—and she starts flipping pages, so I wander to the bathroom, strip off, and climb in. I'm done in fifteen minutes.

"All yours," I call out. When I look up, she's already in the bathroom doorway, completely bare. "Well, you were ready."

"You'd better be ready when I come out," she whispers as she walks by and tweaks one of my nipples. Awww, damn. And then I'll have to shower again. Guess that's okay.

She's only in there for a few minutes and comes out smelling all fresh and flowery. Her towel falls as soon as she gets close to the bed, where I've already taken up residence, and she snaps the sheet back. "Oh. You didn't put on anything either. Guess you're ready."

"Do I look ready?" I ask and grin, then point to my dick.

"Really, really ready." If I wasn't already hard, watching her panther-crawl across the bed toward me would be plenty arousing. She keeps going until she's between my legs, then stops. "Mmmm. Can't wait to taste this." Oh, damn. My balls are aching now, and I pull up to brace myself on my elbows so I can watch.

She doesn't do a warm-up. There's no licking up my shaft or anything like that. She just opens her mouth and takes me right down. "Oh, holy hell. Damn, baby! That's …

wow," I gasp and drop my head back. Oh, fuck, this feels amazing.

"Mmmm-mm-mmmmm," she hums around me, and the vibration makes me suck in a breath. I want this to last, but I don't think it will. It's like she's sucking a climax right out of me, like my cock is a straw and she's drawing out something deep inside me. Just when I think she's got some kind of rhythm, she breaks it, laps around the head, then takes it down even deeper. I can feel her throat close around my hardness and I'm overcome with the sensations.

"Oh, god, Sela." I feel her hands start to corkscrew around my shaft and I know I'm about to lose my battle. It's building painfully. "Fuck, babe. I'm, oh, damn. No, no, no, not yet. Shit. Sela, I ... Oh, babe." Her tongue is stroking up and down my shaft. "Oh, baby, please. Oh, oh, damn, oh, Sela ..." That's the moment I lose my battle.

It takes everything I have not to grab her head and hold her mouth on my cock, but I don't. Unless she asks me to, if she ever does, I'd never do that, but oh, fuck, I really want to. My hips are churning just a bit, but she manages to hold on. "Sela, stop, babe. Sela? Sela, please ... oh, god." I'm beginning to think she's going to torture me, but she finally quits. "Oh, fuck, babe."

"Good, huh?" she asks, a wicked grin stretching her lips.

"Uh, yeah."

"And now I have to do it again," she says in a fake whine.

"Why?"

"You wanna fuck me, right? You have to be hard for that, and that's the best way, right?"

"Uh, yeah, I—"

"One hard cock, comin' right up." I don't get a chance to say anything before she drops that beautiful, sexy mouth back down over me again and I feel myself stiffening instantly.

That only goes on for a couple of minutes and, sure enough, I'm tree-trunk hard. She stops and climbs aboard me like I'm her favorite carnival ride. "How do I look up here?" she asks, her eyes slitted.

"Like the most beautiful, slutty *banrigh* I've ever seen. Damn, girl, those tits are pretty." My hands have already grabbed them, and I squeeze them roughly, sliding my fingers back toward me until I'm gripping only her nipples. There's a gasp from her lips as I twist them, and she smiles salaciously at me. "Like it rough?"

"Oh, yeah. You know I do. Give 'em hell, baby." I pull, twist, and roll between my fingers as hard as I can. Those gasps coming from her tell me she's enjoying it. "More, Miles." Pulled outward as far as I dare, I give her nubs a vicious twist and she cries out, "Oh, damn, yeah! Oh, fuck, more!" Twisted as they are, I give them a hard yank. "Oh, god! Oh, fuck! Yeah! Pull hard! Twist hard! Make 'em hurt! Oh, yeah, so good." I've been so focused on her nipples that I haven't even paid attention to how she's riding me. She's bouncing like crazy, and wild thoughts go through my head, ideas of things I can do to her, ways to make her scream. What I really want in this moment is to force her onto her hands and knees and fuck her so hard that she sees stars, but she's really enjoying herself, and honestly, I am too. "Don't you have some nipple clamps around here?"

"No. Didn't know I was going to be entertaining a pain slut. Want more?" I snarl.

"Oh, god, yeah." Fingers never leaving the left nipple, I slide my right hand downward and start to stroke her clit. "Oh, fuck's sake, Miles. Damn." I watch in wonder as she braces herself with her hands behind her on my thighs and leans back, exposing everything, bouncing on me, giving me a full view of my dick slamming into her. It's amazing. "Oh, fuck, I'm gonna come, Miles. Oh, fuck, oh, fuck."

"Do it, Sela. Come hard, girl. I wanna see you shake." The fingers of my left hand are still tormenting her nipple, and I stretch it out, fold it over my middle finger, and give her whole tit a hard yank.

"Ahhhh! Oh, fuck!" she screams out, her belly spasming and legs shaking. I'm still stroking her clit, and I double down, watching her squirm and shriek, still torturing her nipple and driving her orgasm on. "Oh, god, Miles, stop!"

"No. You'll come again and it'll take you down, Sela. Do it. I want to watch you come apart," I growl at her.

"Oh, god, no. Oh, no. No, no. I can't. Oh, fuck, I can't—"

"Yes you can. Let go, Sela. Come for me. I wanna feel you squeezing my cock again, girl. I know you can."

"Oh, Miles. Oh, fuck me."

"You're gonna get fucked, trust me. But do it again, Sela. Come on. Let go." I speed up my stroking and watch her face, a mixture of fear and desire, knowing when she comes, she'll be at my mercy.

"Oh, oh, damn. Oh, fuck, Miles. Oh, oh, oh!" Her whole body bows, her hips raking her sex up and down on my pubic bone, pussy pulsing and shoulders shaking. The tit I've been mauling is forgotten as I grab her, a hand around the back of her neck, and pull her face down to mine to kiss her hard, my teeth scraping her lips, my tongue searching her mouth, a silent scream breathed into my throat. Her hands have fallen to my chest, pushing against me, and I decide that maybe she's had enough, so I move my fingers from her clit and wait until she collapses on top of me.

I'm still way too hard, but I let her lie there for a couple of minutes, panting and sometimes twitching, on top of me. As soon as she stops jerking, I roll her to the side and pull out of her, then head straight for my closet, my cock bobbing like a flagpole. My toolbox is in there, and I know exactly what I'm looking for …

"What are you doing?" she mumbles as I get to work.

"I'm not finished with you yet," I announce as I snap one pair on.

"Wha … What are those?" Now I've got her attention.

"They're locking pliers." Each little pair is only about three inches long.

"What are you doing?" she shrieks.

I've got a nipple between my thumb and forefinger. "You'd better be still or this is going to be worse."

"Jesus, Miles! What are you doing to me?"

"Isn't it obvious?" I snap the other pair on. "Here we go."

There's a tightening knob on the end of each pair, and I grab the first one and crank about three turns. She moans loudly. "Hurt?"

"God, yeah." So I do the second one. "Oh, shit."

"Yeah. That's doing the trick, right?"

"Oh, hell, Miles. That's a delicious kind of pain," she mumbles, and I smile. I knew she'd like them. I take two more turns on both of them. "Oh, holy fuck. That fucking hurts."

"Want me to take them off?"

"No. I don't think I can take more, but—" I crank down two more times on one of them. "Oh, fuck!" Then I do the other one. "Miles, son of a bitch! That fucking hurts!"

"Yeah. I know. It's bound to." Two more turns and her nipples are turning white. "Just … a little … more." Two more turns apiece and she's howling. "There we go." Without hesitating, I grab them, pull them outward, and then twist.

"OH, FUCK ME!" she screams.

"I'm going to." That gets another twist, and she shrieks. "Hmmm. That looks gorgeous."

Her eyes glance down, then roll back. "Oh, hell, that's fucking scary looking. Can't you find a fucking adult store and, I dunno, get something with rhinestones on them or some shit like that?"

"Look at them, Sela. Just look." As soon as she looks down again, I grab them, pull outward, and twist.

"Oh, fuck you, Miles! That fucking hurts!"

"It's supposed to. Now comes the fun part. Up on your hands and knees." As soon as she moves, she cries out again. "Yeah, they hurt when they move, huh?"

"Yeah. A lot." It takes her some time, but she's finally on her hands and knees. The pliers are swinging underneath her, and she's moaning. I walk around the bed and grab them, then give them a hard pull. "Damn! Oh, fuck!"

"Crawl over here," I order, and she crawls to the edge of the bed. I've already wrapped a hand around my cock. "Suck me."

As she sucks my dick, those pliers swing, and she's moaning and whimpering the whole time. Fuck, I didn't realize how exciting it could be to see her like this, but it really is. She's given me so much shit for so long now, and to see her suffering this way is a little too arousing, but I know she likes it too. She's made no attempt to fight me off or to take them off, so she's getting off on this. After five minutes of sucking, I pull away and step back around the bed, sliding on a condom as I go. "Might want to crawl back a little. Wouldn't want to slam your head into the headboard."

What takes place is the most glorious fucking I've ever given a woman. The whole time I'm pounding into her, those pliers are swinging and she's crying out and screaming. Every time I hear them clank together, I swear I get a little harder. Fuck, I needed this so badly! I pull out for just a second to look, and my cock is huge and purple, so engorged that it's visually throbbing. The sight makes me even harder, and I can't pound her hard enough. "Getting enough cock in you, *banrigh*?"

"Harder. Deeper," she gasps back to me. Damn, I had no idea she'd enjoy it this much. I'm pounding her so hard now that the pliers are constantly clinking together, and I know that's gotta be ridiculously painful. "Oh, god, gonna come. Oh, fuck, more cock. Please, more cock. Oh, god, more cock. Please. Please, please. Twist and pull. Please twist and pull," she mutters, and I know she means her nipples.

"Can't reach 'em, babe. Can you do it?"

"No. I'll fall. Oh, shit," she barks, the pliers banging together again. "Oh, need more hands," she groans. Hmmm. Wonder how she'd feel about me inviting somebody else in with us? The idea of me, her, and another guy fucking her at the same time really appeals to me. That would be amazing. Never thought I'd share a woman with anybody else, but there's so damn much of her that I really need more hands and an extra cock to satisfy her. Much as I love her, she's a heavy-duty fuck, and she needs the attention.

"You realize you're getting an ass fucking after this, right?" I snarl at her back.

She doesn't miss a beat. "Oh, fuck. Yeah. I want it, Miles. Give it to me."

I don't know if she's about to come, and I don't care. I pull out of her pussy and ram right into her ass. She lets out a squeal. "You wanted it, you got it."

"Oh, fuck that ass, babe. Fuck it good," she moans. Jesus! What the hell have I unleashed? "Oh, fuck, my tits hurt. They hurt so good. Oh, damn. Oh, damn," she groans, and I feel her shift. Her right shoulder rises just a little, and I realize what she's doing.

She's stroking her clit. Damn. She's coming apart at the seams, and I'm getting to watch the whole thing. Hell, I'm fucking her into it, and it's better than anything I've ever experienced in my life. I'm just about to the end of my rope when I feel her jerk, and the pliers are swinging wildly as her body turns loose. There's a long, low, "Uhhhhhhhhh," coming from her throat, and I know she's just tipped right over the edge, too far gone to care what I'm doing to her ass.

And there it is—a tiny little bit harder, a tiny little bit longer, and I spill everything I've got into the condom. She's back to both hands on the mattress, and her spine has dropped, her shoulder blades pronounced. As soon as I pull out, I flip her onto her back, and she screams as the pliers clank together. "We've gotta get these off you. Hang on." I turn the knob on one slowly, slowly, slowly, to let the jaws start to open. When they're wide enough, I snap the pliers open and she screams again as blood rushes into the tissue. I do the same for the other one, and she screams again. Without hesitating, I press my mouth over one and she cries out, her hand slapping my head, but in a few seconds, she calms.

I'm exhausted. As soon as my back drops to the mattress, I let out a huge sigh. What the hell just happened here? She's lying beside me, her nipples still dented and purple, her chest heaving, and her eyes closed. This was what my body wanted to do before, but my heart wouldn't let me. Now that I feel more secure in the relationship, I can give her this if she wants, if I want, and I know she understands that I love her. I know she loves me. We can do whatever we want with each other and it'll be okay. It takes me a minute to squeeze out, "You okay, babe?"

"Oh, god. Been years since I was fucked so good."

"Yeah? You like those pliers?"

"Oh, fuck, yeah. God, they fucking hurt so much. It was amazing."

"And the ass fucking?"

"Burns like a motherfucker. I'll walk funny for a week."

"That's a shame. I was gonna do it again in a couple of hours."

"I don't know about the ass fucking part, but you can sure fuck me again. And get those damn pliers ready. Those were fucking *hot*," she says breathlessly.

"You liked that? I thought you wanted something pretty and girly."

"Oh, god, looking at them turned me on so hard."

I lie there for a minute, not sure if I want to bring it up, and then I decide that yeah, maybe this is the right time. "How would you feel about bringing somebody else in here?"

"I don't know what you mean."

"Like me and another guy to both fuck you. Would you like that?"

"A threesome?"

"Yeah. I guess so. *Ménage à trois*. Would you like that?"

"Would you fuck him too?"

"Uh, not sure about that."

"Because I'd love that."

"What? Really? You'd like to watch me fuck another guy?"

"Or him fuck you."

Like that's never happened before. I had enough of that in prison. "I don't think I want another guy fucking me. I've been down that road."

"Oh, yeah. Forgot. Guess that wasn't great."

"Nope. Not too. I'm straight as they come. So that's a no, but I might fuck another guy if he was fucking you too."

"I'm gonna have to think on that." She rolls toward me and bats those big, beautiful eyelashes. "Pinch my nipples again and twist them."

"Right now?" She nods, so I roll toward her, pinch them both between my thumbs and fingers, and then give them a hard twist.

"Ohhh, yeah."

"You want more?" She nods again. "Right now?" Another nod. "Sela, I'm not sure I have it in me."

"Yeah, but I want it in me."

"Damn, girl, you're insatiable!" I say and laugh.

She frowns. "You say that like it's a bad thing."

"Lawd, no. Don't think that. I think it's great. But I'm not sure that's a good idea. I don't want to hurt you—"

"But I *want* you to hurt me," she whines.

"I mean injure you. I don't want to injure you. That's what I meant."

"Oh. Got it. Afraid for me to bleed?"

"I don't want to be the cause of it."

"Uh-huh. Okay. Guess we'll—"

Whatever she was about to say is interrupted by a loud banging on the door. "Who the hell?" I mumble, grab my boxer briefs, and head to the door. And I get a big surprise.

Tony, Steve, and Patch are standing there. "What the—"

"Get your pants on, and get Sela up. We need to talk. Now," Steve orders.

"Uh, okay. Hang on." I take off toward the bedroom and when I'm inside, I close the door behind me. Sela's lying on the bed, stroking herself. I swear to god, she wasn't kidding. She's ready again. "Hey," I whisper softly. "Get your clothes on and get out in the living room."

That makes her stop, and she cranes her head up to look at me. "What's going on? Who was out there?"

"It's Tony, Steve, and Patch."

"I said maybe another guy, not three more," she mutters.

"What? I didn't … No. It's something important. I don't know what. But it's …" I look at the clock for the first time. It's ten after two in the morning. That's a bad omen. "Just get up and put some clothes on."

"Sure you don't want me to go out there just like this?" she asks, fingers gripping her nipples and pulling out on them sharply.

"No. Dressed. Hurry up." I step through the door and back into the living room. "Sorry. She's being stubborn. We weren't exactly expecting guests."

"We weren't exactly expecting to be over here either, but here we are," Tony says, and something in his tone sets me on edge.

"Hey, guys, what's all the fuss?" Sela asks as she steps into the room. She's thankfully put on her pajamas. I was afraid she'd walk out here stark naked.

Tony's face is blank. "I just got off the phone with Angelo, and I've got some really bad news."

"Oh?" Sela says. I can't speak. I'm terrified.

"Yeah. The two guys here in town, the ones you saw today? The cartel don hired those two men to take out you and Natalie. They're supposed to be some kind of extra crazy sumbitches who never quit until the job is done. And some of the things he said are really disturbing."

"Such as?" I ask. Do I really want to know?

"Their orders aren't to kill instantly. They're to torture for at least three days before killing." I watch the big, dark man measure his words. "And I'm not sure killing them will help. He'll only send more."

"So this will be an ongoing threat," Sela says, too much resignation in her voice.

"I'm afraid so. The only way to stop them is to stop Don Julio, and so far, nobody's been able to do that." Then he grins. "But that was before I sicced Angelo on him."

"So you think he can do something to stop this?"

"He's going to try. I'm not going to lie. It was hard for me to make that ask. That's huge. A very dangerous ask, and my *cugino* has a wife and kids. So do most of his men. But if he could neutralize Don Julio during this, it would save a lot of lives in the long run, between the people the asshole kills and the people his drugs kill. It would do the world a huge favor."

Sela nods. "And he's agreed?"

"Says he's ready for it. Been waiting his whole life to take on somebody like this. He's started calling in markers, and operatives from all over the world who owe him are coming to assist. This will be a big operation, but he says he's taking care of it and the only thing *we* have to worry about is keeping everybody here safe."

"As if that's not enough," I mutter.

"It'll be hard, but not impossible. But we do need to enlist local law enforcement and any folks you know who could help—"

"I'm calling Ethan tomorrow. We'll see what he says. He might be able to talk a couple of his guys into coming," Patch says.

"I've got extra guys coming, probably ten or fifteen," Steve says.

Everyone is converging on the farm. I see the magnitude, the ramifications. I'm about to say something when Steve says, "I've already told Tony and Nikki that they have to go. They're high-value targets, and we can't afford that."

Sela's eyes are sad, and I wonder what she's about to say, but I'm floored when the words come out. "Maybe I should just leave."

Tony's head snaps around and his eyes are fiery as he looks at her. "Why? They're after Natalie too. Removing you won't really help, and besides, you belong here now. This is your home."

She shrugs resignedly. "I can go back to Atlanta."

Her hands are limp in her lap, and I reach for one and take it. "Is that what you want?" I ask quietly.

"Does it matter?"

"It matters to me! I don't want you to leave. And I know you don't want to leave. Do you?"

"No."

"Then we fight on." I turn and look at Tony, Steve, and Patch. "We fight on."

Tony stands and steps toward the door. "We fight on. When I learn more, I'll share more. But know that you're not fighting alone. My whole family, everyone and everything, is at your disposal. We won't let you fall. You can depend on that."

"Thank you. This is our place. And we defend it to the end. Nobody leaves here, and nobody dies," Patch says. "My promise to both of you," he says and looks from me to Sela. "You're my people, and no one will hurt you without a fight."

This isn't a battle. It's a war. And for the first time since I found out what was actually going on, I feel like I'm on the winning team.

SELA

I WANT TO BE ELATED. I'VE JUST GOTTEN THE BEST FUCKING of my life. Epic fucking. And a promise of a double fucking.

There aren't enough words to say how happy that idea makes me. Two or three dicks plowing me at the same time? That would be awesome.

And it all had to come crashing down. Just when I should be able to concentrate on the fun of a gang bang, a cartel is after me and Natalie and wants to kill us. My luck.

Miles draws me close in the big bed and I sigh into his chest. "You okay, babe?"

"I wish I could rewind the clock about an hour, go back to when you were fucking the daylights out of me. That was amazing. I don't want to think about this."

"But we have to. We need to start talking about how all of this is going to affect us. How we need to respond. How we're going to change what we're doing to make allowances and stay safe."

"I've already got one."

"Yeah?"

"Wherever Natalie is, I need to be there too. That way, we can concentrate our efforts in one place."

"But don't you think the two of you being somewhat separate would help us divide and conquer?"

I hadn't thought of it that way. Hmmm. Now I've got to rethink that. "Why don't we do some hard fucking while we're thinking about it?"

"Damn, Sela, what's gotten into you? You're like a supreme horn dog. Aren't you tired?"

"Those pliers did something to me. I just want more."

"You're gonna have to wait. I'm exhausted, and my brain is so full that I don't think I could get it up if I had to."

"I can help you with that," I say and spin to sit squatted on the bed, then reach for the sheet.

Miles' hands clamp down across his chest, clutching the sheet. "No. Be serious here. We need to think about this."

"Can't you think and fuck at the same time?"

He lets out an irritated sigh. "Not successfully, no."

"Bummer." I just spin around and lie back down. "You're no fun."

"Fun is highly overrated when you're *dead*," he mutters.

He's got a point there. Never thought about it in those terms before. "Okay. What are we thinking about?"

"I'm thinking how we need to find a way for me to protect you."

"You do. I've seen armored personnel carriers that looked flimsy compared to that body. Look at you! Nobody's gonna fuck with me if you're around."

"No. I mean like a weapon."

"But you're a felon. And that's a federal law," I point out.

"I know."

"What would it take?"

He shrugs. "I dunno. Pardon from the president?"

"Could he do that?"

"Maybe. Never heard about it happening before, but I suppose it could. Wouldn't even know how to go about that or who to approach."

Everything in my brain lights up. "Yes, you do. I do too."

He side-eyes me. "I don't get it."

"Who do we know who's a federal judge?"

"Natalie, but she can't—"

"Not her. One of her federal judge friends. Maybe her boss. And then they take that to the governor, who approaches the president, and—"

"Wait, wait, whoa. How the hell do you think we're going to—"

"Tony!" I shout maybe a little too exuberantly. "Don't you think he could maybe—"

"Oh. I remember them talking about the governor being a

friend of his. Oh, and his sister-in-law was tapped for a spot on a Congressional subcommittee for sexual assault in the military. The president actually called her during a family dinner. So she has connections in Washington."

"Right. We need to put all of this in play. Fast. We need to get every one of you armed as quickly as possible. And the women too."

"What are we going to do about the kids?" Miles asks. That's been on my mind too.

"I'm still thinking about that. There's got to be something we can do."

Miles stares at the ceiling. "We send them home with Sarah and Lenny to Lenny's house. They can take them back and forth to school. I'm thinking if they're gone before the assholes start their operation, they won't even realize there were kids here."

"See? We're figuring this out. Morning will be better. You'll see. Now, about that fucking …"

"Sela …"

"What? You know you want to!"

"No. I don't. Not right this minute."

"I can change that," I say with a grin.

"Sela, stop. This is serious."

"So am I! I like your hard cock all shoved up in me!"

"Gah. My sweet, slutty little horn dog," he says and kisses me on the temple.

"Awww. Nobody's ever called me that before," I coo.

"Yeah, well, you want something hard? Sleep. Because it's going to be hard for me to sleep tonight. I'm way too worried about you."

"Don't worry about me. I'll be fine. Or dead. Either way, you'll be fine."

A finger and thumb capture my chin and he turns my face

to his. "I would *not* be fine if you died. I would never be fine again. I'd be better off dead too, because being without you is unthinkable, Sela. You don't get it, do you?"

My mind goes back to an hour ago. This guy was giving it his all to give me what I need. He backed away the other day. "What changed?"

"Huh?"

"What changed? The other day, you were ready to go after me, but you backed off. Tonight, you went for it. What changed?"

"You. I wasn't sure you really cared that much about me before, and it didn't seem right, turning loose to just do whatever because it felt good. I felt like I was using you."

"And now?"

"You're still here. That means you really do care about me."

"I love you, Miles. I mean that when I say it."

"And I love you too. So yeah, that was about bustin' a nut earlier, but it was about giving you what you need. And did you get what you need?"

"Yeah, but I could use some more," I say again, hopeful.

He sighs and chuckles. "Go to sleep, my horny little *banrigh*. There's more where that came from, but not tonight."

I tweak his nipple again. "Can't blame a girl for trying."

"No. You most certainly cannot."

Now to find another cock. I have no idea where to start, but I'm sure I'll think of something or someone. And I can barely wait.

I KNEW TODAY WOULD BE DIFFERENT, BUT I DIDN'T REALIZE just how different.

We step into the kitchen for breakfast to find a group of men sitting there, eating. Steve's right in the middle of them. "I thought you guys were going," I say as I sit down across from him.

"They did. I insisted Tony and Nikki go on home. You've met Marshall," he says and tips his head toward the big man beside him.

"Yeah, sure have. How's it goin'?" I ask the security agent.

"Pretty good if we can get you over this hump. And we will," Marshall assures me.

"No doubt."

"You'll learn everybody's names in time. Right now, we're just doing some planning and strategizing." I hear the door open again, and I turn.

Natalie's walking in, and she's got two guys with her. I'm certain they're feebs. But she's supposed to be at the court-house. "Hey, what are you doing here?"

"They got a call to bring me here, so here I am. What's going on?" she asks as she sits down beside me. A cup of coffee appears in front of me, and I look up to find Miles smiling down at me.

I point at the two agents. "Who are your friends?"

Instead of answering me, one of them sticks out a hand. "Agent Baldwin?" Well, excuse me for not wanting to take it. He waits a couple of seconds, then withdraws it.

"Not for much longer."

"Gotcha. Sorry to hear that. It'll be the bureau's loss. I'm SSA Tom Mathis, and this is SSA Bob Arterburn. We're Natalie's detail. Andrew told us to be sure to introduce ourselves to you. Sorry about what happened with Morreau and Landrum. They're dickheads."

I stick out my hand to him, and he takes it. Arterburn does likewise. I like these guys. "Yeah, they are. Glad to have somebody different with us. This is Steve McCoy from Citadel Security, and these are his men."

"Glad to be working with you, Mr. McCoy," Arterburn says and stretches out a hand to Steve. Now I *really* like these guys.

"We've got a few more people coming. They'll be here shortly. Have a seat, guys," Steve says, and I see Hollywood, Miles, and Patch hustling to get coffee to everybody. I'm staying right here. My ass is on the line, and I want in on this.

More of the farm's residents—I guess I should say more of us—are filtering in, and all the men take cups of coffee and sit down at the table with all of the men who've come to help. I hear a voice behind me and someone asks, "What can we do to help?" When I turn, I'm shocked.

It's Preston Ramage, Justin Lark, and Marty Lamb from the Hazard Police Department, standing there, hands on their tool belts. "Join us. We're about to start a brainstorming event, and you're invited," Steve says.

"Are we welcome too?" a deep voice says, and behind the three Hazard Police Department officers I see Sheriff Curtis Stafford and two of his deputies, Matt Stegner and Darren Drake.

"We can't have too much help. Have a seat," Steve says and we all wait as they join us.

"Before we get started, can I ask you a question?" I say to Steve.

"Sure."

I motion to Miles. "Is there any way we can get these

guys' rights to firearms reinstated? It would make everything so much simpler."

Steve sits there for a second. "I think it's unlikely or almost impossible, but I can ask. Tony knows the governor, so he could maybe help if he's so inclined, but I'm not sure how fast that could be done. Who out here still can't have a firearm?"

"Priest, Miles, um, Bear, Ghost."

"Gotta say, I'm not optimistic, but I'll sure start asking. They were convicted in other states, so having our governor pardon their convictions is unlikely. Matter of fact, if any of the families of their victims found out, I'm pretty sure that would kill it. But I will ask." He turns his attention to the larger group as my heart sinks. "Okay, everybody, let's get started. Let's see what we come up with."

We talk for over an hour. We've got a commitment of at least eight Hazard Police Department officers and six Knott County Sheriff's Office deputies. Mathis and Arterburn say they think they can get at least eight agents, so that's hopeful. We've got the five guys here who can arm themselves. Steve says he's got fifteen guys easy and probably more if he rotates them out a bit. We're all batting ideas around when Steve excuses himself to answer the phone. When he comes back, his face is drawn and tired. Nobody else seems to notice it, but I do. "What's wrong?"

"That was Tony. Angelo told him they're headed to Colombia to hopefully take out this cartel head and stop the madness. If anybody can, it's Angelo and his team. They're unstoppable. True mercenaries. Our task now is to figure out how to monitor our surroundings here, where the weak spots are, how to protect those, and what to do if they infiltrate, and I do believe that's what they'll do."

That's another hour, complete with Patch producing a

map of the farm and everyone looking at it. Nearing the two-hour mark, I can't take any more, and I slip out the back door where there's some peace and quiet. I haven't been standing there for more than two minutes when the door opens and Miles steps out. What he does next surprises and thrills me.

He doesn't say a word. Instead, he just steps up in front of me, opens his arms, and wraps them around me. As I lean into his chest, he squeezes me tightly against him, and his hugeness makes me feel safe. After all the years of being alone, I realize this was what I missed—the feeling of someone who doesn't need to say words to me, who comforts me just with his presence. That's how I feel—comforted. I'm not alone in this. There's someone else here for me, someone who loves me and wants to see me safe and protected. Miles is that person. In that moment, I understand more than I ever have what true love is, and this is it. Being here with him, having him hold me with no words necessary, fills me with a peace I've never known. Mountains crumble, oceans dry up, the sky turns dark and tornadoes form, but Miles is here, sheltering me, caring for me, protecting me. My arms slide up his sides and my hands cup his shoulders from behind, hanging on, begging him to keep holding me. When he does speak, he whispers, "I'd die for you, *banrigh*. I'd do anything for you."

"And I you, babe. I love you, Miles."

"I love you too. We're going to make it, babe. I know we are." I wish I was so convinced, but I do feel like there's hope now that he's with me. I would've gone this alone before. Now I don't have to.

Patch was on the phone when we came back in, and he turns toward the group. "Just got off the phone with Ethan. Zeke and Drew are coming, and Brock will be standing by if he can do anything to help." I remember Zeke Calhoun and Drew Koopman from some of the things I was invited to out here. Drew was a Virginia State Police trooper, and Zeke was a Green Beret. Those two will be able to help us, I'm sure. "Who is Brock?" I whisper up to Miles.

"Brock Mabrey. U.S. Customs and Border Patrol. If we need him," he explains in a returned whisper.

"I've met those boys. They're good people, and they'll be a lot of help," Preston says, then turns and smiles at me, and I try to return it. I'm feeling more hopeful, but there's so much to do.

Everyone keeps talking, passing around ideas, but I'm numb. I hear Miles' voice say something, and I'm moving. I don't even realize what's happening until I hear the door close behind us, and I'm propelled downward until my ass hits something hard. People are moving around me, and I hear another voice say, "Bend over, Sela. Head between your knees." Something cold and wet hits the back of my neck, and I feel myself suck in a deep breath. "It's okay. You're okay. Just breathe, okay?"

I turn my head just enough to see, and Justin is squatted there beside me. "What happened?"

"You almost fainted."

"I've never fainted in my life, fuck you very much."

"I think you're totally overwhelmed. Bear caught you before you went down." So Miles was the one who led me out here. I take another look around and discover that I'm out back of the kitchen again. "Just stay bent over. You're okay."

"But I don't faint."

"I believe you. Probably just low blood sugar or something." Well, he's being kind to the idiot who probably quit breathing in the kitchen. I could feel myself getting more and more tense, but I didn't realize I was *that* tense.

"Here, babe. Sit up." Miles is sitting beside me, and he hands me a cup. I take one swig and make a face. "No, drink it up. It's peach nectar. Audrey said it's got more sugar in it than anything else she's got in there, and I think you need it."

"I don't understand," I say as I wipe some from my chin where it dribbled out the sides of the glass.

"You're exhausted, *banrigh*. You're not one hundred percent anyway, and this is stressful." He ain't wrong about that. I've done a lot of crazy things in my life, and this is the most stressful thing I've ever been involved in short of the hostage situation. "You should get some rest."

I hear the door open again, and look over to see Preston standing there. "Everybody okay here?"

"Yeah, she's fine. Just worn out," Miles says.

My cup is empty, and Justin hands it to Preston. "Hey, babe, can you refill this for her? She needs some more." What? Babe?

"Sure. What is it?"

"Peach nectar. Audrey gave it to us."

"Yeah. I'll get some more. Just a sec." And Preston disappears.

Did I mention I'm confused? I stare at Justin. "Babe?"

I can see the panic in his eyes. "Oh, shit. I didn't mean to …"

"Wait. Are you two …" Miles starts, pointing back and forth from Justin to the door.

The young officer holds up his hand and points to a small tattoo at the base of his left ring finger on the palm side. "Yeah. A couple of years ago."

"Wow. I mean, that's cool, but wow. How did everybody take that?"

He sighs loudly. "*Everybody* doesn't know. We've kept it really quiet. They all think we're roommates because we can afford a nicer place on the two incomes, but it's more than that."

I'm stunned. My gaydar is usually calibrated pretty well, and I missed this completely. "So you're both gay."

"No. I mean, yeah. I mean, no, we're both bi, but we fell for each other and just decided to make it official. But we both like women too. Just didn't find one we liked as well as we liked each other." That look of panic returns. "Please don't say anything to anybody. Please?"

"No. Neither of us would do that," Miles says decisively, and when he looks at me, I shake my head. "Wouldn't dream of it."

"Yeah. No. Never," I assure him.

"How have you managed to cover this long?" Miles asks, and that's a question I'd like to hear an answer to too.

"We've got this friend, Carmen. Cute girl. Late twenties. She comes over every once in a while and we have a three-some, get our lady lust satisfied. The guys know we do that, so they think we're straight and like to share. That's been good so far. We're hoping they never figure it out."

"Oh. So you don't mind sharing?" Miles asks.

"Hell no. It's fun, the three of us. We both like to watch too, so it works out really well."

I can practically see the gears turning in Miles' brain. "Uh-huh." When he glances at me, I give him a nod only he can see. "So when this is all over, I'd like to talk to you some more about this, if that's okay. Bring Preston into it too."

"I don't …" Justin stops, then glances from me to Miles and back to me. "Oh. Oh! Oh, I get it. You're thinking …" Miles gives him a knowing nod. "Oh, wow. Yeah. That would be … Hell, I can't speak for Preston, but I'm definitely inter-ested. We can talk about it—"

"Talk about what?" I hear Preston's voice ask as he steps back outside.

"You know our arrangement with Carmen?" Justin asks,

and Preston's face goes pale. "Relax. They know, and they're cool."

Preston side-eyes Justin. "What about Carmen?"

Justin just says, "Well, Bear and Sela ..."

Preston stands there for a minute, looking from one to the other of the three of us several times, then chirps, "Oh! Oh, wow. That would be ..." Can't wait to hear the end of this. "Fucking amazing. Here," he says and thrusts the cup toward me. "Gotta go take care of something." And he disappears back inside.

Miles starts to laugh. "Is he—"

"Highly excitable. He definitely is. He needs some privacy. I've got a whole lot more self-control than he does. Apparently more than I realized," Justin says, laughing. "Right now, we've got to keep you safe, doll, but when this is over, yeah. We definitely want to pursue this line of thinking. If that's what you both want."

"It definitely is," Miles says. "Sela?"

My body has started to hum. "The three of you? Awww, hell yeah. That would be awesome."

"Good. Now, I'm going back inside to get my head together and see what's going on. Guess I'd better check on Pres too. He's only got so long in the bathroom before everybody starts to wonder what he's doing." Justin is still chuckling as he heads inside.

"Well, that was a surprise," I hear Miles say under his breath.

"Yeah, for real. So does that intimidate you at all? I mean, they're pretty young and they're both really good-looking."

"Intimidate me? Hell no. The four of us together? Or even five? Damn. I may have to excuse myself too," he says with a grin.

"Or we could go back to your cottage," I offer.

"Sela, this shit is serious. Your life is at stake."

"I know. But I keep thinking about those pliers …" He chuckles again. "Well, I do! That was profound! I mean, it was life-changing!"

"Glad you liked it. We'll do it again, and I'll run to the craft store and get you some rhinestones or crystals or something." That makes me chuckle. "But right now, we've gotta stay focused."

The ground is soft under my shoes as I stand. "You're treating me like I'm not serious about this."

"I'm not. I know you're serious about it. But damn, babe, you've got a one-track mind. Try training it on the problem at hand instead of my dick."

"But I love your dick," I whine.

"And I love your pussy. But if you're dead, I don't have you *or* your pussy, so that's a bit concerning to me." He holds the door open, and I can hear all the voices from inside. "Get in here and eat something. You need it."

Natalie is in the thick of things, and Arterburn and Mathis seem to be engaged as well. It's like everybody is involved. I'm just overwhelmed. Steve looks over at me and smiles before he says, "I need a whiteboard."

"Everybody!" a voice calls out loudly, and the voices all die down as Sheriff Stafford stands. "Be at my office at two o'clock today. We can use the conference room and map out all of this. I've got the whiteboards, markers, stickers, everything we need to get this organized. I think we've got it all covered, but we really need to clarify everything so we all know what's going on."

"That's great," Steve says loudly. "Two o'clock, everybody. Please be there. Everybody will know for sure what they're doing and we'll be ready to fight."

Fight. We're fighting. This time, it's for Natalie's life. It's for my life. Everybody is finishing their food but as they file out, they come by and take my hand or give me a hug. A week ago, I would've recoiled in horror. Today, it feels like I'm finally with my tribe. My platoon. My squadron.

My warriors. This *banrigh* has trained all her life for this. Let the games begin.

CHAPTER 8

BEAR

BY THE TIME WE LEAVE THE KITCHEN, IT'S ALMOST NINE o'clock. The guys all go to the shop, and when Sela and I have finished helping clean up the kitchen, we head to the cottage. Natalie went back to the courthouse with Arterburn and Mathis, and Sarah and Lenny are both busy, so we're the only loose cannons out rolling around.

The door no sooner closes around us than Sela rounds on me and grabs my belt buckle. "Finally alone," she whispers.

"Damn, woman, you're insistent."

"I know what I want. And I want more of this." She's barely gotten my fly down when she sits down in one of the dining chairs, pulls me to her, and runs her mouth down over my cock.

"Shit, babe, you have zero patience," I mutter, then let my head fall back. Standing in the middle of the room with her blowing me might not be such a good idea. If this time is like the last time, I might actually fall down.

Her lips pop as she turns loose, but her hands keep working my hardness. "God, I want you to fuck me. You're definitely hard enough."

Now what am I supposed to do with that? I just point to the bedroom. "Go. Get in there and get naked." I watch her scamper off gleefully and stop in the laundry area on my way past. She's undressing when I get to the bed, so I strip everything off and stand there, lamp post stiff. I surprise her when she turns to face me as I just press my hand into her midsection and force her to fall backward on the bed. She doesn't have a chance to protest before I fall to my knees on the floor, force her legs open, and bury my face in her slit. My tongue deep-dives into her pussy, and then I run it up until it hits her clit.

"Oh, hell," she murmurs.

"Get ready. I'm sending you," I breathe against her skin, then start the torture, my tongue circling and wagging back and forth, sometimes soft, sometimes rough, but never stopping.

"Oh, shit, Miles! Oh, damn! Hey, slow down!"

"Hell no. Just hang on." She's reaching for me but her arms aren't long enough, and I'm happy. She can't slow me down unless she sits up, and that's not going to happen. Even though she tries, I press a hand into her belly and push her back down.

"Miles. Oh, damn, Miles. Oh, fuck, fuck, fuck." The view from here is amazing. I look down, I see that glistening pink pussy. I look up, I see the underside of her tits, her nipples hard, erect, and still raw from last night. It don't get no better than this. When she grips her nipples in her hands and starts pulling and squirming, I almost come undone. I'm so fucking hard that I'm seeing stars, and a one-fingered touch says I've already got precum beaded on the tip of my dick. Listening to her, tasting her sweetness, I think I might actually come with zero stimulation for the first time in my life.

She's tensing, and I can feel it coming. When I run two fingers inside her and stroke the ridges in the front of her vagina, she lets out a squeal. That's what I want. My tongue picks up the pace, and so do my fingers, stroking like crazy. "Oh. Oh, damn, Miles. Ohhhhh, I'm gonna, I'm gonna, no, no, fuuuuuuuck." Her hips are pumping, her tits bouncing, and she's so wet that she's dripping. Damn. It's all I can do to hang on, but I'm still tonguing her like a maniac, and she's still pulsing. A little more, a little more …

Her body bows until her upper torso is almost upright, and she shakes all over. "Miles, oh damn, stop. Babe, please. Oh, god, no. Oh, please, Miles. Please stop? Please." When I do finally stop, she flops back on the bed, limp and spent.

"Oh, no. I'm not finished with you yet. You wanted a fucking, and that's what you're gonna get." She's still lying there, wilted and panting, when I pull out my steals from the laundry area, open them, and clamp them on her nipples. She lets out a scream. "Uh-huh. You're gonna like those."

"Oh, shit! Fuck you, Miles! These hurt!" she says, staring at the white plastic clothespins.

"You like them and you know it," I say, then grab them both and twist.

"Gahhh! Fuck! That hurts!" she shrieks.

"On your hands and knees. Now," I bark and slap her pussy.

"Ohhhh, damn." I watch as she crawls up the bed, her ass to me. That slit is dripping wet and so pink it's almost purple. "Oh, god, Miles. Hurts."

I know my grin is wicked, and I don't care. "Hurts good, huh?"

"Ohhhh, damn. Yeah. Hurts so fucking good. Pound my pussy with that big hard cock," she mumbles.

I slam into her full force. No time for getting used to it right now. She wanted a pounding, she's gonna get one. "Take it, *banrigh*. Take it like the queen you are. Yeah. Just like that. Hard enough?"

"Oh, fuck, harder," she barks. "Damn, I need my tits twisted real hard."

I pull out, grab her, spin and drop her on the mattress, then force her legs up and slam into her again. As soon as I've started pounding, I sit up on my knees, lift her ass, and keep pounding, but I can lean over, grab the clothespins, and twist. I pull them toward me and she screams, "Oh, fuck me! Yeah! Oh, damn, Miles, pound me with that thing."

Never in my life have I exerted such force when I'm fucking. Never. I'm slamming her so hard that every time I hit bottom, her tits stretch out more from the clothespins, and she's screaming and begging for more. I feel like some sadistic maniac tearing a hooker apart, my cock ripping into her, my hands torturing her tits, and all the while, her arms are spread wide in surrender, her hands palms up, asking for rapture. I want to fuck her to oblivion, to fuck her until she's unconscious, and keep fucking her limp body, knowing that it's mine to use as I please. No woman has ever made me feel this way, and I want more, more, a thousand times more. She's a wanton slut, and I'm the stud to give her what she wants. I see Justin and Preston's faces in my mind, and the idea of being here with her, having one of them in her ass and the other in her mouth, while I'm pounding her this way, cranks me up from a ten to a twelve. Oh, fuck, I wanna die fucking this woman.

Fuck it. I want her full of my cum. I want her to drip it from that hot, pink pussy of hers. I want her to know I own her. This woman is mine. I want to watch her being fucked by other men, but I want to know that when the lights go down, I'm the one inside her, powering into her.

"Oh. Oh, damn, Miles. Oh, I'm gonna … I'm gonna … Ohhhhhhhh." She spasms around me, her cunt throbbing, and I can feel myself readying. I twist the clothespins even harder, listen to her scream, then yank outward on them and feel her clamp down even tighter on me.

When I come, I come hard, hunching into her as fast as I can, my hands yanking, pulling, and twisting, and her screaming my name. Heat and wetness fill her and I can feel it dripping down my balls as they slap against her ass. "Ohhhhh, fuck, woman. Yeah. Oh, god, I wanna fuck you again right now," I mumble as I fall on top of her, the clothespins poking into my pecs. I don't even care. I just gave her the fucking of a lifetime, and I hope she appreciated it. Rolling us to our sides, I stare into her face. "Did you get what you wanted?"

"You're so big and hard. I love the feeling of you fucking me that way." She pushes me back with her hands on my shoulders, then grabs the clothespins and twists them herself. "Ooooo, yeah. Hurts so fucking good." Then she opens the jaws on one. "Gah! Oh, son of a bitch! That hurts!"

"Coulda told ya," I tell her, then lean down to take it in my lips.

"Oh, much better." When she snaps the other one off, she shrieks again, and I repeat with sucking on that one. "Yeah. That's much better. Damn, babe, you outdid yourself."

"Yeah, well, you just got about a quart of cum, so you're full."

"Hmmm, nice." Right there in front of me, she dips her finger into her slit, then brings it up and sucks on it. My dick jumps like somebody just hit it with a cattle prod. "You like hurting me, don't you?" she asks, her face smooth and unaccusing.

"I wouldn't say I like hurting you, but something inside me likes knowing you're in pain while I'm fucking you. Does that makes sense?"

"Yeah. And I'll give you that. You're a sadist at heart, and I'm a masochist. That's okay."

That takes me a minute to wrap my head around that statement. I'm a sadist. I never thought of myself that way, but I think back. Did I ever enjoy that with women before? Not that I can recall. Did that happen because of my time in prison? Maybe. I'll have to explore that with Baxter. It's definitely worth looking into. "What time is it?" I eventually ask.

"Ummm." She twists and looks at something. "Looks like it's about ten thirty."

"We were fucking for an hour?"

"Yeah. Didn't think you had it in you, did you?" Her lips are curled into a sick grin. "I bring out the beast in you."

I grin at her. "Yeah. You bring out the beast in me."

"I like that beast. So, do you want kids?"

I shake my head. "Not really. And you do?"

"No. Not really. Never have. I'd rather be free to do whatever I want."

"Me too."

"Or whoever I want."

Uh-oh. Somebody didn't understand the assignment. "Hang on. That's not the agreement."

"Oh, I know. I don't mean any rando walking down the street. I just mean, if we want somebody else involved, then we should be able to do that. And we can't if there are kids."

"Gotcha. Justin and Preston aren't exactly randos," I point out.

"No. And I wonder if Carmen would want to come along for the ride."

I figured I'd have to talk her into that. "Another woman?"

"Yeah. I mean, don't you think I'd like to watch you fuck another woman?"

"You would?"

"Oh, hell yeah, especially if you did the shit to her that you do to me. And even more so if she didn't like or want it."

That's a shock. "So, basically, you'd like to watch me sexually abuse another woman?"

"No. She could *pretend* she didn't want it. I can just see it, me saying, 'Take it, baby, you can take it. He's not gonna stop. He's gonna fuck you hard and you'll love it.' I can see me saying that while she pretends it's too much. Maybe make her eat my pussy at the same time."

"Jesus, Sela, you're hardcore."

"Yeah. I guess I am. So many years being pushed around and pushed down by men. But I like you pushing me down, fucking me, giving it to me hard. It's amazing. I like not feeling like I have any control over what's happening, like I'm in too much pain to fight it. It's freeing, really."

Damn. Baxter and I are going to have a *lot* to unpack. Thank goodness this afternoon is his time to be here. I may miss the two o'clock meeting, but I can't miss that counseling session.

THEY'RE ALL AT THE SHERIFF'S OFFICE, BUT I TOLD PATCH I feel like I need to talk to Baxter, so that's where I am. Now I'm sitting here, trying to figure out how to say everything I'm thinking. It doesn't help that Baxter can read me like a book. "What's going on? You look especially pensive."

"You and the big words," I say under my breath.

"Would you rather I said, 'What's going on? You look like you've fallen in a pile of shit and you're wondering if you should stay or go?' Because that's what I'm left with."

The sofa is comfortable, but I'm not, so I squirm a little. "I have questions."

"Okay."

"So you know Sela is living here with me now."

"Yeah."

"And we have a rather, um, unconventional … sex life." There. That seems like a good way to start.

"Unconventional how?"

"Um, lively?"

"Okay, you're going to have to be more specific. Lively could mean a lot of things."

"So you want to get off to me telling you about my sex life?"

"No. But you seem to have some misgivings about it."

See, this is what I hate about talking to him. It's like I'm wearing a stamp across my forehead that says "PERVERT." I stare at him for a few seconds and I try to collect my thoughts. "So, um, she likes it rough."

"Okay. Rough how? I mean, vigorous penetrative sex? Or something more?"

"Way more. She wants me to pound her hard for hours."

"Okay. Anything else?"

"Uh, yeah. And hurt her."

"Hurt her how?"

"Like, torturing her nipples."

"Hands? Clamps?"

"Locking pliers and clothespins. I mean, she wanted nipple clamps, but I don't have any, so I improvised with what I had."

"Well, that sounds painful for sure."

"It's gotta be. The locking pliers … If they dangle, they hurt. Pulling them, twisting them, that hurts."

"I'm sure. And she likes this? Or you like it and she tolerates it?"

"No. She wants it. She begs for it. She's like on her hands and knees, whining for it. I fu … forcefully and vigorously had anal with her and she was begging for more."

"And how did you feel about that?"

"When we first got together, I didn't want to do that. I felt like I was using her and I didn't really know how she felt about me. But now that I'm sure about our feelings for each other, if that's what she wants, I'm fine with it."

"You're fine with it, or you want it too? Because you don't sound like you're fine with it."

"I …" I don't know how to say this. It sounds so … wrong. "I, um, I like knowing that she's in pain while I'm fu … while we're doing it."

"So you're a sadist."

"That's what she said." He purses his lips and rolls his eyes in exasperation until I add, "No, really. Not joking. That's what she said, that I'm a sadist and she's a masochist."

"How did that make you feel?"

I think for a minute. It's hard to put into words. "I feel … like she called me a name, I guess maybe? I dunno. I'm having to think too hard about how to say these things. It's throwing me."

"Then just use the words you're familiar and comfortable with. I promise it won't offend me." One look at his face tells me he's being honest. He just wants me to be able to talk about it, so why not? He's a big boy.

"Okay." I take a deep breath and blow it out before I start. "So it's like when I know she's in pain, like her tits are hurting and I'm pounding into her as hard as I can, it makes me feel … free. Like I can fuck her however I want and she's going to take it and like it. She's asking for more, so I twist them and she cries out, and that makes me even harder. I know I'm not explaining this very good, but—"

"No, no. You're doing fine. I get what you're saying."

That's a surprise. "You do?"

"Yes. Of course. She's offering you her body to do with as you please, and no matter what you do, good or bad, she wants more. That's very affirming."

Am I on another planet? "It is?"

"Sure! And does the pain seem to arouse her?"

"Oh, hell yeah. She starts talking about me torturing her nipples at the worst possible times, like in a group or whatever, and it's problematic, but she talks about it like everybody does this shit and it's no big deal."

"Bear, there are probably more people doing this stuff out here than you realize. You've got a group of men who've been imprisoned, some repeatedly sexually violated, others the violators, and that doesn't just fade. And with Sela, she's been in a male-dominated world most of her career. She's had to fight for a place at the table. But with you, she knows where her place is, so she can pull off her clothes, offer you her body, and let you use it to satisfy you both, knowing when she puts them back on and stands up, you're going to respect her."

That's when it all begins to make total sense. "Ah. I get it. But the pain. What's that about?"

"Some women just like that. Plus rape fantasy is the number one fantasy women have."

"What? Why?"

"Because it makes them feel like what's happening is out of their control. It's being done to them without their consent, so they're free to enjoy it if they want, and no one can blame them or call them sluts, because it wasn't their choice. Does that makes sense?"

"Huh. Yeah. Since you put it that way. I can see that. She even mentioned bringing in another woman for me to force fuck and torture while she watches. I mean, not really to force. To pretend like she's being forced so Sela can enjoy it and tell her to comply. Wow. I say that out loud and it sounds really sick."

"To you, but not to Sela. She wants to watch you hurt and dominate another woman. That turns her on too, to see you so strong and forceful. Like you said, of course, not really force. You're not a sex offender."

"No! I'm definitely not! No. I don't want anybody thinking that."

"Then if you did that, you'd have to be very, very clear with the other woman. You'd need to make sure that she had a safe word, that she felt free to use it, and that you'd honor it. You'd explain to her that pretending to be non-compliant is what you want, because Sela wants the illusion that you're forcing yourself on this woman. You'd be surprised at how many women would sign up for that, especially with you."

"Especially with me? Why me?"

"In their minds, you're the quintessential bad boy. Big, muscular, strong, hard background. The only thing you're missing for most of them is fifteen tattoos. You get those, they'll be lining up to be your playthings. It's odd to you, I know, but some women like that, the idea of being captured by the pirate lord and forced to bow to his every sexual fantasy."

"That's interesting." All of a sudden, I feel like I can tell this guy anything. So far, there's been zero judgment, just explanations of what's really going on here. "So I mentioned to her that I might like to bring in another guy to watch him with her or to fuck her at the same time I did, and she was all for that."

"Considering what you've just told me, that doesn't surprise me. A woman whose body isn't in her control being sexually plied by two men? She would probably feel almost worshipped."

"Thing is, I think we've found a couple, a married couple of two bisexual men, who acted like they'd be interested. And they have a woman they invite in sometimes, so she could do that. I mean, that's five people. Whaddya think?" My heel is bouncing on the floor because I'm so nervous, and that admission just takes everything over the top.

"I think that's a lot going on at one time and it might be a little overwhelming. Maybe you and the two other guys, and then maybe just you, her and the other woman. Or maybe you, her, the other woman, and one of the men. I dunno. You can figure that out. But I will warn you, if you embark on an actual relationship with her and the other woman, there will be trouble. I see it in virtually every triad I've ever counseled with two women. At some point, one of the women decides she wants the man to herself, and it winds up breaking them up. It's usually the woman who's been brought in later, wanting to rid the equation of the original woman. It's like a show of dominance. I actually think it harks back to ancient times when men impregnated several women to further the species. That automatically thinned out his sexual response to his original mate, who then was less likely to get enough attention to be impregnated again, and the cycle starts over. I think it's a genetic thing and has nothing to do with feelings or that kind of thing. It's a survival instinct. And men have wandering eyes because they could impregnate numerous women and then continue to do so. Just my theory from research over the years."

"That makes sense."

"So you want to watch her with these other men?"

"I think it would be hot."

"And you wouldn't get jealous?"

"They're married. I figure as long as there's a committed relationship, we can keep it fun."

"There's a greater likelihood, yes. And the single woman?"

"Guess we'd have to treat that one with care."

"I'd say. So do you feel better about it now? Do you understand more about the dynamic going on? Because when you walked in here, you looked as though you felt very guilty about having these feelings, very confused about her having these feelings, and really conflicted about giving her what she's asking for."

"I do feel better about it. It kinda makes sense now. But I still think there are times when we need to just make love, to not worry about all of that and just connect. Don't you?"

"If you need it then yes, I do. And she needs to need it too. Or she at least needs to accept that you need it and try to accommodate you. I mean, sounds to me like you're doing all you can to accommodate her."

"I am. It's exhausting, but I want to give her what she wants."

"Then fuck like a stallion." That makes me laugh. "There are others here on the farm that have a similar dynamic."

"Oh? I know you can't tell me who, but really?"

"Yes. And no, I can't tell you. But suffice it to say, the woman doesn't want to be in charge in the bedroom. They're not as aggressive as you and Sela, definitely not masochistic and sadistic, but still very much a power exchange."

Power exchange. That's a term I haven't heard before. "Explain this power exchange."

"When one partner cedes power to the other. So let's say … Let's say Sela is on the bed. Naked. On her knees. You've tied her hands behind her back. You've, um, clamped her nipples and tied the ends of the clamps to the headboard with great tension on the ropes."

"Like stretched out."

"Yeah. Exactly. You've got a big vibrator going in front of her, and you begin to have pretty aggressive anal intercourse with her. Think for a minute. How much power has she ceded to you?"

"All."

"Not exactly. Her mouth is unoccupied, so she can yell for you to stop. Now, let's say you put a ball gag in her mouth. And then you put a hood over her head. And the rope to her bound hands is also bound around her thighs, so she can't even crawl on her knees. And you start with the anal. How much power has she ceded to you?"

I analyze it. Hands are tied. Mouth is full, can't even turn to look at me because of the hood. Thighs are tied so no crawling, there's a vibrator, and I'm behind her. "She has zero power. She's at my mercy."

"Bingo. That's a total power exchange. She's dependent on you to know her, to know her limits, to honor those, to do what you want with her but not to injure her in an extreme way. She has to trust you completely."

"Ah-hah." Now it's all making sense.

"But let me ask you something. Close your eyes." When I don't automatically close them, he orders, "Go on. Close them." As soon as they close, he says, "Now, picture all of that. The binding. The nipples clamped. The gag and the hood. The wrists and the thighs bound. All of it. See it in your mind?"

In my mind, I do. I can see her there on my bed, bound, gagged, and tied, bare and waiting. "Yeah. I see it."

"Now, take a second. How do you feel about what you see?"

How *do* I feel about what I see? It's Sela. I love her. But what I see doesn't really look like Sela. It's just a … body. A bound body waiting for my dick. Nothing more. It could be anybody. It could be nobody. It could be a random stranger. Somebody I paid. It wouldn't have to be her, although I'm pretty sure she'd love that. But me? "Uhhh, it kinda makes me feel … creepy."

"Creepy how?"

"As in she's no longer someone I love, just a random body to stick my dick in. At that point, she's just a thing. A sex toy. An object."

"And does that appeal to you?"

"No. Not really. I mean, I guess in some ways it *looks* sexy, like maybe if it was porn on the internet, but it's something I might do at a drunken party, not in bed with my partner."

Baxter leans out toward me and stares me in the eyes, his hands clasped as his forearms rest on his knees. "That's why it's important for *you* to have limits too, and to enforce them. When something goes farther than *you're* comfortable with, you need to be able to say no, not just cater to her. That's for your safety and your mental health. Otherwise, you'll start to feel a gap open between you, and it'll start to widen, and pretty soon, the feelings will be muddied or gone. Does that makes sense?"

"Makes perfect sense." I see what he's saying. Don't get so wrapped up in the sex that we forget why we're together in the first place. "Wow, Shaggy, you've really made me think about some things."

"Good. I want you to have fun, have a really fulfilling sex life, but not do yourself or your mental health any damage. That's my job. But it's also because I care about you, about Sela, and about this place. You guys are special. I want to see you live good lives and flourish. That's important to me."

"Jesus, Shaggy, don't go gettin' all mushy on me!" I say and laugh.

"I'm not. I'm just being honest with you. My work here is important to me. Every man in this place has grown so much since I've started coming here, and I feel like I've really made a difference."

Even though it's very unlike me, I reach over and place a hand on top of his clasped ones. "You've made a difference for me, and thank you for that."

"You're welcome. Thanks for letting me into your world and listening to me like I actually know what I'm talking about!" he says and laughs.

"Because you do. We value you, Mark. I know we call you Shaggy or Max Baxter and act silly sometimes, but we really do value your input. At least I do."

"Thanks. That makes it all worthwhile. Now, go forth and fuck," he says nonchalantly, "and have a good time at it. But remember your own limits."

"Yes. Remember my own limits," I say and rise. "Thanks again."

"You're very welcome. Do I have any more victims out there?"

"I think they're all at the sheriff's office."

"Yeah, how's that coming? Natalie's really afraid."

"Sela is, but she'd never admit it. I can say we've got plenty of expert help, so I'm hoping for the best."

"Keep hoping. Get this out of your way and you and Sela can have a good life here."

"Thanks. See ya later." Sure enough, when I step outside, there's no one else around, and all the vehicles are gone except for the personal ones. But I somehow feel lighter and more hopeful. I can satisfy Sela and still keep my sanity. I know I can do this.

And I can have a whole lot of fun doing it.

Sela

WHEN MILES STEPS INSIDE, THE AIR SEEMS TO CHANGE. There's something different about him. I don't know what it is, but I'm really curious. "Have a good session?"

"Yeah. We need to talk." Uh-oh. This doesn't sound good. "He made me think about some things."

"Okay. Fire away." There's a hesitation, and I wait. Finally, I say, "Miles, if we can't talk about stuff, there's no point. What is it?"

There's a sadness in his eyes, and I don't know what that means for me. "Sela, I want to give you what you want. I really do. But I can't treat you like a fuck puppet. I just can't."

"Wait, what? What are you talking about?"

"Okay, so there was this philosopher, Immanuel Kant, and—"

"I studied philosophy in college, babe. I know who Kant was."

"So I read his book while I was in prison. *Formula for Humanity*. And he talks about using people as a mere means."

"I'm familiar with it. And you're not using me as a mere means if I consent, if I understand that's what you're doing, or if I want you to do it. It's not the same thing."

"Yeah, but it feels like the same thing to me. Shaggy had me do this thing where I imagined you gagged with a hood over your head, nipples clamped and stretched out and tied to the headboard, hands bound and thighs bound, vibrator on your clit, and me behind you, getting ready to give it to you. And he asked me how that made me feel."

"Ooooo, sounds delicious!" From the look on his face, I can tell that's the wrong answer. "But how did that make you feel?"

"Not good. Creepy."

"Why?"

"Because at that point, you're reduced to a thing. Just an object."

"But if I want you to—"

"Listen to me, Sela. Using your body, yeah. I love it. But I need to see your face, hear your voice. The idea of reducing you to a mute, faceless torso to stick my dick into makes me feel kinda … disgusting."

"Okay, so we won't do that."

"But at some point, I'm betting you're going to want to."

"Maybe. Maybe not. And you still have a say." He's looking at me like he doesn't believe me. "Look, Miles, you're not just a fuckstick for me to ride. You're my partner. I love you."

"I love you too, and I don't want to reduce this to just sex. Because it's not just sex for me. It's a relationship."

"I get it. I feel the same way. And it's okay. Really. We can have a lot of fun without going that far. I'm not trying to go to the farthest point I can before I fall off the edge and into nothingness. I'm just trying to have fun."

"Well, believe it or not, I understand it more now than I did before. I mean, what you want." He stops for a second, then says, "Did you know there's another woman out here who likes for the man to be in control of her in the bedroom?"

"Yeah. Natalie."

His eyes bug. "What? Did she tell you that?"

"Oh, yeah. She told me Paddy's a real hardcore fuck in the bedroom, and she loves it."

"Holy shit. Paddy? He's so quiet and reserved."

"Apparently he's not when her clothes come off," I say with a giggle.

"Never would've guessed. Oh, and I talked to Shaggy about Justin and Preston and their friend."

"And?"

"He said we need to be careful with other women. Something about genetics and survival urges and stuff, but that those relationships tend to get really complicated. Otherwise, he said to have fun and fuck ourselves into oblivion."

"He didn't think the idea with Justin and Preston was bad?"

"He said it could be tricky too, but since they're in a committed relationship, our chances of keeping it just fun are really good."

"That's interesting." So Baxter green-lighted our little *menage a quatro*. That's positive. "Good. Let's get them over here and—"

"Sela! Right now our focus is on keeping you alive! None of that stuff. We'll approach that later."

"Sheesh. That's all you think about."

"It should be all *you* think about," he says, glaring at me.

"All I'm thinking about right now is that rock-hard cock of yours and—"

"Sela! Stop it! Damn, woman. I'll be dead in two years at the rate you're going."

"No. You won't. You think you're muscled up now, you mess with me for two more years and you're going to look like some kind of Greek god. Muscles everywhere from fucking constantly." Now I'm laughing, but he's still scowling. "Oh, come on, babe! Have some fun! Things are serious, but they don't have to be behind our doors here. We can be as free as we want to be." Somebody bangs on the door. "Well, shit. I take that back. So much for fun."

"I'll get it." He strides past me and throws the door open. "Hey."

"Hey. We've got everything under control, Bear. Can I come in?" Patch asks and peers around him.

"Yeah. Come on in."

"Hey, Sela," Patch says and smiles at me.

"Hey. What's up?"

"Everything's being set in motion. We know who's going to be where. Now we just need a reason for them to come out of the woodwork. That's where Sela comes in." His phone rings, and he looks at the screen, then taps ACCEPT and hits the speaker icon. "Hey, bud."

"Patch. How's it going?" I recognize the voice as Tony's.

"I think we've got everything ironed out and ready to go. You know anything?"

"Yeah. Angelo just called me. They're on their way to Colombia, but he had an operative that belonged to another agency who's already managed to infiltrate the compound. I just talked to Steve. Their ETA is tomorrow evening near dark. You've got one more peaceful day, and then all hell is gonna break loose."

"Did he say what he thought was going to happen?"

"Oh, yeah. They're coming to try to kill Sela and Natalie,

and Angelo has to make sure that whatever they do at the compound takes place after we've neutralized these guys. Otherwise, he'll send more. Where are the kids?"

"They're already at Sarah and Lenny's. Martin took the dog with him."

"Perfect. These guys won't bother them there."

"What's going to happen when Angelo and his men get to Colombia?"

"Their objective is to take out Don Julio and all the men protecting him. If they can do that, there's a chance that the cartel will live on—if one of his underlings takes it over—but he dies, and so does the vendetta. They'll know it wasn't you guys who hit his place, but they won't know who it was, so they won't have anybody to go after. That's the eventual goal."

"Makes sense. Anything else I should know?"

"Not that I can think of, but be on your toes. He says these two are slicker'n owl shit. They're not his men—he hired them from an international pool, so nobody really knows where they're from."

"That's great. Just great. I guess anybody can be a hit man these days, huh?"

"Looks like it."

"Thanks, Tony. Please stay in touch."

"I absolutely will. I'll be thinking about all of you. Hang in there. Later."

Patch turns and looks at me. "There's hope. We could have this thing sewn up. That would be best-case scenario. Worst, they take out somebody here before we put it to bed. But law enforcement has our backs, so we'll make it. I want the two of you in the lodge. Priest, Paddy, and Ghost are staying in there too. Izzy will be with the state police. Curtis has gotten them involved, so we've got their air support.

Priest sent Aggie back to her apartment. She was cussing and spitting, but she went. Bulldog took Tinsley and the baby to her parents' house and they're staying there until this is over, and he'll come back to stay with us in the lodge. Audrey went to Sarah and Lenny's to stay with the kids and help out, so Hollywood will be in the lodge too." When he stops to take a breath, the sound of voices outside catches my ear. His and Miles' ears too, from the looks of it. "What the hell is going on …" Patch says and glances out the door behind him. "Well, son of a bitch," I hear him murmur.

He opens the door and we look out across the grass. There, in our big green space, are probably a hundred people, all with shotguns, rifles, and handguns. Preston and Justin are out there, talking to them one by one, and they're nodding and chatting. I watch as Patch pushes the door open and steps out onto the porch, hands on his hips. "Preston, what the hell is going on here?"

The young police officer strides toward us, and when he reaches the steps, he puts one foot up on them and stands there, smiling. "They want to help."

I guess the three of us look really confused. "What?" Patch asks. "What are you talking about?"

"We asked around, and they wanted to help. They want to stand guard and help out."

"Do they have any idea how dangerous this is?" Patch asks, his voice a little louder than I would've liked.

An old man with a white beard steps out of the crowd and looks toward us. "Y'all might not 'member me, but couple-a months ago, ya went out and looked for my Margie. She were off a trail and lost. Y'all found her and brought her home, safe and sound. If I can help ya, I'm-a gonna."

"Yeah, and y'all tole my maw not to worry 'bout me 'cause you'd find me, and ya did. That tree done fell on me, and you cut it up and moved it away, and all I had was a broke leg and some scratches! I weren't even out in the woods after dark 'cause-a y'all and yore searching. I owe ya my life," a young man about twenty-five says.

"We can't never repay you for what you did for our Tim," a middle-aged man says, and I know instantly who he is. Tim was the boy they found in the woods, but not in time. This must be his dad. "I watched y'all. Y'all loved him and he weren't even yores. That meant the world to me and Virginnie," he says, wiping his eyes when he mentions his wife, Virginia. "If-n we can't help you when you need help, we ain't no good fer nuthin'. So we come to help. Virginnie's gonna keep sandwiches and stuff comin' so y'all'll have somethin' to eat, and I'm-a stand guard. We ain't gonna sit by and watch this place be tore apart by some drug guys. Nope. That ain't happenin' on our watch."

The emotion on Patch's face is thick. "Look, y'all, we all really appreciate this. But it's a really dangerous thing. Really dangerous. I don't want any of you hurt."

"That's for us to decide, brother," a man calls out, and I can see his clerical collar in the neck of his denim shirt. "We protect our own 'round these parts, and y'all are our own. Y'all're part of this community. You're our brothers and sisters. Our friends. Our family. And we ain't gonna let nobody come in here and hurt any-a y'all without fightin' back. We know it's dangerous. And we're here to meet it."

I'm totally taken aback when Patch turns to both of us, his eyes full and reddening. "This is your fight. What do you think?"

Miles strides out onto the porch. "We'll take your offer. Thank you for standing with us. Some folks are gonna get hurt. It's a sure thing. And if you leave, we'll understand. But thank you. Thanks from me and Sela." I step out onto the porch and let him wrap an arm around the back of my waist. "I know Paddy and Natalie will thank you too. We always wondered if we'd ever fit in here. We're not wondering anymore. We love y'all," he says, mimicking their speech in a respectful way. "Thanks for being our family." Then he looks down at Preston. "Make sure you know what you're doing when you place them around this property. They are *not* collateral damage."

"Absolutely not, Bear. But thank you for letting them help. They all really wanted to, and I couldn't see telling them no. Their hearts are pure."

"I get that. And mine is touched beyond anything you can imagine."

Preston lets loose a two-fingered whistle and points. "Okay, y'all, we'll sort this all out. Head to the biggest building up there and let's see what we can do."

The door closes as soon as Miles, Patch, and I are inside. "I was not expecting that," Patch says in a coarse whisper.

"Me either, but if they want to, I'll take their help," Miles assures him.

"Y'all carry on. I'm gonna go check on Penny. She and Mavis are going to the work house to stay, and Reboot will be with us in the lodge once they're gone. You guys get your shit together and get on over there." He turns to leave, but then turns back. To my surprise, he hugs Miles tightly, then turns and hugs me. It's like getting a hug from my dad. "I love you both. I want us to all come out of this unscathed. I realize that's wishful thinking, but no matter what, I love you. Just remember that."

"We won't forget, I promise," Miles says, his voice gruff with emotion. "We love you too."

"I won't forget either, Patch. Everybody here is my family now. I love all of you."

"We all want you here, Sela. We get this out of the way and I'm excited about what the future is going to bring. But for right now, as Tony would say, business is business." With that, he heads out the door, and the sound of his boots disappears when he hits the grass below the steps.

"Let's get our stuff packed up and get on over there," Miles orders, and I don't question. I just start packing. We need to be somewhere safe, and that's our safest bet right now.

The lodge or Florida. And I hate Florida but, right now, it's sounding pretty nice.

CHAPTER 9

Sela

ALL OF THE LOCALS ARE PACKED INTO THE BIG GREAT ROOM of the lodge, but we manage to squeeze through and head down the hall. I stop at the entrance to the hallway. "Why are you stopping?" Miles asks.

"Thinking. If we take rooms on the back of the lodge, we're away from the green space. That could be good. But if they're coming through the woods like we think, that could be bad."

"Yeah. I think the green space side. That way, if they try to come in the back side, they've got a room and the hallway between us and them, but if they're trying to come in from the green space, they're totally exposed."

"Yeah. That's my thinking too. Let's find a room." Nobody seems to use those rooms much, probably because they pick up noise from the drive. Frankly, we need to hear those sounds now. The second room is one of the largest. "I think this one. It's plenty big and has a nice bathroom."

"Where are Natalie and Paddy?" Miles asks.

"I dunno. Let me see if I see them anywhere." As I head on down the hallway, I hear voices. "Hey, guys," I call out to Ghost and Priest. "You guys shacking up together?"

"Yeah, we decided it would be best if we were two to a room. You know, not alone," Ghost says.

I nod. "Probably best."

"You got a room?" Priest asks.

"Yeah. Second one on this side. Seen Natalie and Paddy?"

"They're packing. Said they'd be here in a few minutes." I just nod and walk back to our room.

Miles is unpacking stuff and putting it away. "Aren't you gonna put your stuff away?"

"I'm hoping we're only here for about thirty-six hours."

"Me too, but realistically, it might be more." He's hanging up clothes and putting stuff in the bathroom.

There's a rap on the doorframe and I turn to see the sheriff standing here. "Got a minute?"

"Looks like we've got all kinds of time," Miles says.

"This is for you." Sheriff Stafford extends his hand and in it is a handgun, a Glock. Looks like a Glock 19. I reach for it, but he shakes his head. "No. Bear."

Miles' mouth falls open. "I can't—"

"I talked to Steve and the governor. There's no way they can get everything pushed through in time, but you need this." That's when I notice that the grip is wrapped in tape. "Let her rack the first round in. Your fingerprints won't be anywhere on it. Here's two extra magazines. If you have to change one, use your shirttail to rack a round in and throw the empty mag away. Pond, river, somewhere. Just get rid of it."

"We could all go to prison over this," Miles murmurs.

"We could all die without it. I'm not taking that chance.

Priest and Ghost are getting one too. You got your own sidearm?" he asks me.

"Yep. SIG Sauer P226 chambered for three fifty-seven, Rem 870 and Rem 700," I answer, listing my handgun, my pump-action shotgun, and my bolt-action rifle. "And plenty of ammo for everything."

"No nine mil?"

"No."

"Then here." He hands Miles two boxes of ammo. "Now you've got plenty." With that, he just spins and walks away.

My baby just stands there, blinking. "What just happened here?"

"A man in a position of authority told you to protect yourself. Thank goodness for that. Now you can."

"I don't feel comfortable with this, Sela. I could go back to prison for the rest of my life."

"Or your life might not be that long."

"I can't. I won't." He places the handgun carefully on the dresser. "I'll take my chances."

"Fine. Then for god's sake, stay hidden."

We don't say a lot after that. He's made his position clear, and I think I've made mine equally so. I usually love him more for taking what he thinks is the right stand, but he's making a wrong call on this one. We have sandwiches and chips for dinner and some other leftovers. Audrey has plenty of food in the place, so Virginia can feed all of us. The kitchen is so full that we take our food and go back to the lodge, and we're not the only ones with that idea. There are probably twenty other people over here with us.

The evening seems to drag. Everybody is on alert, and everybody is already exhausted. At ten, Miles finally pats my thigh and sighs. "I'm going to bed. Might as well. I can't take it anymore."

"Okay. Right behind you." He stands and reaches for my hand, but I shake my head. "I'm getting a couple of bottles of water. Be there in a minute." As I stand there, he gives me a tiny smile and turns to wander down the hallway and disappear into our room.

I grab the bottles of water, a couple of granola bars, and a few pieces of paper towel, and make my way to the bedroom. I can hear Paddy and Natalie talking down the hallway, but the sound is muffled when I close the door. Miles is in the bathroom, brushing his teeth, so I set everything down and start pulling off clothes. I brought a little cotton gown with me, so I pull that on and wait. When he comes out, I go in, brush my teeth, brush my hair, and hit the head one last time. By the time I get back out there, he's in bed, his bedside lamp turned off and the covers pulled up to his chest. Sliding under them, I scoot up against him, and his arms unfolds, beckoning me into his embrace. With my arm draped across his chest, I sigh, and I feel his lips brush my forehead. "I love you, Sela," he whispers.

"I love you too. We're gonna be okay. I have to believe that."

"I want to. I'm so scared for you."

"I'm scared for us all." He squeezes me tighter, and I kiss his pec and stroke a finger down through the hair on his chest. Lying here with him, I feel completely safe.

But I know better.

I sit bolt upright in bed when I hear the tone. "What the fuck?"

"Shit." Miles' slippers are on and he's headed up the

hallway in his pajama pants. I slip on my slippers and hurry that direction.

Out in the big room, Ghost is already standing there in front of the call box, and he pushes the button. "This is App STAR base. Go ahead, central dispatch. Over."

"Roger, App STAR base. We've got a report of a child lost on Moss Holler Trail. Repeat, report of a child lost on Moss Holler Trail. Over."

Ghost looks around at Miles, Paddy, and Priest. "What the hell do we do?"

We all pivot when the door opens and Patch strides in. "Well? What do you want to do?" he asks the four men.

"What do you mean, what do we want to do? We're already under a red alert and we're supposed to do this?" Paddy snaps.

"This *is* our responsibility," Priest reminds him.

"But Natalie is here, and so is Sela. And if we leave—"

Patch runs a hand through his close-cropped hair. "Yeah, but Priest is right. And the women are as safe here with the rest of us as they would be if you were here."

Miles straightens. "I disagree with that statement, but I do agree that this is our responsibility. Those people out there with guns surrounding our home here, they're here because we've taken our responsibility to this community seriously. Every physical body we add to this place is an added layer of security, but we still have to do what we're asked to do for this community. I'm with Priest. Paddy, if you really feel you should stay here, that's your call, and I won't fault you for it, brother. We all have our own decisions to make. But I'm going. Priest?"

The shorter man nods. "With ya."

"Ghost?"

"That kid needs findin', and I'm here to help."

Miles turns and looks at Paddy. "Brother? What say ye?"

I feel bad for Paddy. He loves Natalie, but he wants to do the right thing. "Okay. Let's go."

"If you're not all in, it would be better if you stayed here."

"No. I'm all in. And I've got most of my EMT training and you might need that, plus I'm the only one of the four of us who can carry a weapon, and we might need that."

"True. Let's go. Everybody suited up. At the Jeeps in ten."

As they stream toward the door, Miles is bringing up the rear, and Patch catches him by the arm. "Be very careful out there. Those guys might already be in the woods. If they recognize you as one of us, you could become a bargaining chip, and we don't need that."

"Understood, chief. We'll keep watch." He's about to step through the door when he turns and looks back at me. "I love you, *banrigh*. Do what Patch and Steve tell you and stay safe."

Instead of answering him, I run straight for him, and he catches me and lifts me off my feet to kiss me. When he pulls back, he smiles down into my face. "There's more where that came from. Be a good girl." Then, with a peck on my lips, he's gone.

Something inside me torques, and for the first time since all of this started, I'm terrified. I just want him to come back, for everything to go back to normal, for us to curl up in his big bed and sleep peacefully, knowing that our world is okay. My chest is heaving and so is my stomach. They've no more than made it out the door when Patch's phone rings. It's three in the morning, and I wonder who would be calling.

"Uh-huh. Okay. Good. Thanks for letting me know. I'll pass it along to everybody. Thanks."

"News?"

Patch nods. "Angelo. His inside guy says one of the assassins here called Don Julio to let him know they know where Sela and Natalie are and they're getting ready to do the deed." Hearing them called assassins for the first time makes my skin crawl and sets up a burning in the pit of my stomach.

"When?"

"He's sure they'll wait until dark this evening. That gives us some time, but puts us at a disadvantage. They'll be watching us prepare, so we've got to be really careful about what we're up to. It's got to be business as usual. But it does give us some time to get some trackers out into the woods and try to find them before they can take a shot."

"True. I'll get on the phone and find out about the FBI agents as soon as it's light out."

Patch nods. "Steve's got guys who'll go out there and work the hills. Hollywood, Bulldog, Reboot, and I can help them since we know a lot of the territory."

"Sounds good." It's all churning in my mind, and I'm overwhelmed. "I need some sleep if I can get any." That's the moment I hear the sound of the Jeep racing out the drive. My eyes close and my heart starts to pound. "Please tell me—"

"They'll be fine, Sela. They're well-trained and alert. They'll make it back in one piece."

"I hope you're right. Night." That's it. I'm done. There's nothing more for me to do until it gets light outside.

And there's no telling what will happen at nightfall.

BEAR

.   .   .

WELL, THAT WAS QUICK. IT TOOK US LESS THAN AN HOUR TO find the kid. He was hiding in a small overhang under some rocks, and the only reason we found him so quickly was because he giggled as we walked by. He's nine and developmentally delayed, so he's more like a toddler. His parents have a terrible time keeping him in the house, and he managed to get the slip on them. They wouldn't have known he was gone except that the dog woke them up jumping on their bed—a dog that sleeps outside at night. He left the door wide open when he went out, and the dog seemed to have waited a little while before he went in.

Now we're out, it's getting light, and I want to alert Patch that we're on our way back. As soon as we pull in, we all head straight for the lodge. Virginia catches us on our way by. "Breakfast is ready anytime you guys are, such as it is." I know what that means. She fixed what she had, and that's fine. It's food.

"Thanks, Ms. Virginnie. We'll be right back," I promise her as I follow the other three guys.

I slip off my clothes and slide under the covers to cuddle Sela. "Oh, god, you're back," she whispers, her voice coarse with sleep.

"Yeah. Just got back. Showering and going to the kitchen. You coming?"

"You get in. I'll get in when you get out." And she rolls back over. That makes me smile, and I kiss the back of her neck before I climb out and wander to the bathroom.

We're all in the kitchen, dozens of people trying to eat and get back outside, when the door opens and a short, stout guy with shoulder-length blond dreads steps in, dressed in gray-toned urban camo. Everybody turns, and he looks a bit startled. "I'm, um, looking for Steve McCoy."

Patch is already on his feet. "And you are?"

The man holds out a hand confidently and when Patch takes it, I can see his firm grip. "Peyton Flores-Stokes. I work for Tony Walters. He asked me to come."

"Oh! I'm Patch Scott, the farm's owner."

"Yeah, I've heard all about you!" the man says, his smile warm. "Army MEDEVAC/CASEVAC." He points to Patch's patch. "Afghanistan, right?"

"Yep."

Peyton lifts his left pantleg where his prosthesis is clearly visible. "Fallujah."

Patch pats him on the shoulder. "We're brothers in more ways than one! Um, Steve's around here somewhere. Probably in the lodge. He didn't tell me you were coming."

"He didn't know. Tony said my expertise might be useful." We're all listening intently. "Former Ranger sharpshooter. Need to find a vantage point and dig in." Holy shit. Might be useful? Fuck yeah, I reckon so.

"Hey, y'all, reinforcements are here!" a voice calls out as Zeke steps in, Drew right behind him.

"Glad to see you guys!" Patch says and gives Zeke a bro hug, followed by Drew. "You know all of our guys, but these are community members who've volunteered to help us keep watch," Patch says, sweeping an arm out. "And we've just met this fella here. Zeke Calhoun and Drew Koopman, meet Peyton Flores-Stokes, former Ranger sharpshooter." We watch as Zeke and Drew greet Peyton. I feel better already just knowing that these guys are here, and this Peyton guy must really be something for Tony to send him. "Please, help each other as best you can."

"Yeah, I need some guidance. You guys have been here before, so maybe you can help me find the best vantage point," Peyton says.

"Absolutely. We'll get our heads together," Drew assures him. "Where are all the feebs and KSP?"

"We don't have that many, but they're down the road at the other farm we just bought, using it as a covert staging area. They figured too much of a presence in broad daylight would tip our hand," Patch explains.

"Probably best. Can we get them on the phone?" Zeke asks.

Patch nods. "Absolutely. We all need to coordinate. You guys can have our office over in the lodge." Just as quickly as they appeared, the three men disappear out the door with Patch leading them.

"Wow. Army Ranger sharpshooter," I murmur.

Sela's eyes are still wide. "They're bringing out the big guns."

"Yeah. We're gonna need 'em." I swallow my last bite of pimento cheese sandwich—hey, it's something, and something's better than nothing, even for breakfast—and stand. "I'm going over there with them. I want to know what's going on. You coming?"

"No. I can't. I just … can't. My brain is shutting down."

Her temple is soft and her hair smells like lilacs when I lean down and press a little kiss to it. "I get it. Just watch your back—always."

"Yep. Absolutely." Something about the way she answers me makes me a little afraid. It's almost like she's given up. That can't happen.

Steve's on the phone when I step into the office. "Uh-huh. Okay. Let us know. Yeah, I knew it would take something like that, but I'm glad they've at least got it underway. Sure. Right. Okay. And thanks for sending Peyton. Bye." Steve hangs up and sits there, motionless, for a few seconds while everybody else waits. Finally, he says, "You guys need to know, it's killing him to not be here with you."

What did we do to make these people care about us so much? We are beyond blessed to have them supporting us and to call them friends. "He can't be here. There's too much risk, and he's got a lot of businesses to think about and people who depend on him," Patch says.

"I know. That's what I told him."

"You should go too, Steve," Peyton says. "We've got this. Go home to Kelly and CJ."

"No. I've never really done shit with my life, and this is my chance."

"Don't say that. You gave me a chance when nobody else would. Everything I have now, my job, my home, Molly, José, the kids, I have all of that because of you." Peyton stands there, arms folded across his chest, but a look of compassion in his eyes. "Your life has made an enormous difference to a lot of people. Go home. Let us handle this."

"No. I'm here for the duration." Steve sighs heavily, but the next words from his mouth take me by surprise. "He called about Angelo. They managed to get three more guys inside the compound. Apparently there's a tunnel, and they found it. They planted explosives all through it, so tonight at nightfall, the whole compound is coming down as soon as I let them know our marks here have been neutralized."

"Seriously?" Zeke asks.

"Yeah. Absolutely. I know you have no idea what I'm talking about, but Patch can fill you in. Let's just say the guys here? Their boss is going to die tonight, and his vendetta will die with him. But that won't stop them. Future strikes, yes. This one, no. It's already been set in motion, so we have to run with what we're doing." His phone rings, and he hits ACCEPT, then speaker. "McCoy."

"Mr. McCoy, our agents are in place completely around the perimeter about a mile out," a voice says.

"Thank you, SSA Mathis."

"Yes, sir."

Before he stops, he hits a contact and the voice on the other end says, "Yeah, boss."

"You guys ready?"

"Yes, sir. We're set up between the FBI agents, some farther out and some closer in. Did Tony send Peyton?"

"Hey, Marshall!" Peyton calls out. "Yeah, I'm here."

"Hey, buddy! Boy, it's good to hear your voice! I've got some ideas on where you might want to plant yourself."

"Yeah, Zeke Calhoun and Drew Koopman are here with us, and I want their input too," Peyton announces, and the two Eagle Point men nod.

"Good deal. Let's put our heads together in about an hour, if you want."

Peyton grins. "Absolutely. Thanks, Marshall. Glad you're on board."

"Wouldn't have it any other way. Later."

"Okay. We all know what we're doing. We all know where we're going. Except for you," Steve says, pointing at Peyton, "but I know whatever you figure out, it'll be right."

Peyton gives him a knowing nod. "I know what I'm looking for, and so do they. We'll be fine."

Steve's text tone goes off, and he looks down at his phone. "According to one of Preston's guys, they've spotted the vehicle at a sporting goods store up in town. Once they leave, he's going to go in and question the employees, see what they bought. Most likely ammo, I'd say. It's go time, folks. Let's head to the kitchen and talk to the locals."

I let them all file out the door, but I turn toward the hallway. The door opens quietly when I turn the knob, and she rolls over and looks at me. "Thought I didn't see you, huh?" I ask with a smile as I close the door behind me and sit down on the side of the bed.

"Didn't think you noticed."

"If it's you, I'm always going to notice."

"Uh-huh." She scoots toward me, then takes my hand and kisses the back of it. That's something she's never done before. "I just … I can't. My brain is so scrambled."

"I get it, baby. Want me to stay?"

"Would you?"

"Of course. Nothing I'd like better."

"Don't you have an assignment?" she asks as I slip my boots off.

"Nope. I don't have a gun, remember? One of Preston's people just saw the car that followed you. They were at the sporting goods store, stocking up, or at least that's what Steve thinks."

"Yeah. I heard you guys talking. Can I just go to sleep now?"

"Yes. Let's." Lying here with her in my arms, everything is fine. Our world is intact and safe. I know that's not going to be the case in a few hours. There's no telling what tonight will bring, but for now, we're okay.

I'll take what I can get.

WE'RE LATE TO LUNCH, WHICH IS MORE OF AN EARLY DINNER, and as we're leaving the lodge to go to the kitchen, Paddy strides in. "Guess you heard the good news."

"Good news?"

"Yeah. KSP brought in an MRAP. If they need to remove Sela and Natalie in a pinch, they've got the ability to do that."

Most of law enforcement has at least one of the mine-resistant ambush-protected vehicles for their tactical teams now, and it would take some kind of heavy firepower for them to hurt Natalie and me if they evacuate us in that thing.

"Yeah, and KSP's sending ten tactical foot soldiers. We've got a lot of help," Steve says. "We've got roughly five more hours. You guys make sure you know exactly where you're supposed to be. And Sela?"

"Yeah?"

"We've got your back, lady. Nothing to worry about. You couldn't be safer."

"Thanks."

If she didn't have confirmation before, she should now. Everybody's here for her and Natalie. And we won't quit until it's done.

I practically order her to finish lunch, and I'm hoping nobody interrupts us. Virginia set two huge pieces of apple pie aside for us, and we get those down with some tea. Before long we're the only two people in here except Virginia, and when we finish, we thank her and head back to the lodge.

That's when I see them. There's a man with a gun at every door and every window. I'm not talking about Steve's guys, or KSP, or FBI, or local law enforcement. I'm talking about our neighbors, the men of the community. They're standing guard, and I know they've probably worked out a schedule so that every entrance is covered at every moment. Our family is rallying around us, not the family we were born into, but the ones we've chosen. The ones who've chosen us. We stop and hug the guys by the door before we go in, then make our way inside.

As we lie there in the quiet, listening to the voices of the men in the great room, I sigh. There's a current running through everything today, and I realize what it feels like to me. An apocalypse. We're running out of time. "We're running out of time."

"What, babe?"

Shit. I didn't realize I'd whispered it out loud. "I said, we're running out of time."

"No, we're not."

She's either totally in denial or she's truly stronger under pressure. Not sure which it is, but apparently she's not feeling the fear I am. "It feels that way to me. Did you see Peyton?"

"Yeah. He's on the roof of the kitchen with a Lapua."

"A what?"

"A Lapua. A three thirty-eight Lapua. It's a sniper rifle."

"Wow." I hear a sound from outside, something both familiar and strange. "What was that?"

"Sounded like gunfire." I'm on my feet and moving in a split second.

"This is command base. Sniper one, got one in sight?" I hear Steve ask into the radio.

"Negative on that," a voice answers, and I know it's Peyton.

"Roger, sniper one. Keep me apprised every five minutes, over."

"Roger that, command base. Over."

"All agents, all agents, who fired? Over," Steve asks.

There's some crackling and finally a voice answers, "Command base, this is Smith. That was a local LEO. We've got one pinned down on the side of the mountain out here. He'll have to shoot his way out, and I'm not sure he can do that where he is. Over."

"Roger that. Any sign of the other? Over."

"Negative. Over."

"Keep us apprised, Smith. Command base, over."

I'm panicked. "What's going on?"

Steve sighs. "It's already started. They've got one pinned down. And they don't know where the other one is."

"Shit. I thought you said dark."

"I was wrong. We all were. But it's damn near dark anyway, will be totally dark in thirty minutes. All we can do is use an educated guess, and these guys had a different idea. It's under control, Bear. I promise, but we need to be ready."

There's a lot of cross-chatter on the radio, and I listen intently. It's heating up out there, and everyone is reporting back and forth on what's happening, what they're seeing, who's moving where. Patch and Steve are looking at the maps on the table and they know where everybody is, but I'm growing more confused by the minute. At some point, Patch looks up and catches my eye. "You okay?"

"Yeah. Trying not to panic."

"You should check on Sela," he says.

"But she's standing …" I turn and look. She's not right beside me, but I thought she came out of the bedroom with me. She's probably back there on the bed, still curled up. My feet are barely touching the floor when I run to our room, but my heart skips a few beats when I realize she's not there.

She has to be with Natalie. When I slide to a stop in front of their room, Natalie looks up at me. "Was that gunfire?"

"Yeah. Where's Sela?"

"I have no idea. Haven't seen her. I thought she was with you."

A quick check tells me she's not in the office, and I glance at my watch and try to remember … It's been almost an hour since I actually saw her myself. As I turn to go back, I notice something. The door on the other side of the hall from the office is open just a crack, and I open it the rest of the way and flip on the light switch. The window in that bedroom is closed.

But the curtain is closed in it. Fuck. I slide it open and look out. Even in the near-darkness I can see a man with a gun sitting there outside the window, his head cocked back and his mouth wide open. It sounds like somebody's running a chainsaw.

I know Sela. Tiptoeing past him would've been nothing for her. My whole body tenses, and I feel my heartbeat double. What has she done?

And I'm almost certain I know exactly where she is.

SELA

PATCH REALLY NEEDS TO WORK ON SECURITY AROUND HERE. It was way too easy for me to crawl through that window in the last bedroom on the back side of the lodge. Even with my weapons and ammo, it was no challenge. And my guard back there? He has no idea I stepped right over him. Bless their hearts, they mean well, but they're certainly not professionals.

This is my fight. They want me to hide and wait, to let the boys do the heavy lifting, but that's not who I am. Watching the tree line, I dart from one building to another until I finally reach our cottage. The cottage faces the green space and away from the forest, so I slip through the front door and close and lock it behind me. After I've smoothed out the covers on the bed, I start laying out everything. Handgun, rifle, shotgun. Ammo next to each. I load the weapons, then check all the magazines. Everything is full. I'm ready.

It's so quiet. Occasionally I hear a couple of muffled voices, but I can't tell where they're coming from. Fuck it, I wish I had a radio! The way these cottages are situated, I'm sheltered from the forest behind us, and also the wooded area toward the road. An hour has passed, and it's dark now. If I go out that way, no one can see me, but I can peer around, so I pull on my gray sweats, gray sweatshirt, and pull the hood up. When I open the front door just a crack, I can see Peyton on the roof of the kitchen, flat on his belly with his rifle in a tripod. No one from the tree line could possibly spot him, but I can from here. I slink toward the edge of the porch, then drop quietly and creep along the side.

And I wait, letting the darkness deepen. I occasionally peer around the back corner of the cottage, but I see nothing and no one. I know some of our men are out there, but I can't tell where. When I flatten my back against the side wall, I look up. Yeah, Peyton's seen me, and he's none too happy. I'll be ratted out in under thirty seconds. But I've got a gun, so what are they gonna do? *Make* me come back to the lodge?

Fuck that shit.

Bear

Everybody turns to stare. "She's not here! She went out a window in the back!"

Steve glares at me. "Yeah, no shit. She's at your cottage."

"What?"

"Sniper one, you can still see her?" Steve barks into the radio.

"Roger that, boss. She's up against the side of the cottage. Over."

He rounds on me, his eyes blazing. "Uh-huh. She's decided to play cowgirl. Bear, you had one job—"

"How the hell was I supposed to guess she'd pull this?" I scream. "Of all the dumbass, shit-stained, motherfucking crazy … I'm going after her." Two men step in front of the door.

"We can't let you do that," one of them says.

"You're not going to *let* me do anything. I'm going out there."

"No, you're not," Steve calls to me. "You're sitting your ass down here and waiting. I'll send a couple of men out there to get her."

"No. She won't come back with them. She'll only come back with me." I don't know if it's true or not, but I'm afraid it might be.

"Yes, she will. We'll make a compelling argument and—"

"No. She won't. I'm going out there." I step closer, and the two of them close ranks. "Look, I don't want to have to beat your asses, but I will if you don't move out of my way."

A voice I know all too well says, "Let him go," and I wheel around. Patch walks straight up to me. "Don't do this, Bear. Please. I beg you."

"I have to. You know I have to. If it was Penny, you'd do the same."

"I know. That's why I'm not going to let them hold you here, but I really wish you wouldn't. Please."

"I have to."

Patch nods at the men, and they step away from the door. "Then stay out of the line of fire."

"I will." One of them opens the door for me, and I look through to the outside. The green space, usually filled with laughter and chatter, is silent and dark. As I step out, I head around the corner of the building, slide along the side of the kitchen, and keep going. I can't see Sela from where I'm standing, partially hidden by some of the cottages, and I pray that wherever he is, that guy with the gun can't see me. As for Sela, I know where she is. And now I have to get to her. There are so many things I want to say to her.

I just hope I get a chance to say them.

When I round the back corner of the cottage next to ours, she's right there, and I step out toward her. But I hear a sound behind me, and I don't even turn. The look on her face as she spins and sees him is all I need to know. There's only one choice, one right one. Over thirty years ago, I chose violence. Over and over again in prison, I chose violence. I marked myself as a dangerous man, a violent man, a man whose only goal was mayhem. That's not my choice today.

Today, no matter what it costs me, in this place and at this moment, I choose love.

SELA

THE ORGAN MUSIC IS DISCONCERTING TO ME. I DIDN'T GO TO church growing up, and I find it unpleasant. I'm also surprised at the smell. It's like the flowers are in my lap, they're so strong. The casket at the front is draped in red roses, and somebody said they were from community members, that a bunch of people got together and paid for them. That's quite a sacrifice, considering most of the residents here are below the poverty level. They appreciated his service, the things he did for them, and they wanted to pay their respects. Their gratitude has been evident throughout all of this.

After listening to the pastor drone on for a bit, everyone is invited to get up and say a few words. Several people do, plus Priest, Bulldog, and Ghost. Patch finally stands and makes his way up, but my mind is elsewhere.

All I can think about is that night. I relive it constantly.

I can see movement in the trees, but by watching it, I can tell it's some of our people. They're not nearly as stealthy as an assassin, and I should know. I've dealt with a few of those in my time. Out of habit, I check my SIG's chamber, then double grip it, slide to my chest. It's quiet, so quiet, and then I hear something and turn.

I'm looking straight into a gun barrel, but I don't get a chance to lift my gun before something blocks my vision and I hear a shot, then another from a distance. I'm lying on the ground, something heavy on top of me, and I realize it's probably the man Peyton just shot who was aiming at me. But then it occurs to me—there were two shots. Who …

It takes some effort to push whatever it is off me, and when it rolls away, I sit up and look around. The man with the gun is about twenty feet from me, and I can hear Peyton yelling something into his comm. If that wasn't him on top of me …

The light is dimming as I look to see who's beside me on the ground, and when I do, my heart freezes. Miles is lying there, a stain on his shirt and a trickle of blood coming from the corner of his mouth. "Miles! What the fuck—"

"I stopped him. You're safe. You're safe, Sela. I did it." I rolled him, so he started out face down on me. No. No, no, no. It only takes me a second to slightly roll him so I can look at his back, and when I look under him, there's blood everywhere. He took the shot in the back. All around me, shots are ringing out, and there's no way for me to get help to him. I can hear someone yelling something in a foreign language, and that's when I see it—the door to the crawl space under the cottage. There's a turn stick on the top, and I twist it so the little door falls open. He's heavy as lead, but I manage to drag him into the opening with me, then grab the door and pull it up until it's resting in place. It's black as pitch in here, but I pull out my phone and turn on the flashlight feature. The whole crawl space lights up, and there we are. "Miles, oh my god. Miles, talk to me. It's gonna be okay."

"Sela? Babe, are you okay? Please, Sela …" His voice trails off, and my hands start to shake.

"I'm right here, baby. Right here. Don't talk. Save your strength." My hands are shaking so hard that I'm having trouble hitting the right spots on the face of my phone.

"Where the hell are you?" a voice bellows in my ear.

"We're in the crawl space under the cottage! Miles has been shot! Patch, please help us!"

"We'll get to you as fast as we can, but we've got our hands full trying to get to the other guy. Just hang in there. Apply pressure and hang on, Sela. We'll get to you, I promise."

"Please, hurry! Please? Oh, god, please—"

A voice outside yells, "Sela!" There's the sounds of feet everywhere, and I wonder what's going on. Yelling is coming from farther away too, and I'm panicking and trying to figure out what's happening when the door falls open and a face partially obscured by full tactical gear says, "Agent Baldwin?"

"Yes! Oh my god, yes!"

"I'm Lieutenant Jonathan Morgan of the Kentucky State Police Tactical Response Team. You have a man injured here, correct?"

"Yes! Oh, god, please, don't worry about me! Just get him out of here and get him some help!" I'm crying so hard that

I'm having trouble talking, and I watch as Miles slides out through the opening and disappears. I'm crawling right behind him.

"We've got one wounded on the north side of one of the cottages. Need medical assistance ASAP, over," Morgan says into his radio. "Ma'am, are you hurt?"

That's when I look down at myself and for the first time, I realize I'm covered in blood. "Uh, no. I don't think so. I think that's all his."

Morgan hits his radio again. "We've got a critical response on this man down. Repeat, critical response on the man down, over."

"Roger that, tactical. EMTs are on their way. Over."

The words are no more than out into the air when Bulldog and Drew come into view. "Holy shit, Sela, what happened?" Bulldog snaps.

"That guy," I say, pointing at the downed man as I sob, "was going to kill me. Miles knocked me out of the way."

"Let me see what we … Holy shit."

"How bad is it?" another voice asks, and I look up to see Paddy there.

"It's bad." Bulldog reaches for his shoulder comm. "Patch, you there?"

"Yeah. Go ahead."

"We need the bird. We've gotta get Bear out of here."

"I can get it, but Izzy's already in the air. KSP five, report. Over."

Izzy's voice is crystal clear, and I can hear the rotors somewhere nearby. "Roger that, App STAR base. I hear you. Down in two. Over.

"In the meantime, fluids?" Paddy asks.

"Yeah, IV push. And let me see if I can pack this."

They're working like crazy over Miles, and all I can do is wring my hands and cry.

I'm the reason.

I'm the reason he's lying here bleeding and dying. If I'd just kept my ass in the lodge … If I'd just listened to orders … If I'd just done what I knew I was supposed to do …

What have I done? I've blown my life apart. I've made a mess. I've hurt Miles. "Is he—"

"I don't know, Sela. I really … There's Izzy. Go tell her where we are." I can hear the sound of their big Sikorsky whining off to the back of the cottages, and I know she's landing the bird.

"But the shooters—"

"They're both neutralized. Peyton got this one, and Preston's men finally got the other. Go get her! Now!"

My feet are flying across the grass and when I reach the bird, Reboot and Zeke are converging on it too. "Far side of your cottage?" Reboot asks.

"Yeah. Hurry!"

In minutes, Miles is on a backboard and headed to the bird. I can't do anything but stand and watch as they load him up. Reboot and Bulldog climb onboard with him, and in a flash, they're gone.

There I stand, in the grass, blood covering me, Paddy beside me, Zeke and Drew nearby, and a body lying twenty feet away. KSP officers have already surrounded it, and I know the FBI agents are somewhere in the woods, taking care of the body there. And now I don't know what to do. There's a handgun lying nearby, and for a split second, I think about picking it up and blowing my brains out. This is all my fault, not the whole thing, but what's happened to Miles is definitely my fault. I have nobody to blame for that but myself. If he doesn't make it ... "What do I do now?" I ask in a tiny voice to no one in particular.

Paddy's arm wraps around my shoulders. "You go get cleaned up and somebody will take you to the hospital. Come on. Let's go."

The lawn is full of guys in tactical gear, camo, and uniforms. We walk on past and head straight for the lodge, Paddy propelling me along and Zeke and Drew flanking us. As we walk, I keep thinking about those words Miles said to me: "I'd die for you, *banrigh*. I'd do anything for you." He meant them. He lived them. Now he's going to die for them.

When we reach the lodge, two big burly guys open the doors and I step through. Steve, Patch, and Preston are standing there, and they all turn. Patch doesn't speak. Steve glares at me. "Sela."

That's my breaking point. "I'm so, so sorry. I just didn't want to sit here like a huge target and—"

"We told you it was under control. All you had to do was wait, and you couldn't. Do you realize what you've done?" he hisses.

I look down at myself, Miles' blood drying on my clothes, and wail, "Look at me! Don't you think I know? Don't you think I want to die? I want to die! I don't deserve to live!"

I don't remember a lot after that. I know Paddy gave me a sedative at Patch's instruction because I got so wild and out of hand. My next really clear memory was the moment the doctor stepped through the doorway of the waiting area, blood all over his hands and his gown, and asked for the McMillan family. It felt like my body weighed ten tons and my legs weren't strong enough for me to stand, but I did. Everybody was still mad at me, but I remember Penny taking my hand on one side and Mavis taking the other, and how my knees buckled as the doctor spoke. I ran outside and hit my knees on the pavement, not caring if anybody saw me, screaming at the sky, begging for one more chance, a chance I knew I wasn't going to get.

But here in the church, I'm shaken from that nightmare by warmth on my hand, and his big bear paw grasps mine and holds it tightly as he leans over to me and whispers, "You okay, *banrigh*?"

I look up into those big brown eyes and see my own reflection, but that's not all I see. I see gentleness, and kindness, and love that I've never known before. My life was spared by his sacrifice. His life was spared by whatever it is these people in this place believe in, a higher power or a universal energy or sheer mercy or pure luck. I don't know. I don't pretend to know these things. All I know is that I have a second chance with this man, a man who by all rights should be dead, a man who made a split-second decision that allows me to sit here beside him today. I'm going to make the most of it every fucking day. No exceptions. The tear trailing down my face tickles as I nod gently to him, and his hand leaves mine, only to wrap around my shoulder as his arm stretches across the back of the pew and pulls me closer until I'm leaning into his side, a place I want to be for the rest of my life.

Careful not to smear my makeup as I blot my tears, I listen as Patch speaks. "I'm sure when he made that stop last Saturday, he never dreamed it would be his last. Every man on my team has dealt with Curtis at some time, and every man on my team found him to be fair, honest, and dependable, not to mention one of the smartest people I've ever met who also had an enormous amount of common sense. It's usually one or the other, folks. Most smart people don't have a lot of common sense." Everyone chuckles. "And yet, Curtis did. His deputies all looked up to him and respected him, and he shepherded them and taught them like a father. I do want to say to Matt and Darren," Patch says, turning toward the two younger men sitting on the front row, their jaws clenched as they fight tears, "Curtis was extremely proud of the two of you. He knew he could always count on you. He respected you as men and loved you like sons." Matt's head drops, and I know he's just lost his battle. "I'm thankful, this community is thankful, that you're here to carry on his legacy.

"In the coming weeks and months, there's going to be an arraignment. I don't know how that's going to turn out. But I do want to remind this community of something. The young man who committed the despicable act that led to us being here today … His family still lives in this community. They're scarred and broken too. He made a bad choice, several bad choices, in fact. He did a horrible thing. He robbed a woman of her husband, children of their father, grandchildren of their grandfather, and a community of a man they loved, respected, and trusted. But let me remind you of this. Out there on that farm with me are seven men who found themselves in a similar position once. One in particular found himself in a nearly identical situation." I know he's talking about Miles. "Today, they're contributing community members. They've paid their debts, done their time, worked hard, and rejoined society to help others. They've saved lives right here in this community, dozens of lives. When the young man whose path led us here today finishes whatever his penance is, I hope all of you will follow Curtis' lead and help us to lift him up, not tear him down again and again. It's what Curtis would want, for us to help him, and for us to pray for his family, that they might find peace. Wrap your arms around them. They need us now more than ever." He stops for a second, steps around the podium, and places his hand on the casket. "Thank you for your service, Curtis. You were my friend, and I'll miss spending time with you." Then he sits down beside Penny in a pew, head bowed. I know Patch. There are tears on his face, just like the faces of all the men in this room, strong men who aren't afraid to show people that they feel love and loss.

The ride to the cemetery is quiet until Miles says something that I don't catch. "What, babe?"

"He handed me that gun."

"What? You mean in the lodge that night?"

"Yeah. He handed me that gun. He wanted me to be safe. He didn't care that I was an ex-con. He just wanted me to be safe, for me to keep you safe. He knew he could get into trouble, and he didn't care. He was only thinking of us."

"I know. He was a great man. We were lucky to have him for as long as we did."

"Yeah. I made up my mind that I'm going down to the jail to talk to that kid next week. He needs to know that somebody sees more than just his deed. They see his addiction and his weaknesses, but they see his heart. I don't believe he's a bad person."

"It was the meth and fentanyl. It makes people do crazy things," I say, staring out the window to look at all the tombstones scattered across the cemetery. People are gathering under a tent nearby, and I see the pallbearers carrying the casket, a huge, mahogany monstrosity with brass fittings, toward the bier.

After the pastor has spoken, Aggie stands and steps up to the front, places her hand on the casket, then begins to sing. I was told that she sang a different song at the little boy's graveside service. This time, she sings "Amazing Grace," and it's truly beautiful. We stand outside the tent space, Miles behind me, his arms wrapped around my waist and my hands on his clasped ones. When she's finished and everyone starts to walk away, he makes his way to Matt first and then Darren to hug them both and tell them how much he appreciates them. Every Knott County deputy is here, and most of the Hazard Police Department. Every municipal worker from Knott County is here, from the fire and rescue department all the way down to the road crew, and a huge contingency of KSP from this end of the state is here. Izzy is standing nearby with Ghost beside her, her uniform neat and crisp. All of our guys are wearing suits and ties at Patch's order. He wanted them to look respectable and respectful, and they're an incredibly handsome bunch.

As we start away, I hear somebody say, "Hey, Bear!" Before we can turn, Ghost catches up to us. "Hey, can I catch a ride? Izzy's going back to the post."

Miles turns and smiles at him. "Sure." And there it is.

I love that smile. That smile means everything to me. He's absolutely everything to me. If I never, never see anything again in my entire life, I'll die a happy woman just because I saw that smile.

CHAPTER 10

BEAR

"AND NOW WE GET TO DO SOMETHING I WASN'T SURE WE could ever do. Thanks to Tony and Nikki, it's a possibility, and when they pulled Steve into the mix, he encouraged it. We had eight cottages. Fiona took Hollywood's. Then we got the four others enlarged and Paddy, Bulldog, and Reboot took one of them apiece. That leaves us with one big one and four smaller ones. Plus I think Fi's going to take the spare bedroom at the work house once she starts college," Patch says, talking about Penny's grandparents' house down the road where she and Mavis work, "so we'll have five of the smaller ones available."

He starts passing out packets of papers as the rest of the women and I look on. "Take these back to your cottages with you and look them over. And yes, ladies, you get a say too. These are men with whom you'll have to live and work, so you should be able to have a say. Each couple should agree on three possibilities, and we'll all get back together. Bring those three. We'll sort them out and the pile with the most returned is the one. We'll keep the others in order of selection and maybe revisit them after this one is settled. And thanks, everybody. I don't know about you guys, but this is exciting for me. I had to make the original choices, and that's a heavy burden to bear. Thankfully, I did good with every one of you, but having some help is nice."

"Listen, if we get to give somebody else the chance we've been given here, I think it's awesome," Priest says, and the other voices rise in agreement, mine included. This is super exciting to me. We'll get a new brother. I couldn't be happier.

That excitement gets tamped down once Sela and I start going through the possibilities. There are so many. "Well, I like this guy. He was a mechanic on the outside. We could use one of those," she says from the other side of the table.

"Yeah, and I like this guy here." I hold up a sheet. "Did time for manslaughter. Killed his wife and her sister in an accident while he was driving drunk, but according to the paperwork, he's not an alcoholic. It was an isolated incident. And he's the kind of guy we like offering second chances to."

"Does he have a skill set?"

"Mmmm." I roll down through the details. "Not that I can see. Looks like he was a truck driver. In town, not long haul. Deliveries. Worked there for fourteen years, so he had job longevity. What have you got over there?"

"This one is interesting. Take a look." She hands it to me, and I scan the page.

The first thing that catches my eye is his conviction. First degree hard time in max for the murder of a police officer. And then the conviction overturned after twenty-two years when they did DNA testing and discovered he wasn't the shooter. Prior to that, he'd worked for five years as ... "A welder."

She nods. "Yeah. A guy who understands metallurgy. Talk about a good fit."

"Yup. Says he did some electrical classes in prison. He could really help out in the shop."

"That's what I was thinking."

I lay the paper on the table and sit there for a minute, my brain racing, trying to put my thoughts into words. "Doesn't it seem wrong?"

"What?"

"Sitting here, deciding a man's fate? I mean, we choose one, but the others are all deserving in some way. What happens to them? I mean, who are we to make those decisions?"

"Miles." Sela stands, walks around the table, and kneels beside my chair, her hands on my thigh. "Baby, we can't save the whole world. But the man we choose, we can change his world, and he in turn changes the whole world with his actions. It's not a splash. It's a ripple. But that ripple extends out past where we can see. Remember the kid at the funeral who stood up and said if Curtis hadn't arrested him, he never would've gone to jail, and if he hadn't gone to jail, he never would've learned to read? And by learning to read, he got a job when he got out, and now he's making a living for his family. That's the kind of change we're making. And this guy would give as good as he gets."

"True. And that doesn't mean we can't choose some of the others on down the line." But I know the truth. If those guys are aimless for the next few years, their chances of going back to prison increase exponentially. My mind is rolling when she takes my hand, and everything stops.

"Babe, no matter what we do, we do the right thing. We give a guy a chance he didn't have before. And to that one guy, that's everything." She's right. I'm living proof.

To that one guy, that's everything.

"This one," I say and drop my free hand onto the paper. "This is the guy."

"I agree."

I guess tomorrow will tell the tale. For tonight, we choose two more, and then it's bedtime. There are no pliers. There is no craziness. We just make love, and it's glorious, her skin against mine, the softness of her hair, and the sweetness of her lips. "I love you, my *banrigh*," I whisper into her crown.

"I love you too, my *righ*," she whispers back as I feel her relax against me, naked and warm.

"*Righ*? You know what that means?" I ask with a grin.

"Yeah. You might have Grandpa, but I have Google. And you are my *righ*. You're my king." The happiness in my heart with her beside me is something I've never had before, and it's more than enough.

For the first time in my life, I'm whole.

DINNER IS OVER, EVERYTHING IS CLEANED UP, AND WE'VE moved to the big table in the lodge. We sit at the table, and the women stand behind us, their hands on our shoulders. When Sela's fall onto me, I pat the back of the left one as I slide the papers out with my right. Patch starts to sort them, and we all watch, wondering who it'll be.

One pile has one. Two have three sheets. One has four, and one has five. But one has eight. Every couple picked the same man, and I can feel my heart pounding as we wait. The first seven go back into a stack on their own, and then patch picks up the stack with four sheets. "Okay. Third choice, manslaughter conviction for DUI with two fatalities. Truck driver." That was one of ours. He sets that stack aside and picks up the stack of five. "Second choice, production with intent to distribute. Prior work as a mechanic. Has completed all drug and alcohol rehab and did great." Our other one. Then he sets that stack aside and picks up the big one.

"Convicted of first-degree murder for the killing of an officer of the law. Conviction overturned after twenty-two years with new DNA evidence. Prior work as a welder. This stack has eight sheets in it. That means every one of you picked this man as one of the best candidates, including Penny and me, and he was definitely my first choice. For every household at this table, stand if this man was your first choice." The sounds of chair legs on the floor is deafening as every man at this table stands. "The choice is unanimous. Tony, Steve, and I will be contacting him this week. He's living in a halfway house in ..." Patch looks down at the sheet, but I remember. "Provo, Utah. The other two will stay in their own files and hopefully we can make some kind of offers to them in the very near future. Good work, brothers. Our family is growing, and I couldn't be happier."

There's a lot of handshaking, back-slapping, and hugging, but the smiling faces are enough. We're getting a new brother. Iron Oak Farms is growing. And with it, our search and rescue capabilities.

We are the Appalachian STAR team—search, train, assess, and rescue. We will fulfill our duties to our community and our families, and we'll gladly risk our lives to bring the lost home. It's our vow. It's what we do. It's who we are. It's my family.

And I couldn't be prouder.

BUT WAIT! THERE'S MORE! WOULD YOU LIKE TO KNOW what happens next? It'll surprise you, I promise! Just click for more: https://deanndrawrites.com/ADangerousManBONUS CONTENT. Or if you're reading in a paperback, scan the QR code and get your copy!

Curious about Tony, Nikki, Vic, Laura, Steve, and Kelly? You can find them all in the Bluegrass Dynasty series here.

Have you met Ethan Watson and the men of Eagle Point SAR? You can find Susan Stoker's Eagle Point SAR series here.

Want more Kentucky romance and suspense? Grab the Bluegrass Bravery books in Susan Stoker's Operation Alpha: Police and Fire world. They're all here, and some of the guys will show up in the Appalachian STAR series too! Just click here.

This is the last book in the Appalachian STAR series, but is it the last book ever for this team of brave men? Should there be more? Reach out if you'd like more of Patch and his team! Just email me at Deanndra@DeanndraHall.com and let me know what you think. Your opinion really does matter to me!

ALSO BY DEANNDRA HALL

<u>Books included in Susan Stoker's</u>

<u>Special Forces: Operation Alpha World,</u>

<u>Eagle Point Search and Rescue</u>

The Appalachian STAR Series

A Desperate Man (Book 1)

A Bitter Man (Book 2)

A Broken Man (Book 3)

A Twisted Man (Book 4)

A Furious Man (Book 5)

A Tormented Man (Book 6)

A Fierce Man (Book 7)

A Dangerous Man (Book 8)

<u>Bluegrass Dynasty Series</u>

<u>Bluegrass Dynasty:</u>

<u>The Love Under Construction Novels</u>

Laying a Foundation (Book 1)

Tearing Down Walls (Book 2)

Renovating a Heart (Book 3)

Planning an Addition (Book 4)

<u>Bluegrass Dynasty:</u>

<u>The Citadel Novels</u>

One Simple Mistake (Book 5)

One Broken Promise (Book 6)

One Poor Choice (Book 7)

One Wrong Glance (Book 8)

<u>Bluegrass Dynasty:</u>

<u>The Legacy Novels</u>

Atonement (Book 9)

Legacy of Pride (Book 10)

Legacy of Freedom (Book 11)

Legacy of Faithfulness (Book 12)

Legacy of Hope (Book 13)

Legacy of Memories (Book 14)

Legacy of Love (Book 15)

<u>Bluegrass Dynasty:</u>

<u>The Moonlight & Moonshine Novels</u>

Kindred Spirits (Book 16)

High Proof (Book 17)

Angel's Share (Book 18)

<u>**The Bliss Series**</u>

Adventurous Me (Book 1)

Unforgettable You (Book 2)

Incredible Us (Book 3)

Completely Mine (Book 4)

Undeniably His (Book 5)

Eternally Yours (Book 6)

Blissfully Hers (Book 7)

<u>**The Harper's Cove Series**</u>

Karen and Brett at 326 Harper's Cove (Book 1)

Becca and Greg at 314 Harper's Cove (Book 2)

Donna and Connor at 228 Harper's Cove (Book 3)

Savannah and Martin at 219 Harper's Cove (Book 4)

Cheryl and Samuel at 323 Harper's Cove (Book 5)

Tasha and Davis at 333 Harper's Cove (Book 6)

Lily and Brock at 343 Harper's Cove (Book 7)

Siobhán and Gabhain at 241 Harper's Cove (Book 8)

<u>**The Witch of Endor Series**</u>

Laid Bare (Book 1)

Ripped Open (Book 2)

Torn Apart (Book 3)

Bound Together (Book 4)

<u>**The Silent Cove Series**</u>

Awakening (Book 1)

<u>**Independent Novels**</u>

My Last Dom

The Celtic Fan

Rough Stock

<u>**Books included in Susan Stoker's**</u>

<u>**Police and Fire: Operation Alpha World,**</u>

<u>**Badge of Honor**</u>

<u>Bluegrass Bravery Series</u>

Shelter for Sharla (Book 1)

Justice for Aleta (Book 2)

Shelter for Martina (Book 3)

Justice for Daesha (Book 4)

Shelter for Jerrica (Book 5)

Justice for Landee (Book 6)

Shelter for Tanna (Book 7)

Justice for Liella (Book 8)

Justice for Maisey (Book 9)

Shelter for Nita (Book 10)

Justice for JoElla (Book 11)

Refuge for Flora (Book 12)

Refuge for Phaedra (Book 13)

Refuge for Cherilyn (Book 14)

Refuge for Ailsa (Book 15)

Justice for Samara (Book 16)

<u>Tarpley Volunteer Fire Department Series</u>

Fighting for Carly (Book 2)

Tarpley Volunteer Fire Department Series 2

Fighting for Lorna (Book 4)

Fighting for Amethyst: A Tarpley VFD Novel

ABOUT THE AUTHOR

Deanndra Hall is a working author living in far western Kentucky with her partner of 30+ years, crazy little dogs, and maybe a snake or two. She's written for business, industry, religious institutions, non-profits, and owned her own graphic design business, as well as working as a fiber and textile artist. When she's not writing all things romance from sweet, simple plots to explicit, erotic suspense, she can be found working out at the local gym, hiking, kayaking, reading (of course), or working on a healthy recipe. And wherever she is, chocolate is sure to be nearby.

On the Web: deanndrahall.com
Email: Deanndra@DeanndraHall.com
Amazon: amazon.com/Deanndra-Hall
Bookbub: bookbub.com/authors/deanndra-hall
Facebook: facebook.com/deanndra.hall
Goodreads: goodreads.com/deanndrahall
Instagram: instagram.com/deanndra_hall/
Newsletter: Subscribe!
Pinterest: pinterest.com/deanndrahall
Mailing address:
P.O. Box 3722
Paducah, KY 42002-3722

There are many more books in this fan fiction world than listed here, for an up-to-date list go to www.AcesPress.com

You can also visit our Amazon page at:
http://www.amazon.com/author/operationalpha

Special Forces: Operation Alpha World
Christie Adams: Charity's Heart
Elizabella Baker: Challenging Luke
Linzi Baxter: Dangerous Rescue
Misha Blake: Flash
Anna Blakely: Rescuing Gracelynn
Julia Bright: Saving Lorelei
Cara Carnes: Protecting Mari
Kendra Mei Chailyn: Beast
Melissa Kay Clarke: Rescuing Annabeth
Gia Cobie: Saved from Revenge
Samantha Cole: Handling Haven
KaLyn Cooper: Spring Unveiled
Jordan Dane: Redemption for Avery
D.M. Earl: Claire's Guardian
Riley Edwards: Protecting Olivia
Dorothy Ewels: Knight's Queen
Lila Ferrari: Protecting Joy
Nicole Flockton: Protecting Maria
Amy Gamet: Guarded by the SEAL
Lea Griffith: Finding Ava
Desiree Holt: Protecting Maddie
Danielle M. Haas: Crossroads of Betrayal
Bree Hera: Trusting the Team
Jesse Jacobson: Protecting Honor
Rayne Lewis: Justice for Mary

Ireland Lorelei: The Detective
Kristin Lynn: Worth the Risk
JM Madden: Rescuing Olivia
A.M. Mahler: Griffin
Ellie Masters: Sybil's Protector
Trish McCallan: Hero Under Fire
Naomi McKay: Twist
Rachel McNeely: The SEAL's Surprise Baby
KD Michaels: Saving Laura
Olivia Michaels: Protecting Harper
Annie Miller: Securing Willow
MJ Nightingale: Protecting Beauty
C.K. O'Connor: Delaney's Bodyguard
Melinda Owens: Betraying Katie
Victoria Paige: Reclaiming Izabel
Danielle Pays: Defending Sarina
Lainey Reese: Protecting New York
KeKe Renée: Protecting Bria
Taryn Rivers: Savage Cove
TL Reeve and Michele Ryan: Extracting Mateo
Ariana Rose: Chasing Paige
Deanna L. Rowley: Saving Veronica
Angela Rush: Charlotte
E.M. Shue: Discovering Tyler
Rose Smith: Saving Satin
Tyler Anne Snell: Cowboy Heat
Dee Stewart: Fighting for Brielle
Lynne St. James: SEAL's Spitfire
Bella Stone: Rexar
Jen Talty: Protecting Ainsley
Reina Torres, Rescuing Hi'ilani
LJ Vickery: Circus Comes to Town
R. C. Wynne: Shadows Renewed

Delta Team Three Series
Lori Ryan: Nori's Delta
Becca Jameson: Destiny's Delta
Lynne St James, Gwen's Delta
Elle James: Ivy's Delta
Riley Edwards: Hope's Delta

Police and Fire: Operation Alpha World
Freya Barker: Burning for Autumn
B.P. Beth: Scott
Jane Blythe: Salvaging Marigold
Julia Bright: Justice for Amber
Gia Cobie: Saved from Revenge
Hadley Finn: Exton
Danielle M. Haas: Crossroads of Betrayal
Deanndra Hall: Shelter for Sharla
Jenna Harte: Dead But Not Forgotten
India Kells: Game Master
Amber Kuhlman: Protecting Paisley
Reina Torres: Justice for Sloane
Aubree Valentine, Justice for Danielle

Tarpley VFD Series
Silver James, Fighting for Elena
Deanndra Hall, Fighting for Carly
Haven Rose, Fighting for Calliope
MJ Nightingale, Fighting for Jemma
TL Reeve, Fighting for Brittney
Nicole Flockton, Fighting for Nadia

As you know, this book included at least one character from Susan Stoker's books. To check out more, see below.

SEAL of Protection: Alliance Series

Protecting Remi
Protecting Wren (Nov 5, 2024)
Protecting Josie (Mar 4, 2025)
Protecting Maggie (Apr 1, 2025)
Protecting Addison (May 6, 2025)
Protecting Kelli (TBA)
Protecting Bree (TBA)

The Refuge Series

Deserving Alaska
Deserving Henley
Deserving Reese
Deserving Cora
Deserving Lara
Deserving Maisy (Oct 1, 2024)
Deserving Ryleigh (Jan 7, 2025)

SEAL Team Hawaii Series

Finding Elodie
Finding Lexie
Finding Kenna
Finding Monica
Finding Carly
Finding Ashlyn
Finding Jodelle

Eagle Point Search & Rescue

Searching for Lilly

Searching for Elsie
Searching for Bristol
Searching for Caryn
Searching for Finley
Searching for Heather
Searching for Khloe

Delta Team Two Series
Shielding Gillian
Shielding Kinley
Shielding Aspen
Shielding Jayme (novella)
Shielding Riley
Shielding Devyn
Shielding Ember
Shielding Sierra

SEAL of Protection: Legacy Series
Securing Caite (FREE!)
Securing Brenae (novella)
Securing Sidney
Securing Piper
Securing Zoey
Securing Avery
Securing Kalee
Securing Jane

Delta Force Heroes Series
Rescuing Rayne (FREE!)
Rescuing Aimee (novella)
Rescuing Emily
Rescuing Harley
Marrying Emily (novella)

Rescuing Kassie
Rescuing Bryn
Rescuing Casey
Rescuing Sadie (novella)
Rescuing Wendy
Rescuing Mary
Rescuing Macie (novella)
Rescuing Annie

Badge of Honor: Texas Heroes Series
Justice for Mackenzie (FREE!)
Justice for Mickie
Justice for Corrie
Justice for Laine (novella)
Shelter for Elizabeth
Justice for Boone
Shelter for Adeline
Shelter for Sophie
Justice for Erin
Justice for Milena
Shelter for Blythe
Justice for Hope
Shelter for Quinn
Shelter for Koren
Shelter for Penelope

SEAL of Protection Series
Protecting Caroline (FREE!)
Protecting Alabama
Protecting Fiona
Marrying Caroline (novella)
Protecting Summer
Protecting Cheyenne

Protecting Jessyka
Protecting Julie (novella)
Protecting Melody
Protecting the Future
Protecting Kiera (novella)
Protecting Alabama's Kids (novella)
Protecting Dakota

New York Times, USA Today and *Wall Street Journal* Bestselling Author Susan Stoker has a heart as big as the state of Tennessee where she lives, but this all American girl has also spent the last fourteen years living in Missouri, California, Colorado, Indiana, and Texas. She's married to a retired Army man who now gets to follow *her* around the country.

www.stokeraces.com
www.AcesPress.com
susan@stokeraces.com

Made in the USA
Monee, IL
20 May 2025

17800570R00154